Trail of Broken Chains

David Burton Flint

Dedication

To all the courageous yet anonymous men and women who started and ran the Underground Railroad, whose daring missions sent them deep into the Southern states to free the poor people held captive as slaves from a life of bondage. Their valiant efforts forged trails of freedom to the North through hundreds of miles of unknown land to local safe houses known only as stations.

Foreword

David Burton Flint has a good feeling for the early times of our nation with interesting character development. The author uses vernacular of the late 1780s, which helps the story line flow as the two friends, Robert Flint and Joshua Wells, delve into a thrilling new adventure after their beloved grandfathers die. The two young men decide to move into wide-open spaces and seek their own fame and fortune. Unfortunately, life in the early country was anything but civilized, and those with the biggest guns ruled most of the time. All sorts of wonderful adventures are in store for the curious young men. There are new people to meet, new places to see, but there are also people with evil intentions, robbers, and those who do not hesitate to kill. These brave young men were told to stand back to back when danger appears, just as their grandfathers once did. Their loyal companion, a young wolf pup, helps them with his animal instinct. Will they safely drive the valuable cargo entrusted to them into the new lands? It won't be easy! This historical novel shines with excitement and adventure as it tells the story of two eager young men. A good read.

AJ Berry

Preface

After completing my first book, *The Life and Times of Robert Flint, the Pioneer*, I was convinced there was another story to be told of the descendants of Robert Flint and his dear friend Ben Wells.

We all have ancestors who at one time or another have just packed up everything they owned and moved on, maybe for a better life or another dream, or to see what lies across the valleys and rivers. This is what Robert Flint's grandson Robert did, along with his close friend, Joshua Wells, grandson of Ben Wells.

Their friendship was as strong as their grandfathers. These two young men also had their grandfathers urge to explore the wilderness. This is their story, a portrayal of the way they helped to settle the new West and came to the aid of many a poor soul.

David Burton Flint

Restless

Seventeen eighty-three was a difficult year for all of us Flints. In early spring, my grandfather Robert Flint died. He was surrounded by my father, Robert Flint Jr.; my uncles; and, of course, his closest friend Ben Wells. My father told me that my grandfather wanted to see me and to hurry along. I remember that day as if it were yesterday.

It was April 18, 1783. The fields were turning green from all the spring rain, and the livestock were in the fields eating the ankle-deep grass. I was sitting on my grandfather's old cabin porch, the one he had built more than fifty years ago. Joshua was there with me, and we were talking about our grandfathers and how close they had been since 1739.

Joshua said, "I heard my grandfather talking the other day and he said to my father, 'If old Robert dies, then I'll be right behind him.'"

"I believe he is right, Joshua," I replied. "He doesn't want to live without Grandpa not being here. They've been together for so long and have done so much together. I know I would feel the same way if you up and died on me. We've been friends since we were five years old."

"Robert, another thing has been bothering me lately," Joshua said. "Your father said he may sell the farm and move out to Wyoming County. Are ya going with him if he does?"

"No, I ain't," I told him. "I want to go out West. Maybe we'll go see the Mississippi River. They say it's pretty long and wide. I heard my grandpa talk about it once in a while. He said it goes from the far north of this country, winds, and flows south through this wilderness all the way to the ocean, and is wild all the way there. But I don't know. I just ain't going with my father; he knows how I feel about it. I told him I'm nineteen now and it's time for me to go and find my own trail, like Grandpa did and told me to do."

My father walked up to Joshua and me sitting on the old porch.

"Robert, your grandpa is asking for you and Joshua," he said. "He and Joshua's grandfather want to talk to you both alone."

"What does Grandpa want us for, Father?"

"He didn't say, just that you should get yourselves over there quick."

Everyone was there when we entered the house. All my cousins, aunts, and uncles were sitting around the table. Some were crying and some were just plain talking.

Joshua and I walked into the bedroom; Joshua's grandfather was sitting on an old chair they both had made years ago. Grandma smiled at me and left the room.

Grandpa took a pint of ale from Ben, drank a big swallow, and set it down on the table. He smiled at me and said, "Well, Robert, looks like your old grandpa has got to move on and find another trail to follow. But I must tell you and Joshua what old Ben here and I have been talking about. Your father promised me many years ago he would move out to the western part of the state after I died. Well, he has kept his word to me, so now he has my blessing to go. Hell, I don't blame him for going. He is getting up there in age also, and he has done very well here on the farm. Now my question to you is what are *you* gonna do now?"

"Well," I answered, "Joshua and I were talking about heading out West, maybe seeing the Mississippi River, but who knows what or where we'll end up."

"Old Ben here and I were hoping that you two would continue like we have been doing for fifty years," Grandpa said. "We know there ain't any damn wars and Indians to fight, but there is a land out West that has hardly seen a white man before. If we were your ages, we'd be heading southwest, and who in hell knows what we'd get into."

Ben broke out into his old laugh and said, "That's for damn sure, Robert. Every time we wandered away from this house we got into some damn trouble. But we always did make it through all right, didn't we?"

"That's for damn sure," Grandpa agreed. "We were lucky, I guess, or it was the beads that our old friend Coppernol gave us many years ago. That's one reason we wanted you two here."

Grandpa reached for an old box next to his bed. He opened the top and pulled out two long strands of colored beads. He handed one to the other and me to Joshua.

"Here are those beads that Coppernol gave old Ben and me many years ago. I've talked to your father, Robert, and he told me that they should go to you instead of him. He knows the power they have, and he said you would need them more than he would. So take these beads and carry them around your neck. Never lose them or forget them somewhere. They will protect you in any fights that you get into. The same goes for you, Joshua."

"That's right," Ben confirmed. "Your father told me the same darn thing. He wanted you to have them."

I took the beads and put them over my head. They draped down my chest. They were beautiful, and it was funny, but I could feel a mysterious power going through my body.

"Grandpa, I feel this strange energy going through my body. I hope I ain't getting sick."

"Hell, no," Grandpa said with a laugh. "It's the beads and the power they have. Ben and I felt the same thing many years ago. Coppernol told us that they came from warrior spirits entering our bodies. They will protect you both."

"But you need them more then I do, Grandpa."

"No, Robert. My days are few. You have your whole life ahead of you, and I know you'll need all the power and protection you can get. It's a whole big world out there now. You two will be seeing all kinds of different places and meeting so many different people. You'll be fine, but always remember to help the good people when you can and kick the devil out of the other ones who want to do you wrong."

Ben grabbed the jug of ale on the table, put it to his mouth, and chugged until it was all gone. He set it down and reached for a new one at his side. He pulled the cork and said; "Now the four of us will drink. Then we will talk a bit more. After that, I want you two to walk out that door. Don't come back inside. Robert and I have more to talk about."

We each took turns and drank almost the whole jug. I had never drunk that much before, and I was feeling a little strange.

Robert got out of his chair slowly and walked over to a tall wooden case that stood against the wall. He opened it, reached inside, and brought out his beautiful old musket. He turned toward me and said, "I want you to have this. I ain't fired it since we last fought at Fort Herkimer. I have killed many Indians and Tories with this. Now it is yours. I want you to take care of it, and keep it as nice and clean as I have over these many years. She can shoot a man one hundred feet away."

Ben got up, walked to the case, took out his old musket, and gave it to Joshua. He smiled and said, "Now, this is my old musket, and it too is the best one I ever owned. It can shoot a man one hundred and ten feet away."

Robert looked at Ben and said, "Well, you old son of a gun. You know damn well my old musket can outshoot yours."

Joshua and I held these beautiful old muskets and laughed. Grandpa and Ben were really giving it to each other. They turned, looked at us, and started to laugh along with us.

My Grandmother Joanna came in and said, "Now you two had better quit raising so much noise in here. Robert, you know what the doctor said to you. You have to take it easy and rest."

Grandpa smiled at my grandmother. "You know, Joanna, I'll be dead within a week," he remarked. "Why should I worry about resting? Hell, I can rest up on the hill behind us for the rest of eternity. For now I'll laugh and enjoy my old friend Ben here and my grandson. He is taking over where I have left off. And Joshua here is doing the same after his old grandfather Ben here. They are heading west and who-knows-where, and I feel damn good about it. Now I can die knowing my blood is heading west and has the same damn feelings I had seventy-six years ago in Flintshire, Wales. So don't you worry, Joanna. I just may stay around and wait to see how his life turns out."

Joanna shook her head and said, "You're right, Robert. I know you have seen your favorite grandson take the life you have had. That is good, I know, but you must still take it easy a little."

Robert smiled and said, "You're right, as always, Joanna. I will calm down, but what these two young men will see and do together is exciting."

Ben spoke up. "Don't worry, Joanna. The boys are leaving now."

Joanna smiled and walked out, closing the door behind her. Grandpa Flint and Ben just stood there. I could see tears in their eyes. I knew this would be the last time I would see them both. I was choked up and couldn't say a word. Neither could Joshua.

It was dead quiet in that room. The sun cast an eerie light upon both of the old men. I saw them smile at us. I walked over to Grandpa, put my arms around him, and held him tight, as he did me for a minute or so. I backed up and said, "Grandpa, I love you, and I will always remember you. I'll wear these beads and hang onto your musket until I die with it in my hands."

Joshua also hugged his grandpa and thanked him. Then we both turned and walked out the door, closing it behind us. We didn't say a word to anybody; we just walked out the front door and headed for the old stockade. We sat on some empty barrels and pulled out a jug of ale that we had kept hidden. I grabbed the jug and said, "I don't know about you, but I feel like I just lost a good friend. I'm going to miss that man and your grandpa. There ain't never gonna be nobody like them ever again."

Joshua wiped his nose on his shirt and said, "You got that right, Robert. I don't wanna stay around here anymore. I know my grandpa will die soon."

"Well, Joshua, I don't either, but we must. We just gotta be here to see them bury Grandpa. Then we will leave. We'll take our horses, a couple of packhorses, and some supplies and just head southwest like Grandpa told us to."

"Good," Joshua approved. "We'll leave after they are both buried. What do you think it will be like out there, Robert?"

"Well, I think we'll see a lot of towns being built," I answered, "and if we get into the Allegheny Mountains in Pennsylvania, we won't see many people at all. I heard that

Kentucky is still wilderness. Then we can move further west and see the Ohio River. I guess it goes into the Mississippi River. We had better see what happens first out there. My grandpa told me about his uncle and how he bought this ship. He was going to buy a big farm in Virginia. He always wanted to go there, but he never did because of the wars here. Maybe we can go down that way and see if we can find any of his kinfolk. I know there are big farms there; they call them plantations, I think."

"Damn, Robert. We sure got a lot of trails to follow, don't we? But let's go see the Mississippi River first. Then we can go look for your kin."

"All right, then," I declared. "Let's do that first, and maybe we can work enough to help pay our way there. But for now, we will stay here and get what we need. I know Father will let us have some supplies and some money."

"I have some money from working on Nelson's farm, so we'll be okay for a while," Joshua added.

"Well, Joshua, sounds like our grandpas were right about us," I said with a laugh. "We have the itch, and I know they will be watching over us."

"I believe you're right, Robert," Joshua said with a nod. "I truly do."

George Washington's Tour of the Valley

During the summer of 1783, word spread quickly that General George Washington was coming to the valley. He wanted to see the Mohawk Valley where so many brave men had died fighting for our freedom. Joshua and I knew we had to go to Canajoharie and see this great man. We had heard that he would be there on the seventeenth of September, so we made sure we would be there also. I only wished my Grandfather Robert could've ridden with us, but he was not strong enough anymore to leave his bed. I wanted to see him again, but my grandmother told me that it wasn't what he wanted. I knew he wouldn't live much longer.

The day we all hated to see came on September 10, 1783, when Robert Flint passed away in his sleep. I wanted to cry, but I knew he wouldn't want that from me, so I stayed strong and kept my chin up. We buried my grandfather as he wished, behind the old log cabin on the hill. We also placed the huge boulder over his grave, which was the only marker he wanted. We put a new split rail fence around the old cemetery and made sure none of the livestock could get inside. Every day Ben would walk up that hill, sit on that boulder and just talk to my grandfather like he was sitting there with him. I guess maybe he was. I knew Grandpa was happy and spending time with Coppernol, General Herkimer, and his old friend Sir William Johnson. Sometimes I could hear Ben half drunk yelling, "Robert, you old son-of-a-gun, I'll be with ya all soon. Just wait a little longer."

I knew Ben wanted to die soon. He was a changed man after Grandpa died. He would walk to the old stockade or to the furniture shop that they had built years ago and talk away to himself.

My Grandmother Joanna took it well. She was a strong woman, always busy with my cousins and their children. She would say to me, "Robert, when are you and Joshua going to leave and head west?"

I told her, "Joshua and I are going to see George Washington first. Then we're heading out to Kentucky and Tennessee."

She had mixed feelings about us going, but she knew that Joshua and I were just like our grandpas.

My father wanted to move to the western part of the state by fall. He had bought some land, and there was a house there already, so he was all excited about that.

My father was happy for me and said, "You just remember what your grandfather told you and Joshua. You also know how I feel about it. Just be very careful about who you meet and talk to. The world is changing and there are many men who will try to take all that you own or worse."

"I know, Father," I assured him. "We won't trust a soul until we have known them for some time. We will be fine."

The day came to say good-bye to my family. Joshua and I had our horses and packhorses ready to go. It was hard to leave, but we knew that we had to go our own way. I told them we would see George Washington in Canajoharie, and then we would head toward Albany and then south-west. I told my father, "I'll come back here to see every-body someday, and then we'll come out and see you, Father."

"That's what your grandfather said to his family many years ago," Father laughed, "and he never did."

"But you aren't all the way across the ocean like he was," I pointed out.

"No, I won't be," he agreed, "but once you and Joshua get south or wherever, it will seem like you are. Try to write once in a while and let me know where you're at or if you need me."

"I will, Father, but I can't promise you a letter every year."

"I know, but damn it, it'll be hard for me to get used to you being gone and on your own." My father grabbed me by the shoulders and said, "Make us proud, son, and make your grandfather proud too. He will be watching over you both, I'm sure of that. And I know old Ben will be there with him before the first frost. He is ready to die, and he is even looking forward to it. He is one hell of a man."

We hugged each other, then Joshua got on his horse, and

we waved and yelled good-bye to everyone.

We turned the horses and had started down the road when we heard a shot. We looked, as everybody did, toward the cemetery, and there was old Ben wearing his old buckskins, standing next to Grandpa's grave. He raised his musket over his head and yelled, "You boys be damn careful. If ya have to fight, remember to stand back to back. Don't worry. Old Robert and I will be watching over you for the rest of your lives."

Joshua and I raised our muskets over our heads also and waved them toward Ben.

"We know you will, Ben."

We turned the horses back toward the dirt road, started a trot, and never looked back.

Joshua and I didn't say a word for a mile or so. We both were thinking about our folks and families and old Ben.

I finally broke the silence. "Well, here we go, Joshua. A whole new country is out there, and we will see what we can find."

"I'm glad we're finally going," Joshua replied. "I'll miss everyone, but they all are happy being there and that's good. As for you and me, we're different. Each day I feel like there is something out there that we must do, but I'll be damned if I know what it is yet."

"I know what you're saying," I said with a nod. "I also have a feeling that we are supposed to do something somewhere, but I'll be damned if I know what it is either. I guess the time will come when we'll find out, but for now we'll just keep going until we reach it."

We arrived in Canajoharie late in the afternoon. We rode

into town and tried to find out when General Washington would be coming through. We tied the horses at the edge of town where they could drink and eat some tall grass in the field. The farmer said we could stay there for the night, so we thanked him and walked into town.

The town was as busy as I had ever seen it before. People were hanging flags out on the stores and building a small stage by the new hotel that had just opened. It was a two-story wooden building, set up where all the dirt roads came into one. There were so many people running here and there trying to clean up the streets. We even saw a small band playing on one corner.

"Well, look at this, Joshua," I said.

"Yeah, I ain't never seen so many flags at once," he replied. "I've never seen a band like that either."

"Can ya imagine how big Albany is?" I gasped. "There are a lot of people here, and they say that Albany is twice the size of this town. I don't know if I could be around so many people at once for too long. How about you?"

"No, not me either," Joshua answered, "but it is fun to watch them all running around. Let's walk around some and see when George Washington will be coming into town."

"Let's go into that old trading store down across the street and see if they have anything we may need later."

We walked across the street and into the store. There were many people buying goods and talking to the owner. This was a much larger store than the one in Cherry Valley. It had just about anything a man would want. We decided we wanted some hard candy, so we bought two pieces and were about to pay the storeowner when he said, "You young men are not from around here, are ya?"

I answered, "No, sir, we're from Sprout Brook, and we are heading west, but we want to see General Washington before we move on."

"You look like two men I knew years ago," he stated. "Could ya be related to Robert Flint and Ben Wells?"

"Well, they are our grandfathers. I'm Robert Flint the Third, and this here is Ben Well's grandson, Joshua. My grandfather Robert Flint died the other day, and Ben Wells is old and will not live much longer."

"Well, I'll be damned," the man gasped. "I thought you might be kin to them great men. Hell, we fought together many years ago. Those two men and that Mohawk Indian could really fight. I hope Robert is at peace now. He did so much for all these people, even if they don't know him."

"How much for the hard candy, sir?" Joshua asked.

"You boys don't owe me a cent," the man insisted. "Here, take a big handful and don't worry about it. It is the least I can do for two young men whose grandpas were my good friends."

"Thank you, sir," I said, "and we will enjoy this candy on the trail going west."

"Well, you two just be darn careful out there," he warned. "It is still pretty wild country, and there is always somebody who will try and take advantage of you. You do as your grandfathers used to do."

"What is that, sir?" I wondered.

"I heard them say it many a time before a fight," he recalled. "Robert would tell Ben, 'If all hell lets loose and they start coming at us, just stand back to back.' And ya know, boys, they would do just that, and they both would come out of it without a scratch. So you just remember that. When the going gets tough, just stand back to back and fight like hell."

Joshua and I listened to this man, and we told him we would do just that if the time comes. We thanked him for the candy, said good-bye, and walked out of his store. We headed over to a huge old oak tree and sat down next to it in the shade.

I said, "Well, he was a nice man. I'm sure glad for all this hard candy he gave us. I hope all the men we meet are as nice as he is, but I doubt they will be."

Joshua was sucking on his rock candy. He took it out of his mouth and said, "That is something, what he said about our grandpas. They must have been a couple of mountain lions when they were our age. Hell, with them fighting like they did, it's a wonder they weren't killed by them Indians and all."

"Well, you heard the man say how they stood back to back and fought. I guess it works. They sure were never hurt too badly that I know of."

We sat there sucking on that rock candy for an hour, watching all the people doing their daily chores. We decided to walk back down the street and try to find out what time General Washington was coming the next day. We heard people saying that the general would arrive by eleven o'clock, and that he was going to stand in the center of town and make a speech to the people. Joshua and I looked for a tree or something to stand on so we could get a better view of this American hero. We found a large tree that would be a great place to see and hear him, and we decided we would get there early with the horses. When he left, we could head downstream by the Mohawk.

"Joshua, what do you think the general will say to all these people?" I asked.

"I bet ya he'll tell them how thankful he was for all their fightin' and helping to keep the British from setting up a stronghold around here," Joshua answered.

"Yeah, I can hear him speaking real loud and telling everyone how hard we all fought through the years. I wish our grandpas were here to see him and even talk to him."

Joshua broke out into a laugh just like his grandpa always did and said, "Maybe that ain't a good thing for them to do. If Robert was still alive and Grandpa Ben being the way he is, they would be talking the general's ears off with all their years' worth of stories about fighting. They would end up complaining like crazy to General Washington about how he should have fought the war."

We sat up in that old oak tree and laughed for nearly ten minutes. The sun was starting to set over the Mohawk River and disappear into the hills on the other side. We decided we had better get a small fire started and cook up some rabbit we had shot earlier. We hoped we could still find small game along our way to wherever we were heading. We had some money, but we knew we had to be careful about how we spent it. We hoped we could find some work along the way that would earn enough money to keep us in powder, shot, flour, and maybe even some sugar.

Joshua had the rabbit about cooked through, and it sure

smelled good. We knew it might be a day before we could go and shoot some turkey or rabbit again. Small game was hard to find in this area. The war had people over-hunting along the river, and it was going to take a few years for things to get back to the way they were.

As we sat next to the warm fire, we finished the last of the rabbit and shared some rock candy.

Joshua said, "Well, Robert, here we are. Our first night together and on our own. Don't it seem funny not seeing our family around or being in our homes?"

"Yeah, I have been thinking of that too," I agreed. "But ya know, we have been talking about this ever since we were about ten years old. We are finally going where we want to. It'll be hard for a while, but we'll be fine. There is so much to see and do out West. I know that somewhere there is something for us, and we'll have to decide then and there if we want to do it. I sure wish to hell I knew what it was, but I guess I'm like my Grandpa Robert. He always knew that there was something waiting for him to do. Well, I guess I have the same feelings deep inside. When we come across it, we'll sure know it."

"Maybe I got my crazy old grandpa's instinct in me too," Joshua replied. "Oh, Robert, can ya even think that we may be like them?"

"Damn, ya know, Joshua, I'm beginning to think that," I said with a laugh. "If that is so, then we'll be in all kinds of trouble. Every time our grandpas were together they would get into all kinds of crazy situations. But the good side is that it was never their fault. Those two and old Coppernol sure as hell got out of it one way or the other."

We both laughed for a long time. We started telling each other all the stories that had been passed down from our grandpas to our fathers. We both wondered how it was back then. Those must have been some rough times, but those stories made us feel strong and wise.

The fire was really putting out the heat, and we decided we had better get some sleep. We knew the morning would bring some fine day, and the story would be told over and over for years.

We were awakened early by the sounds of people coming down the dirt road in wagons and on horseback. Children were yelling, all excited about seeing and hearing General George Washington.

Joshua stood up, still covered in his blanket, and said, "Well, Robert, this is the big day for everybody."

"Yes, Joshua," I agreed. "I'm a little excited myself. You know, Washington coming here will be good for the valley. They fought and had hard times for so many years. They will start feeling that their lives will finally get back to normal."

"We'd better get some breakfast and get up in this tree," Joshua replied.

We ate our breakfast of ham and eggs that we had brought from the farm. We had hoped that we could eat like this on our travels, but we both knew that there might be times we'd be going without. But we didn't worry about that for too long. We knew we could survive one way or the other.

It was about eleven o'clock in the morning, and the September sun was feeling mighty good after a chilly night under that old oak tree. We were sitting up in the tree with a great view of the place where Washington would be speaking to the people. Off in the distance we heard a few muskets fire, and we knew that meant Washington and some of his regulars were coming into town. Within a few minutes we heard the fifes and drums becoming louder and louder. We could see the dust from the dry road rising above a few cabins near the center of town.

Then Joshua yelled out, "Here they come, Robert! Look over there!"

"I see them," I said. "Just look at those fifes and drums. There must be twenty men playing there."

"I can see maybe thirty regulars behind them now," Joshua said. "There he is! I see General Washington. He's riding his big white horse. He is sure a tall man in that saddle, Robert."

The fifes and drums had turned the corner near the old store, followed by the regular army. They wore their blue uniforms and marched in step. I hadn't ever seen anything like this before. Then came General Washington, riding his beautiful white horse. He was waving to all the people on both sides of the street. There was a wagon in the center of the street that he was to stand upon when he spoke to the people. The fifes and drums took their positions around the wagon. The regulars made a complete circle around it as well. Then General Washington got off his horse and walked very slowly toward the wagon.

"Robert, did ya ever think that General Washington was so tall?" Joshua asked.

"No, I didn't," I replied, "but he sure looks great in that

fancy uniform."

General Washington climbed the steps to the wagon and took off his hat and waved it around in circles above his head. All the people became quiet. The general put his hat back on and one of his aides gave him a paper to read.

"My dear true friends," he began, "I'm so very happy and honored to be here with you on this fine September day. I have been waiting for many years to come to this beautiful Mohawk Valley. I've been told every one of you fought and many died in this valley for our freedom. We could never have gained our freedom if it hadn't been for the men in this valley. You fought with hardly any powder and shot, and there were times many of you had no food to eat. But I knew when I was in the South that you strong people would survive and help turn the tide of this war.

"Now your time has come. We have our own country. We can rebuild our homes, restock our shops, and get this great country growing. The new age is upon us, and every one of you here today can be proud of it. We all must begin to help this country grow strong. We must never let any other foreign power come onto our land and try to take it from us. We are a new nation, and we will always be a strong nation because of people like you.

"I also have here a letter signed by many generals who had fought in this valley. They told me of two men who were the heart and soul of this valley. They fought in the French and Indian War here. Their names are Robert Flint and Ben Wells, and their Mohawk Indian friend and brother Coppernol. Are these men here?"

Joshua and I both yelled from the tree we were sitting in.

General Washington looked toward us in the tree and said, "You two young men come here."

Joshua and I climbed down the tree and ran over to the wagon.

General Washington asked, "Do you know these three men of whom I speak?"

"Yes sir, General, they were our grandpas," I said proudly. "I'm Robert Flint the Third, grandson of Robert Flint, and this here is Ben Wells grandson, Joshua Wells."

"I have heard stories of your grandfathers and how they had fought with General Herkimer and Sir William Johnson," General Washington told us. "They are legends. How are they both doing?"

"My Grandpa Robert died a few days ago," I told the general, "but Ben Wells is still alive and just as crazy as he ever was, but in a good way. Coppernol died some years back."

"I'm sorry to hear that," General Washington said, "but I knew they were quite old. I want to give you two young men these Medals of Honor. Your grandfathers were great men, and I sense that you two have their spirit. Please accept these medals on behalf of your grandfathers."

General Washington handed the medals to us, shook our hands, and saluted us. The people all cheered. Joshua and I didn't know what to say.

Finally, I said, "We thank you for this honor, sir, but Joshua and I will not be going back home. We are heading west to make our own life somewhere, so we really shouldn't accept the medals."

General Washington shook his head. "You're wrong

about that. Your grandfathers would be proud of you for keeping these medals for them. They know that you are also pioneers, and that every day you look at them you will remember how they helped this country. Keep them and be proud. Young men like you are the new pioneers of this country. You are the new blood of this nation, and you know what is right and wrong when you come upon it. You have their blood in your veins and that, Joshua and Robert, is what will guide you through life."

Joshua and I looked into this great man's eyes, and we knew he was speaking the truth. We had this strange feeling going through our bodies, and we both knew that something had changed within us. We knew that out there in the West, or wherever we went, there was something we had to do. We didn't know what it was, but we'd discover it when we came upon it.

We shook General Washington's hand and thanked him again. As we walked down the steps, the people cheered us and slapped us on our backs. We were almost across the street when we heard General Washington say to the people, "Now, my dear friends, there goes our future, and may God bless them and all of you."

Joshua and I turned around and watched General Washington climb off the wagon. The fifes and drums started to play again, and the regulars took their positions. The general got back on his beautiful white horse, looked over to where we were standing, and saluted us again. He then turned his horse toward the road heading up to Fort Plain. As he rode out of town, the dust from the road lifted up over the small buildings. Within a few minutes they were gone from sight, but we could still hear the fifes and drums in the distance.

As we stood there in the middle of the street, the old shopkeeper walked over to us and said, "Well, my friends, there goes the greatest man this country has ever known. We'll never see him again, but we will read about him until the day we die. You two must feel honored by the general's words and those great medals."

"We don't know what to say," I answered. "We are very honored by all of this. We never dreamed something like this would happen to us. We're only nineteen years old."

The old shopkeeper said, "Well, your grandpas said that same thing many years ago. They knew this country was going to be free one day, and they both lived to see it, just like I did. But you two have other paths to follow, not fighting for the nation's freedom, but for another freedom to be won. I don't know what it is, but something tells me that you will find it someday."

I said, "That's the hard part. What is it that we will do?"

The old storekeeper smiled. "God will let you know in time," he assured us. "You see, that's what life is all about. You'll always wonder what you should do and when. Let your heart and soul tell you, and follow what they say. Your gut feelings are always right. So what are you two going to do now?"

Joshua and I looked at each other, then at the man. "We're heading southeast, then maybe into Virginia," I told him. "I had a great, great uncle may have had a large farm there. My grandfather always wanted to see his uncle, but all the wars he fought in kept him from going and finding him. So we'll try and locate his family."

"You two already have a mission to accomplish," the shopkeeper stated. "You must go and do it, and maybe by then you'll know what your purpose in life is."

Joshua turned to me and said, "You know, Robert, he's right. Maybe this is what we must do. Maybe we will find it down south, and maybe your great, great uncle has kin still living there."

"You're right, Joshua," I concurred. "Then it is decided here and now. We'll head down to Virginia and find him or his kinfolk."

The old shopkeeper nodded. "That is a long way to travel," he said. "I'll tell you what I'm going to do for you two. Come into my shop, and I'll give you both plenty of food, powder, shot, and whatever else you may need. And don't you worry about paying me a cent. I want to do this for you two; your grandfathers did so much for me. I have no sons and no one to give the shop to, so I don't give a damn about the money. I will feel better knowing that I gave supplies to people I know rather than to some strangers. Bring your horses around back. I don't want everybody in town knowing I'm giving you all these supplies for nothing."

We walked over to where we were keeping the horses and packed up all our gear.

"You know, Robert, this shopkeeper is a good man," Joshua said. "I feel kind of funny letting him give us these supplies for nothing."

We got the horses tied out back of the store and went inside. The old shopkeeper had just about everything a man would want for supplies. He stood there with a big smile on his face and said, "Well, there you go, men. If it ain't in there, then I ain't got it." He let out a hardy laugh.

"We don't know what to say to your kindness," I said. "There are enough supplies here to take us clear across the Mississippi River."

"Hell, boys, you never know," the old man replied. "Maybe you will have to go across the Mississippi to get out of trouble. Your grandpas had to circle many miles to go around trouble, but half the time they just stood there and fought their way out."

We got all the supplies loaded onto the packhorses. When it was time to leave I said to the shopkeeper, "We can never repay you for all of these supplies."

The old shopkeeper scratched his chin, smiled, and said, "You already have. You two coming into my shop telling me you're Robert Flint's and Ben Wells's grandsons is all I needed. You see, I never had the chance to tell your grandfathers how thankful I was for them saving my scalp so many years ago. Now I can pay my debt to them by helping you. You two go and make your way to Virginia. Start making your own lives and many stories to come, so when ya get old like me you can sit around and remember the old days. May God bless you two and may you trust each other to the end."

The old storekeeper had tears running down into his gray beard. He took each of our hands and gave us a leather pouch of silver. He then turned and went inside the store so quickly that we never had a chance to thank him or say good-bye.

Albany

We didn't say a word for nearly an hour after we left the old storekeeper. Our minds were busy thinking about all that had taken place that day. The horses kept walking along the road, heading south out of Canajoharie toward Albany. We followed the Mohawk River down, planning to branch off to Albany. The sun was starting to feel much warmer, and we knew it was close to two o'clock in the afternoon. The sun moved in and out of the huge clouds in the sky. There was no sign of rain, and we were glad about that.

I picked up the pace of my horse and came up alongside Joshua. "Do you believe this?" I laughed. "We've got hundreds of pounds of supplies and pockets full of silver, and we ain't never been this far from home before."

"I know," Joshua said with a nod. "I've been thinking about that since we left town. I know we are doing the right thing and all, but sometimes I can't help but wonder."

"Well, I look at it this way," I said. "My father is moving out to the western part of New York, and he sure don't need me there. There isn't any adventure out there for me."

"You're right, Robert," Joshua agreed. "There isn't anything back home for me either. I'm not a farmer, and I sure as hell get bored easy. Maybe the old storekeeper was right about us. He said we have our grandfathers' blood in our veins, and they sure as hell didn't sit around the farms too much."

As we talked and rode along the river, we saw many boats and people heading north. They rode in wagons, stringing their cows behind them as the passed us by on the Old Kings Highway.

"Joshua, look at all these people heading up the road and river," I pointed out. "They will be building new houses and farms all over up there. I don't know if I would like that too much, but our families own a lot of land, so they ain't gonna be next to them."

"I bet ya old Grandpa Ben will be complaining about that," Joshua said with a smirk. "He ain't the type of man who likes too many people around him."

We both laughed out loud.

"He'll run up to where Grandpa Robert is buried and start telling him about all these people coming in," I remarked. "He'll go on and on for an hour about that."

Again, we laughed and Joshua said, "Hell, I feel pretty damn good now. How about you?"

"I do now," I told him. "I will never ask if we are doing the right thing or not again."

"Me neither, Robert," he promised. "Let's just think about our future down the road and let whatever happens

happen. We always know that our grandpas are watching over us."

We kept up the slow trot as we had done since we'd left Canajoharie. Our whole lives were ahead of us, and we were in no damn hurry to get there.

It was getting close to late afternoon when we decided to set up camp near the Mohawk River. It seemed pretty quiet off the main dirt road and away from people traveling on the east. Joshua got the fire started, and I began making some biscuits. I added some dried beef to one of the new large cast iron pots that the old shopkeeper had given us. I knew I would have to cure the new black cooking pot, but I would do that some other night.

We were almost done eating when Joshua said, "Well, Robert, which way will we be heading tomorrow?"

"I was thinking about following the Mohawk River until when we get into Albany, and then following the Hudson River to New York," I suggested. "Then if we can follow the Rareton River, it will get us to Trenton. After that, we could head south until we can maybe get a canoe or raft and go down the Chesapeake Bay, which will finally get us into Norfolk, Virginia."

"That sounds fine with me," Joshua replied. "How long do ya think it'll take to get to Norfolk?"

"Well, according to my Grandpa Robert, he and my uncle had horses and they left Norfolk and got to Albany in one month. But hell, Joshua, that was way back in 1723 or so. I bet the old road or path is a lot faster now than when they came to Albany."

"So maybe by first frost we can be there?"

"That is what I had been figuring on."

"That would be good. I don't want to get caught in an early snow up here. But they say it is warmer down that way, and that I would like. I don't care for that bone-chilling cold anymore."

We were just about done with our supper when we heard a noise coming from the brush near the river

I turned to Joshua and said, "Get your musket ready just in case it's somebody who travels this road and robs people."

Joshua held up his musket, ready for anything. I grabbed one of the burning sticks from the fire and edged my way toward the riverbank. Joshua was right behind me, calm as could be. As I got closer to the riverbank, I saw a dog or part wolf pup limping down along the water's edge.

"It's only a dog or wolf," I said. "I can't tell yet. Bring that torch down closer to me."

Joshua sat down next to me, and we could see that it was a young wolf pup. He was whimpering and looked like he was in bad shape. I carefully scooped the little animal up in my arms.

"Let's get him back to fire and look him over."

When Joshua and I got back to the campfire, we could see him more clearly. He was barely one year old, and he had a beautiful gray coat of fur. He was not cut and nothing seemed broken, but he looked almost starved to death.

Joshua lit one of the oil lamps. I took my blanket and laid it on the ground next to the fire and placed the pup on it.

"Look at him, Robert," Joshua said, awestruck. "He's

beautiful, and he's not afraid of us at all. I bet ya he got separated from his mother up in those rocky cliffs. He's probably thirsty and hungry."

While I was looking him over real good, Joshua got some food and put it in a tin bowl. He put the bowl down in front of the pup, and as soon as he did, the pup got the smell of it and started to eat. Joshua and I just sat there watching this little wolf pup eating and making all kinds of noise.

We both started to laugh. The pup gobbled up everything that was in the bowl and then looked over at us, begging for more.

"That is enough for you tonight," I told him. "We'll feed ya some more in the morning."

"Well, Robert," Joshua commented, "it looks like we have our first new friend. What should we do with this little guy?"

"I decided as soon as I picked him up that we would keep him," I answered. "He will be treated real well, and we can train him to protect us and our supplies. He is little now, but I bet he'll get real big and strong."

We took turns petting our new companion and then watched him walk around.

It was getting late, and we decided we had better get some sleep. We covered the wolf to keep him warm and hoped he would still be there in the morning. We figured if he spent the night with us, he would never leave us.

The fire grew smaller, but the embers kept us plenty warm throughout the night.

We awoke to another beautiful September day. It was already warm, and it was only about seven o'clock. I could tell it would be a hot day, but we were close to the river, so we could always jump in for a quick swim to cool off.

I sat up and looked at Joshua. He had a big grin on his face.

"What are you all smiles about this morning, Joshua?"

He pointed down by my feet. I looked down and saw the wolf pup with just his head sticking out from under my blanket.

"Well, I'll be damned," I said. "He did stay with us all night. I never felt him move."

"Looks like we have a new traveling partner," Joshua remarked. "Now we have to give him a name."

"I ain't even thought about that," I said. "Have you got a name figured out for him?"

Joshua sat there for a few minutes, thinking real hard. I could always tell when Joshua got to really thinking; he would get this look on his face like he was in another world. I always thought it was funny how he did that. He looked just like his Grandpa Ben.

"I got it!" he finally shouted. "We'll call him Half-moon."

"Where did ya come up with a name like that?" I wondered.

"Well, the moon was half full last night," Joshua explained, "and I think we are near this place they call Half-moon. So I figured, why not?"

I let out a laugh. "You do come up with some good ideas, Joshua, and this is the best one yet. Then it is settled."

I picked Halfmoon up, raised him high over my head, and yelled out, "From this day on, you will be called Halfmoon. And you will be with us until the end of time. You will be our protector, and in return, we will love you, feed you, and take care of you like Joshua and I take care of each other."

Halfmoon let out his first bark. He must have sensed what all this was about. He started to wag his tail and bark even louder. I put him back down on the blanket, and he jumped around looking so happy.

Joshua had gotten some food for Halfmoon to eat and the pup waited patiently until it was put in a small tin bowl. The bowl was really too big for him, but we knew that he would grow into it. Joshua and I sat and played with him for nearly an hour.

"Well, we'd better get packed up here and get going," I said.

"I'll keep Halfmoon in this big side basket we've got here," Joshua suggested. "He is too small to walk for a long time now. Later, we'll get him to follow us for a while. He'll need to get use to how we do things and all."

Joshua put Halfmoon in the big side basket on the pack horse, and the pup sat in there with his front paws hanging over the top, looking like he had been doing this forever. He saw us getting on our horses and let out a few barks, telling us he was ready and he knew he had found a home.

Joshua and I laughed every time we looked back at him; he was so darn cute sitting in that big basket.

"Joshua, I think Halfmoon thinks he is some kind of a special wolf."

"I'll bet he does," Joshua agreed. "I got this gut instinct that the three of us will be spending many years together."

It was late in the afternoon when we finally reached the edge of Albany.

I asked Joshua, "Do you want to find a place in town or should we stay on the outskirts for the night?"

"I think we'd be better off staying out here," he answered. "I ain't much on too many people around, and we need to get Halfmoon used to us first without all the strange noises of the town and all."

We rode a bit closer to Albany and found a quiet place next to the river. We knew further down river the current got real swift, and that there were some rapids before it entered the Hudson River. We started a campfire and cooked the last of the fresh meat we had brought with us. We knew we would have to kill a rabbit or turkey in a day or so, but we could always buy fresh meat in the many trading posts along the roads.

Halfmoon sat there licking his chops. He knew he was going to eat again, and we knew we could never fill his stomach. He was like any animal—they always eat and never get full.

While we were eating and Halfmoon was licking the last of his food, Joshua said, "I wonder how much he weighs."

"I don't really know," I replied. "I'd say he is near fifteen pounds. Maybe we can find some scales in one of the trading posts tomorrow and weigh him."

"I wonder how big he'll get."

"Grandpa Robert told me once that when he and Ben were in the North Mountains they saw some wolves that must have weighed a hundred pounds or better."

"That's pretty big," Joshua commented. "We won't be able to feed him enough, will we?"

"We will do our best, but he'll hunt on his own in time. I'd rather feed him, though. I don't want him running too far away from us. You never know when some hunters might see him and shoot him just for the fun of it."

"That better not happen," Joshua warned. "I will kill any man who tries to kill or even hurt him."

"I'd be right there with ya, that's for damn sure."

We settled in for the night. The moon was almost full, and the sky was very clear. Halfmoon crawled under my blanket and curled up next to my feet. He had already started to adjust to our routine. I looked over at Joshua and said, "I'll bet this wolf was a gift from Coppernol. Maybe old Coppernol has come back to life as this here wolf. I would hope so. Maybe Grandpa Robert met up with Coppernol and told him what the two of us were doing."

"I was kind of wondering that also," Joshua stated. "Now we have Halfmoon and the stones our Grandpas gave us. We should be really protected."

I patted Halfmoon on his head and he sort of groaned. I knew he felt safe and content.

The early morning sun didn't stay out too long. Thick clouds started to form right after we got the horses packed and ready to move.

"I hope the rain holds off until we get into Albany," I said. "We might have to rent a place in a stable for the night if there's a downpour."

We tied up Halfmoon in his basket and made sure he wouldn't jump out. I didn't think he would, but being a young wolf pup, it was hard to be sure what he'd do.

As we rode into Albany, we saw that the place was busy. There were horses hooked up to wagons that were full of supplies from the boats on the river. We rode near the water and saw at least twenty ships tied up at the old docks.

"You know, Joshua, my grandpa and grandma started the first delivery service here," I stated. "My grandfather once told me that when he was sixteen, he and my Great Uncle John built the shop and warehouse. But looking at all these buildings now, he wouldn't even know which one it was."

"I wonder what it looked like way back then," Joshua said. "I can't imagine what this place was like with all these buildings not here."

We started to ride up the street and were about to turn the corner when I saw an old sign on the side of a building that said FLINT'S SUPPLIES AND DELIVERY SERVICE. I yelled to Joshua, "Look at that sign! That it has to be where Grandpa Robert had his store. Let's go over there and see what we can find out."

We wove our way through the crowded streets and finally got to the front of the store. Joshua stayed with Halfmoon and the horses while I went inside.

I walked inside the store and looked around. A man about my age approached me and said, "May I help you find something?"

"I sure hope so," I replied. "My friend and I noticed the old sign on the side of the building here saying it was

Flint's Supply and Delivery Service. By any chance was this store owned by Robert Flint many years ago?"

"Why, yes it was," he answered. "Mr. Flint sold it to my grandfather way back in 1739, and it's been in the family ever since then. I own it now. Why do you ask?"

"My name is Robert Flint the Third; I'm the grandson of Robert Flint, the one who used to own it."

"Well, I'll be darned. My name is Patrick O'Riley. It is sure good to meet you, Robert. I tell you, business is really booming now that the war is over. There are people coming up this way all the time and heading into the Mohawk Valley to settle and start farming. I'm trying to get as many supplies as I can from New York, but it's a little slow. I got a few men who want some supplies taken to the lower Susquehanna River. They are opening up a big trading post there. They tell me that many new settlers are coming up the river there, going into the western part of Pennsylvania, and moving up into New York."

"Why don't they just come up the Hudson and overland to the Mohawk River?" I wondered.

"They tell me they can save a lot of time and money by coming the other way," he explained. "I don't know. I've never been out of Albany."

We talked for a few more minutes, then Joshua walked in and said, "Oh, there you are, Robert. I thought ya got lost or something."

"No, I just have been here talking to Patrick. He was telling me that my grandfather sold this business to Patrick's grandfather back in 1739. So the sign we saw on the building was my grandfather's."

"Well, that is something. We are here where it all started for your grandfather."

"Patrick was telling me how busy he is, and about a few men who have a new trading post company out in Pennsylvania. They are starting up a good-sized business out there, and they can only get supplies from up here in Albany."

Patrick shook hands with Joshua. "So where are you fellows heading?" Patrick asked.

"We're thinking about going to the same place you have been telling me about, then heading down into Virginia," I answered. "We're gonna try to locate the place where my great uncle lived and see if he has kinfolk that may still be there. But nothing's set in stone. Why do you ask?"

"I was thinking that if you two were heading that way, you might like to work for me," Patrick said. "Maybe you could take two large wagonloads of supplies to these men. They have plenty of money, and I can pay you half of the cost to haul everything there. When you arrive, they could pay you the other half. They've already given me five hundred dollars to get someone to make the trip there, but there isn't anyone around here who wants to head out in that wild country now that the war is over. They just want to go up the Mohawk and start a new life."

Joshua asked, "Why don't anyone want to move away from all these people and this hectic life?"

"Well, there are rumors that there are thieves and just plain nasty men who sometimes attack the lonely settlers and all," Patrick explained. "Those are just rumors, but I guess they could be true."

"Well, there is always danger lurking someplace," I remarked. "But the money does sound real good to me. What do you think, Joshua?"

"I don't know," he answered. "Maybe we had better sleep on it for the night before we decide. We'll let you know tomorrow, Patrick."

"That sounds fair to me," he acknowledged. "Do you two have a place to stay the night?"

"No, we just got into town and haven't had a chance to decide where to bed down," I told him. "We may look for a stable someplace, I guess."

"To heck with the stables," Patrick scoffed. "You two will stay here for the night. Up above the store are two beds and everything you'll need. Plus there is room for your horses and packhorses out back."

Joshua smiled. "Now that is the best news we've had in a few days," he said. "Heck, yes, we'll stay here."

All of a sudden we heard Halfmoon let out a loud bark. We ran outside and saw a man looking at him and our horses. He had a rough and a funny way about him.

I yelled out to him, "What in hell are you doing by our horses, mister?"

"I was just looking," he muttered. "I ain't gonna steal nothin' from ya."

Joshua walked off the store porch and approached him. "Now that is for damn sure," he snapped. "You'd better get away from these horses and our wolf or you'll be sorry."

"You ain't gonna tell me to do a damn thing, boy!" the man growled back. "You'd better mind your tongue or I'll cut it out of your head."

As the man reached behind his back to grab his knife,

Halfmoon broke loose from his rope, jumped out of his basket, and lunged straight for the man's neck. He had his young teeth into his throat before any of us could stop him. He knocked the man to the ground, and he was snarling like hell.

I quickly ran over and yelled, "Let go, Halfmoon. Sit!"

Halfmoon let go of the man's neck, sat back, and growled at him. The man was reaching for his knife again, but Joshua stomped hard with his boot onto the man's hand. We could hear the bones break as he did it. Joshua weighed close to two hundred pounds, and he was big and strong like his Grandfather Ben.

Joshua spoke calmly to the man, "I told you, mister, to leave and not start any trouble with us. Now you'd better get to your feet and be gone, or I'll let the wolf finish what he started."

The man got to his feet slowly, and when he stood up, he looked at us and said, "You two have made a deadly mistake. I'll remember this and that damn wolf of yours. Someday I'll kill all three of you real slow."

I'd had enough of this miserable man. I leaned back and came straight down on his nose with the handle of my grandfather's large bowie knife. Blood flew in all directions. The man grabbed his bloody broken nose and ran down the dusty street, swearing and yelling at us.

By then, there were a dozen men standing around, watching all the commotion. One man stepped forward and said, "Damn, you two are a scrapping bunch, aren't ya? Hell, you remind me of a couple of old friends of mine that I fought with in the early wars. They were a fighting bunch

50

just like you two young fellas."

I looked at the man and saw he was near the same age as Ben and my grandfather.

"Well, we hardly ever get into fights," I said, "but when somebody is thinking about stealing from us or hurting our wolf, we will kick somebody's ass if we have to. And I'll tell ya right now, that no good son –of a gun was going to do it."

Another man walked over to us and said he was the town constable. "I saw the whole thing from across the street," he told us. "I've had my eyes on that guy for a few days now. He is known to steal and kill a man for the clothes on his back, but I could never arrest him. He is a slick weasel. I knew he was about to steal from you, and if he did, I would've had the goods on him to put him in jail. But you two took matters into your own hands. He wasn't expecting any of what happened to him, and I tell you, neither was I. There aren't too many men around here who would have done that to him, but I can see you two aren't from around here, are you?"

"No sir," I answered, "We come up by Cherry Valley way. We were just passing through."

"I guess it's true what they say about men like you that have lived up that way."

"What's that?" Joshua wanted to know.

"They say men like you are a tough lot, and that whole valley was a hard fight for the Indians and the British. Hell, they never could control it."

The older man spoke again. "Well, I'll tell ya all something. I fought up there with two men and a Mohawk Indian; the Indian's name was Coppernol. The two men were called Robert Flint and Ben Wells. They were the toughest bastards I ever saw fight, and I tell ya this, I've fought in many battles with them three."

Joshua and I smiled.

"Well, sir," I said, "Robert Flint was my grandfather and Ben Wells is Joshua's grandfather."

The old man let out a crusty old laugh and yelled, "Well, I'll be damned. I told ya all they fought like them."

The constable smiled. "Well, you two did what you had to do. I will not be arresting you. You were just protecting what is yours. And I don't know where you got that wolf from, but after what I saw him do, I'm sure he'll protect you both to his death. I must be on my way now. Don't worry about that man you beat up. I'll try to find him and arrest him, but knowing his kind, he has headed out of Albany and back into the wilderness."

The constable walked away and the crowd dispersed. The old man was the only one left standing there.

"I thought I'd never see two men fight like you two did again," he said wearing a wide grin. "It is good to know that there are still men like you around. Nowadays, the men back off or look the other way. They are too damn busy trying to become rich. They have no grit in themselves. But you two have made me feel damn good about the future in this new country. Your grandfathers must be proud of you. I just want to shake your hands before I leave."

The old man reached out his worn, oversized hand. He still had a hell of a grip. He shook our hands and smiled. "Be strong and God bless both of you," he said, "and even that wolf you got."

He turned and walked away. We could still hear him laughing and talking to himself as he disappeared down the road.

Patrick looked at us and said, "I have never met anybody like you two before. I'll tell you what I'm going to do. I will pay you both another one hundred dollars to take those supplies to Pennsylvania. I know that they will get there, and I'm sure the men there will be very happy with you two. They will want more from me later on, so I'll be able to recoup my wages to you now. The main thing is to get a supply route from here to there. In time it'll be safer for whoever delivers them. This first trip may be tough, but after seeing you two take on, hell, there isn't a question in my mind now. So what do you think about that?"

Joshua and I were petting Halfmoon. We looked at each other and smiled. We both knew that we would do it.

I stood up and extended my hand to Patrick. "Well, Patrick, it looks like you got two men and a wolf to take your supplies to Pennsylvania."

Patrick smiled from ear to ear. "Now that is great," he approved. "Let's close up the shop, go to the inn down the street, and have some good food and a few pints of ale."

Joshua said, "Like my grandfather used to say, that is the best damn news I have heard all day."

We all laughed and Halfmoon barked with excitement.

We led the horses back behind the store and made sure they had water and feed to eat. Patrick showed us the upstairs where we'd be staying for a week or so until all the supplies arrived and were ready to be loaded onto the wagons.

"Well, it has been one hell of day, Joshua," I said. "Here we are where it all started for my grandfather. I wonder what he is saying now about all that happened today."

"I bet ya he is laughing like crazy," Joshua replied. "He and Grandpa Ben are having some ale and saying, 'Well, that's our grandsons for ya.' I can't believe Patrick gave us a job and all that money. The good thing about it is that we were going that way anyway. Now we have a job and money to get us there. Who knows what may happen when we get there? Maybe those men will want us to work for them doing the same thing."

"That's what I have been thinking," I said. "You know, it's funny how things turn out. We were just passing through Albany, and all this has happened in the past three hours. I wonder if our grandfathers ever went through this."

"Knowing them and some of the stories we've heard throughout the years, I wouldn't be surprised."

Patrick came back upstairs and asked us if we were ready to go to the inn. We told him that we were and that we'd leave Halfmoon in the room.

"Good idea," Patrick stated. "The people around here don't know that he is sort of a tame wolf."

Joshua said to Halfmoon, "You stay here. Lie down and relax. We'll be back soon."

Halfmoon walked over to the blanket we had given him and lay down.

As the three of us reached the bottom of the stairs, we could see the streets were finally clearing out. All the merchants that had been there earlier had gone home for the evening. Oil lights hung from each post along the street. An old man was making his way from one light to the next, until they were all lit. I couldn't imagine doing a task like that each night and morning, but I guessed one had to do whatever he could to put food on the table. Still, I knew that this type of work or living in such a large town wasn't for me, and I knew darn well that Joshua would never stay in a town any more than a week. He needed the open spaces just to breathe and be free.

We walked down the dusty street, turned the corner, and found the inn.

"Now you two try to stay out of trouble," Patrick warned as we walked inside. "There are some shady characters that drink in here. Just pay them no mind and there won't be any problems."

Joshua and I laughed and agreed that we would behave.

We found a table and sat down. The place was very busy with all sorts of men. Many were merchants and dock-workers. We could overhear them swearing and complaining about one thing or another.

Joshua said, "This is one reason I don't like to be around so many people. They're always complaining about something. You would think they would all be happy since we are now free from wars and the damned British. I guess most men are never happy about anything."

Patrick laughed. "You aren't used to all this. I grew up hearing it day in and day out. It's nothing. It's just human nature to complain, I guess. They are happy, but when they stop complaining then there is trouble."

The innkeeper came to our table and asked us what we

wanted to eat and drink. He seemed real pleasant as he took our order. He disappeared back to where they were cooking the food and a minute later brought us three large pewter mugs of ale. It didn't take long for us to drink them down and order three more. In the meantime, Patrick got out a map.

"This is the route you will have to take into Pennsylvania," he explained. "It's the only way you can take the wagons. The small town is called Station Point. It is near the Juliana River; the Susquehanna River feeds from this river. The names of the men you are taking the supplies to are Henry Simmons and Luke Roberts. They purchased this land during the war, and now they own maybe two thousand acres there. From what I understand, there are no more than one hundred and twenty people living there, but they seem to think that this whole area will open up soon. With all the new surveys and boundaries being drawn, a man never really knows where anything is. Our new government is working on it as I speak, so it is very critical that you follow the map. There are no signs, or if they were there once, they will be gone by the time you get there."

"How long will it take to get there, Patrick?" I needed to know.

"I've been told it is about one month or so by wagon," he answered. "That's if the weather is good, so it is very important to get there before the first snow falls. In that country you never know how bad things can get. They have given me eight horses to pull the two wagons and they are great horses. They are just down the street at the livery stable. The wagons are the newest that we could find. They are well built and will have everything you'll need for the journey. I also have plenty of food, powder, and shot for you. Now do you have any questions?"

Joshua and I sat there drinking our ale and taking in all the information.

I said, "Well, I can't think of anything right now. How about you, Joshua?"

"There is one small detail," Joshua answered. "I know there ain't no law out there, so what happens if robbers or some wild Indians attack us?"

Patrick smiled. "Well, based on what I saw from you two this afternoon, I truly believe you won't need to find a constable. I'm sure you'll take care of any problems your own way."

The supper we ordered finally came, along with another pint of ale. It sure was good to have a great meal after so many days on the road. None of us talked much more about the upcoming job, but we all had it in the back of our minds.

We got to know more about Patrick. He was a down-to-earth sort of fellow. I knew Joshua liked him from the beginning. He seemed honest in what he told us and he could be trusted, which was all that counted with Joshua and me.

The evening went by without any problems with any of the drunken men at the bar. We didn't pay much attention to all their comments about everybody who walked in. That was just as well. We'd had enough excitement for one day.

It was way after nine o'clock when we finally got back to our room above the shop. Patrick gave us a key for the shop and said he was going home. He'd be back in the morning around seven o'clock. We said our goodnights and parted.

As we entered the room, we heard Halfmoon starting to growl.

"Wait a minute, Joshua," I said. "We'd better start calling Halfmoon by his name so he'll know who in hell we are. I ain't about to just walk in there. He would be on us in a second."

"Halfmoon! Halfmoon!" I called. "It's just us, boy."

He stopped growling and barked, so we were sure that he knew who was on the other side of the door. When we entered, he was very excited and happy to see us again. I had saved some meat for him and he instantly picked up the scent of it.

"You'd better put it in his tin bowl right away, Robert," Joshua told me. "If ya don't, he'll take half your fingers with it."

"Wait a minute, boy," I instructed.

Halfmoon sat down and waited. He was already licking his chops. The meat hardly hit the bottom of his tin bowl before it was gone. In the meantime, Joshua had gotten some more food for our wolf. That was when he finally slowed down to enjoy it.

"I tell ya, Robert," Joshua said. "I'm gonna weigh him tomorrow on Patrick's scales in the store. I think he is gaining a few pounds each day."

"I'm sure he has," I agreed. "I'll tell ya something, Joshua. We'd better have a lot of food for him on this trip. He'll be eating like there is no tomorrow all the time."

We sat in the old chairs, laughing and watching our pet.

When Halfmoon was done eating, he lay down between us on the floor, wagging his tail.

"Now there is a happy wolf," I commented. "I still can't believe he got loose today and was on that stinking thief's throat before I could even blink."

"He sure surprised the hell out of me too," Joshua replied. "He'll have to be tied up real good on a short rope so we can handle him when we are out and around. Once we get out of town with the wagons we can let him walk by himself. He ain't gonna go too far from us now. After what we saw today, it's safe to say he'll be near us all the time."

"That's for sure," I agreed. "He has proven to us even as young as he is that he is our protector. Well, I guess we'd better get to bed now. Tomorrow is going to be a long day. We'll have to see what supplies we'll be taking with us. I know Patrick will want us to help him get everything together and see what we are missing."

"Well, it can rain all night now," Joshua said. "We will be warm and dry for once. I still think it'll rain tonight; I can feel it in the air."

I turned out the oil lamp and told Halfmoon to go to sleep. He was a little uneasy sleeping inside for the first time, but I knew he would have to get used to it sooner or later. I watched him for a minute, and he finally went next to the door and lay down.

"Look at Halfmoon," I said with a laugh. "He ain't taking any chances of somebody coming in here tonight."

Joshua got out of bed and took the blanket that Halfmoon had been sleeping on and set it down by the door. Halfmoon lay down upon it and went to sleep.

It was early morning and I could hear the heavy rain hitting the roof. It was really coming down hard, just as Joshua had expected. I don't know how he knew about the changes in weather, but he was always right. Little did I know how useful this gift would be in the years ahead.

I looked over at the door and there was Halfmoon. He was awake, waiting for us to get up. He was becoming our good friend. I called to him, and he ran over to me and rested his head on my leg. He looked like he had grown just overnight. I had never seen any animal take to us the way he did. I told Halfmoon to go over and wake up Joshua. He looked at me and then jumped on top of Joshua's stomach. I burst out laughing. Joshua tried to sit up, but Halfmoon didn't move.

Joshua yelled out, "Halfmoon, you're too darn big to sit on me! Did Robert teach ya that trick?"

Halfmoon jumped back onto the floor and wagged his tail. Joshua grabbed him around his chest and gave him a big hug.

He then turned to me. "I hope we ain't gotta work out in this rain for too long today."

"I'm sure Patrick won't have us out in this," I stated. "He needs to keep us healthy for this supply train."

I looked around the room and wondered what my grandfather thought about when he lived here. I noticed some writing on the outside wall. "Joshua, come here. Look at this."

Joshua walked across the room. There were my grandfather's and grandmother's names carved into the beam.

Robert Flint and Joanna Bowman
June 1735

"I can't believe what I'm seeing," I gasped. "They came here together way back then. I bet they both forgot they'd carved their names here."

"I bet you they didn't, Robert," Joshua laughed. "This was their private place to go and be alone."

"If these walls could talk," I sighed. "I bet they both talked about their future together here."

"I'm sure they did just that," Joshua agreed. "I think it is great that they had this place to go and get away from everyone."

By the time we ate breakfast and had our coffee, we heard Patrick calling us from downstairs.

I yelled back to him, "We'll be there in a minute."

We made a collar for Halfmoon and attached it to a six-foot rope so we could handle him. We went downstairs and found Patrick busy doing paperwork on some supplies he was checking in.

"Good morning, Robert, Joshua," he greeted. "And good morning to you, Halfmoon. I hope you all slept well and kept warm."

"That's for sure," I replied. "It was good to be in a bed again, warm and dry. Even Halfmoon slept great."

"I've got good news for you," he informed us. "Everything that we need for the trip is in except for some sacks of flour, but they should be here sometime today."

"Does that mean we'll be leaving here in a day or two?" I asked.

"Yes, and that is good for all of us. You'll have a chance of getting there before the first snow if it comes early."

Joshua smiled and said, "That would sure as hell please me. You know I ain't much on this big town life."

"What you can do today is go down to the livery stable and check out those wagons," Patrick told us. "See if they are all right for you. And if you need to do something more to them, just go ahead and do it."

Joshua led Halfmoon over to where the scales were. We finally got him to sit still so we could weigh him.

"Well, I'll be damned, Joshua. How much do ya think he weighs now?"

"I don't know, maybe forty pounds?"

"What kind of wolf have we got here anyway?" I wondered. "He isn't even full-grown yet."

"The only thing I can say is that he has to be sent from Coppernol," Joshua insisted. "After yesterday, how he has understood everything we've said, and now his weight, he must be Coppernol's spirit and our protector."

"Well, no matter what we have here, we both know it is something special, and we will have many stories to tell our grandchildren someday," I declared.

The rain had let up some, so the walk to the stables was not so bad. The mud in the streets was already ankle deep.

When we walked into the stable, an old man came toward us. We told him who we were and what we were there for.

The old man saw Halfmoon and stopped dead in his tracks. "What in hell is that?" he gasped.

"Oh, he is our spirit protector," I answered with a smile.

"Well, you'd better keep him close to you," he said nervously. "He looks mean as hell."

"No, Halfmoon is gentle," I assured him. "Just don't make him mad."

"Well, you sure as hell ain't gotta worry about that. I'll go get me some breakfast and make sure I'm far away from him."

The old man left quickly and Joshua and I laughed. Halfmoon let out a bark.

"We sure can clear a room in a hurry with Halfmoon here, can't we, Joshua?" I remarked.

"We'll never fight again with him around," he replied.

We saw the two wagons, and they were just as Patrick had described them. They were the finest we had ever seen. They were solid oak, and all the steel that kept them together was heavy, extra wide, and well made. They had huge wooden wheels and all the spokes were strong. The canvas covering the wagon was hand-stitched and very tough.

"I have never seen a wagon like this," I responded. "Our grandfathers had strong-built wagons, but these two are so well made that we won't have any problems with them breaking down."

We walked all around the wagons to make sure we were happy with them. Joshua even crawled underneath them, looking for anything that might give us problems down the road.

"They are well-built and very strong," Joshua announced as he got back to his feet. "I think it would be wise if we made a gun rack right behind where we'll be sitting with the reins. We'll need to be able to grab one musket after another to fire if we run into any trouble. I want to be able to fire without reloading."

"Good idea," I agreed. "Let's look around and see if we can find some lumber to build something that will work for us."

It didn't take us long to find some scrap wood lying about the livery. In about three hours, we had cut and set the racks right behind the seats. It was a hell of a good idea, and later we would find out just how good of an idea it was. We also made up two boxes for each wagon where we could store powder and shot, designed to fit tightly under the seat so they would be easy to get at.

While Joshua and I were getting these things ready, we stopped for a minute and watched Halfmoon. He had walked over to where the eight horses stood and was just lying there.

"Well, I'll be," I commented. "The horses are not even afraid of him; this wolf never stops amazing me. I thought for sure that he would spook them, but they are calm as can be."

"I keep telling you, Robert, Halfmoon isn't normal," Joshua replied. "I truly believe he is Coppernol's spirit."

"I think you're right," I told him. "I'll never question that again."

We both laughed and then walked in with the horses and Halfmoon. They were great horses, and it was a good time for all of us to get used to one another. We spent the next hour with them and we even brushed them. They knew we were all going to get along real well.

The old man who ran the livery stable returned.

"Well, I'll be damned," he gasped. "I'm sixty-five years old, and I thought I had seen just about everything, but looking at you two and the horses and that damn wolf ya got all in the same place, well, it ain't natural. I've never seen horses come that close to a wolf before. They can smell wolves a mile away, and then they start to get nervous and take off in the other direction. This is something else."

"Well, sir, we ain't never seen it either, but I tell you something," I said, "I'm damn glad that we all get along. We have a long road to travel, and we'll have to be close and take care of each other."

"When do you want to get the horses and wagons all set to go?" he asked.

"We would like to have them at the store tomorrow," I answered. "Would that be time enough?"

"I don't see any problem with that. I'll be there around seven in the morning."

Joshua and I started to leave, and we called Halfmoon to come with us. He ran to our side and wagged his tail. He seemed excited to be going back to the store, probably because he knew he was going to be fed again.

The rain had finally moved out to the east, and the sun was starting to shine. The streets were still muddy, but the people were moving about. The road would get even muddier with all the foot traffic.

When we got back to the store, Patrick was busy getting all the supplies together.

"Well, what do you think of the wagons and horses?" he asked.

"The wagons are the best we've ever seen," I replied, "and the horses are very strong and healthy. We added a couple of things to the wagons, but all in all, they are just what we'll need. I told the liveryman to have the horses and wagons here tomorrow morning at seven. I figure by the time we load them and get ready to leave, it'll be afternoon. We'll still have good daylight left to be on our way."

"That's all settled then," Patrick announced. "Now I won't have to worry about getting the wagons here along with everything else."

We all helped making sure we had all the supplies and that we had everything we would need for this journey. It was early evening when we decided that we had done all that we could do until the wagons arrived. Patrick was tired and told us he was going straight home. We said goodnight to him and went upstairs to our room.

"Well, Joshua, tomorrow is the day," I said. "I know we are ready to go, and I think Halfmoon is too."

"Why don't we eat here tonight?" Joshua asked "I don't want to go back to the inn. It is all right there, but I just want to stay in tonight."

"I feel the same way," I agreed. "We have plenty to eat, and it is a lot warmer in here than in that drafty inn. Halfmoon would like it better if we stayed here too."

We had the wood stove really throwing out the heat by the time we were ready to eat. It felt good to both of us knowing where we were going and how long it would take to get there.

"You know, Joshua," I said, "after looking at the wagons and horses today, I feel much better knowing they are the best. We ain't gonna have no problems with the wagons or horses."

"That is a load off my mind too," he replied. "Now we need to think of ways we can protect ourselves on the way there. I got this damn feeling that we'll run into trouble with some thieves or worse along the way."

"Well, all we can do is keep alert and make damn sure that we have the extra muskets loaded behind us," I stated.

Joshua clearly had something on his mind. "Robert," he finally said, "I have been thinking about what we should do if more than two people attack us. We'll jump off the wagons and get under them. I made damn sure that the reins are long enough. I added a strong metal keep under the wagon, so we could tie the reins to them. This way the horses won't take off running if they feel there isn't any strain on their reins."

"I was wondering what you were doing under the wagons for so long," I said. "That's a good idea. We'll be safe under the wagons, and we'll still be able to hold the team of horses together and fire our muskets. I was thinking we could make some type of holder under the wagon for the muskets just in case we needed another shot."

"We can do that," Joshua stated. "I'll take care of it as soon as the liveryman brings the wagons and horses tomorrow."

"I want to have all the advantage I can get if we are attacked," I maintained. "They'll be surprised and sorry if they try."

"Well, I think we'd better get some sleep and be up at the crack of dawn tomorrow morning," Joshua said. "There is a lot more to do, and the sooner we get out of Albany the better I'll feel."

"Yeah," I agreed, "it's getting late and Halfmoon looks tired also. Let's enjoy our last night in a warm building, because from here on out, it'll be damn cold and hard sleeping on the ground again."

I lay in the dark thinking of what might lie ahead for us. I had ideas running through my head of all sorts of trouble. I knew this trip would be tough and that I had better get used to the fact that it would probably change our lives, but I knew if we survived this, we could handle anything that would come along in the future. Little did I know what would be waiting for us in the years to come.

Joshua, Halfmoon, and I were up at the first light of day. We knew it was going to be a long hot day. The liveryman had brought the two teams of horses and wagons at seven o'clock, just as he promised. Patrick was already loading the wagons with all the supplies that we were to take to Carlyle, Pennsylvania.

It was almost nine o'clock when the last of the supplies were put into the wagons. Patrick walked over to us and said, "Well, that is the last of it. Now they are yours to protect and deliver to Henry and Luke. I know you will do it. I have this gut feeling about you two, and I know darn well no thief will be able to take them from you. With Halfmoon growing like he is, a man would be a damn fool to even try. Unfortunately, there are a lot of fools out in that wild coun-

try, but you three will handle it. Here is the money I promised you, and when the supplies are delivered, they will pay
you the other half."

Patrick handed each of us a small canvas bag, and we
could feel the weight of the silver inside. We both looked at
each other and smiled.

Joshua said, "This is the most money I have ever seen.
And I tell ya what, Robert, there ain't no thief going to take
it from me while I'm alive."

"Damn right," I confirmed. "It is our future, and we'll
fight any man to keep it."

As soon as I said that, Halfmoon let out a growl and
barked.

Patrick said, "The more I'm around this wolf, the more I
think he understands what we are saying."

We all laughed.

"Well," Patrick said, "we'd better say our good-byes
now. I know you two want to get started since you have a
long way to travel. You will never know how much this
means to me and to all the new settlers moving out into that
wilderness. I hope you can write me once in a while. I
know it'll be a few years and all, but I do want to hear from
you great friends again. I will help you in whatever way I
can, so please always remember that."

We both shook Patrick's hand. Joshua climbed up on his
wagon, and I climbed up on mine. Halfmoon barked and
Joshua yelled to him, "Well, get up here with me if ya want
to ride. You can ride with Robert later down the road."

Halfmoon jumped up and sat next to Joshua, barking
like crazy. I yelled to Joshua, "Well, let's get these wagons

moving before they arrest us for disturbing the peace with this crazy wolf."

We directed the teams of horses out of Albany, heading southwest. We glanced back and saw Patrick still standing in the middle of the street, waving good-bye.

The road out of Albany was very good and busy with people coming into town and heading south to New York. I only wished it could be like this to Station Point on the border of New York and Pennsylvania. I knew in one day's time we would turn and head southwest. From where the road forked, the roads we'd have to use would only get worse.

We stayed behind each other as we traveled south along the busy dirt road. There were so many people heading north and south, there was never a time when we could travel side by side. We had driven the horses for almost three hours when we decided to stop at a small settlement to feed and water them.

An older man at the livery stale was very nice to us. "You can have all the water you need," he said. "I haven't seen a good-looking team of horses like you boys have in a long time. Where ya all heading?"

"We are taking these supplies to Station Point, then on to Carlyle, Pennsylvania, to a trading post," I answered.

"Damn, that is a long and dangerous trip."

"What do you mean by that?" Joshua asked.

"Well, I hear that it is rough out that way," he explained. "I also heard that a few men were killed out there. I guess they were trying to do like you fellows are doing, delivering supplies from Albany."

"Well, there ain't a damn thief going to do that to us," Joshua stated.

The old man looked at Joshua and me, and then saw Halfmoon. "Well, by looking at you two and that wolf, I reckon there ain't no man going to try that. But if he does, I feel sorry for him. You two look like you got fighting blood in ya. I reckon your fathers had too."

"We come from a fighting stock of people," I told him. "Our grandfathers fought in the French and Indian War and also in the American Revolution up in the Mohawk Valley."

"Yeah, I heard about how the men fought up that way," the old man said. "They are a tough lot, they say. Anyway, help yourselves to the water, rest your teams, and go when you are ready. I got chores to do."

The old man walked away, talking to himself. Neither Joshua nor I could hear what he was saying. Maybe it was for the best that we couldn't.

Halfmoon jumped off the wagon, went over to where the horses were drinking, and joined them.

"Robert, just look at him," Joshua said. "The horses just love him."

We both laughed and decided to get some water from the large wooden oak barrels that were hooked to the sides of the wagons. We took our time drinking, and Joshua said, "Well, what do ya think about what that old man was saying?"

"He was a strange one all right," I answered. "As soon as he knew where we were from he didn't say a damn thing more. I don't believe half the talk we hear from anybody

71

anymore. Maybe he was telling the truth about the men getting killed out there, but you know damn well how gossip can start and spread. I just let it go in one ear and out the other. If we listened to everything we have heard since we left the farm, we would've gone crazy by now. To heck with them all. We'll know soon enough what's true and what isn't. We'll just deal with it as it comes, like our grandfathers did."

Joshua nodded confidently.

"Hey, Joshua," I then said. "What do you think about going until about four o'clock, then finding a place for the night?"

"That would be the smart thing to do," he approved. "We don't want to tire out these fine horses by pushing them too long. We'll find a stream or a place where they can drink their fill for the night."

I climbed back up on my wagon and called Halfmoon. He jumped up on the seat next to me, all excited about moving down the road again. He just loved to keep moving and seeing different areas.

Not much was said as the next few hours went by. The never-ending flow of wagons and people on horseback had slowed down quite a bit from early that morning. There wasn't a lot of settling out this way; I guessed that the land was very rocky by looking out at some of the open fields. Every once in a while we could see the remains of an old house that had burned down and was forgotten. Again, nature was reclaiming the fields with her underbrush and tall weeds. I often wondered who these early settlers had been and how hard they had worked to clear this land. My

Grandpa Robert sure had some great fertile land back in Sprout Brook. He knew it could grow almost anything with some hard work.

It was almost four o'clock when Joshua hollered back to me, "Hey, Robert, let's pull off the road up there by those tall elm trees. I think there is a small stream running near there. It'll be a good place to camp for the night."

"Sounds damn good to me, Joshua," I replied. "My backside is getting sore from this hard seat. I'll fix it to-night before I sit here again."

I could hear Joshua laughing at me, so I laughed with him. We pulled the wagons way off the dirt road and un-hooked the team of horses for the night. Halfmoon was al-ready looking around, sniffing the air and ground around us.

"Robert, looks like old Halfmoon is making sure this spot is safe for us tonight," Joshua said with a laugh.

"He sure is, and I think this is a good spot also."

By the time we got the horses tied up and let them drink on their own, the sun was starting to drop behind the tall woods in the west. We still had plenty of daylight to get set up and start cooking some food. We pitched our canvas tent between the two wagons. It would protect us from any wind or rain that might come during the night. Joshua and I had been camping ever since we were young boys, so we knew what worked and what didn't. With this set up, we could last through a damn blizzard. We had canvas rigged up on both sides of the wagons, so when we made camp at night, all we had to do was unroll the canvas down the sides of the wagons and tie it off from inside. This made very comfortable lodging in any weather. We always had a fire going between the wagons so we could keep warm and out of any bad weather.

"Look at Halfmoon," I said as we settled in. "He's claimed his spot between the wagons near the fire. He'll lie out there in all kinds of weather, and I know he'll be listening and watching all night. It's a good place for him; he'll let us know if anybody or anything is around."

"That's for sure," Joshua agreed. "I feel so much better knowing I can sleep without somebody sneaking up on us. If they do, we'll just grab the muskets we have tied up under these wagons and blow them away."

"I took some old feed bags and stuffed them with some others we had. I'll use them on that hard wagon bench. My skinny ass is too bony to sit all day on it."

"You see, Robert, that is the Flint in you," Joshua remarked. "You all are skinny. I'm glad that I take after Grandpa Ben. He was big and had more fat than my father."

We both laughed. Halfmoon looked at us and barked. He knew what we were talking about for sure. Joshua and I talked for another hour about the trip and what may lie ahead. We knew we would be fine and that tomorrow would be another day.

Station Point

It was September 30, 1783. The sun was coming up over the large oak trees, and by the way they were turned upward, we knew we would be getting some bad weather.

Joshua looked at the leaves on the trees. "There is a bad storm coming today, Robert," he warned. "We'd better try to get on the trail to Station Point. This map that Patrick gave us shows some small streams we'll have to cross, and if we get all this damn rain before we get to them, we may have to wait a few days before the water is low enough to reach the other side."

We hurried, got the horses hitched up, and headed out on the road again. It was almost two o'clock in the afternoon when we came to the split in the road. There was a sign posted there that wasn't very old. One arrow pointed to Albany and New York, and the other pointed to Station Point.

"Well, Joshua, here we are," I announced. "I hope this road is in good shape. If we get hit with them dark clouds back to the east, we'll be in mud and ruts."

"We ain't got a choice now," Joshua grumbled. "Let's just hope we can get across that stream before it starts raining like hell just let loose."

We turned the wagons down the road, and the further we traveled, the narrower it became. There was enough room for the wagons, but it would be hard if we met another wagon coming back toward us. It was almost four o'clock by the time we came across the first stream. It was low, and for the time being, the rain was holding.

"Well, Joshua, let's get across this one while we can," I said. "Hopefully the next two streams will be low like this one."

We drove the wagons for another hour when we started to feel the rain coming down. I yelled up to Joshua, "Is there any type of clearing ahead of you where we can pull off?"

"There is a small field just ahead," he answered. "Let's pull in there for the night."

We guided the horses into the field until we reached a burned-out cabin that was once a farm-sitting close by. The roof and sidewalls had collapsed; it had burned down long ago. The rain had let up long enough for us to get the horses to cover under a grove of trees. We started a fire and stretched the canvas down along the sides of the wagons. We closed the front and back of the wagons to protect the supplies from the wind and rain. We took more canvas and covered the wagons from front to back to keep the fire from going out. We also made sure we got the wagons on high ground so no water or flash floods would come under them during the night.

While we were eating, the sky lit up as if it were daytime. The lightning was the worst that I had seen in a long time. The thunder sounded like a hundred cannons being fired at once.

"I hope the horses are all right," I yelled. "I tied them up real tight. I hope they don't get spooked and break loose."

I had just gotten the words out of my mouth when Half-moon took off like running toward the horses.

"Where in hell is he going, Joshua?" I shouted

With the next flash of lightning we could see that Half-moon was with the horses, sitting there and watching them.

"Well, I'll be damned, Robert," Joshua laughed. "Half-moon went right with those horses. I think he is keeping them calm during this storm. They trust him, and maybe with him there they will stay calm."

I shook my head in disbelief. "I tell ya, Joshua, that wolf ain't normal. If he isn't the spirit of Coppernol then I'll crawl all the way to Station Point."

We didn't say another word to each other for the next four hours. The thunder was so loud we couldn't talk even if we'd wanted to. The storm seemed to linger right over our heads. There were times when the lightning hit so close that we thought it might strike us dead.

The next four hours seemed like ten. Suddenly the storm passed by as fast as it had come. The rain was letting up, and we still had the fire hot enough to start drying us out. We were damp and cold, and the heat was finally starting to feel good against our wet clothes. Joshua took a lantern and walked over to where the horses and Halfmoon were waiting.

"Halfmoon, are you still here, boy?" he called out.

Halfmoon let out a couple of strong barks, letting us know that he was all right. Within a few minutes, Joshua came back under the canvas with Halfmoon right on his heels. He brought down the canvas to keep the wind from blowing in and sat down next to the fire.

"Well, we are lucky, Robert," he told me. "All the horses are alive. They're just soaking wet. They'll be fine. But old Halfmoon here is really soaked to the bone."

I reached up into the wagon, grabbed an old wool blanket, and started to dry him off. He groaned and happily wagged his tail. I wrapped the blanket around him, and he lay down next to the fire and went to sleep.

"He'll be fine now, Joshua," I said. "We'd better get some sleep before dawn. It'll be here in a few hours. I sure hope the sun comes out and warms things up."

"The road out there will be deep in mud," Joshua groaned. "I hope we can make some headway through it tomorrow."

"We'll do the best we can and just keep heading southwest to Station Point," I said. "I was hoping we'd get there in five days, but now who knows."

It seemed like we had only slept a few minutes when we were both up walking around the wagons. There was no damage, but it was just like we'd figured—the road looked like a small stream.

"Well, Robert, what do you think?" Joshua asked.

"Let's get the horses fed, hook them up to the wagons,

and see what the road looks like farther down," I suggested. "We'll just take it slow and easy."

Within an hour we were on the road or what had been a road the day before. Six inches of water followed the old wagon tracks, taking all the dirt with it and exposing the rocks underneath. For the next five miles, we could see the once small stream the road followed was now flowing to the top of its banks. We would be all right until it started to overflow.

We had traveled another five miles when we heard a loud roar coming from over the next hill.

I yelled back to Joshua, "Hold the wagons here. I don't like the sound up ahead."

"I hear it too," Joshua confirmed. "I'll be there in a minute."

Joshua, Halfmoon, and I trekked through the mud toward the rise of the hill. When we got to the top we looked down. The narrow crossing we had to pass was completely under water.

"Damn it!" Joshua yelled. "I knew this would happen. It'll be at least another day before we can get across that river."

"You sure as hell can say that again," I replied. "It is really pounding through there."

Halfmoon took off down the bank and started downstream, barking like hell. Joshua and I knew something was wrong. We half slid down the muddy road and near the bank of the roaring river. There we saw what was left of a wagon. It was all busted up and half under the water, caught on a large tree that was ripped from its roots into the river. Halfmoon had found something or somebody. We maneuvered our way toward him, and there hanging from a tree limb was a young woman and a Negro man trying to hang onto her so the river wouldn't take her away. We grabbed hold of the woman and then the young Negro and pulled them to safety onto shore.

"Good boy, Halfmoon. Good boy," Joshua praised.

Halfmoon barked and wagged his tail.

Within a few minutes, the Negro started to cough and spit out the water that he had sucked into his lungs. He looked to be about twenty or so, stood about six feet tall, and had a big chest. His arms were like small limbs on a tree.

Joshua said, "Damn, Robert, he is one big man. The only thing that saved them was his strength."

As he rolled onto his stomach, we saw that his shirt was just about ripped to shreds from being in the water for so long. Then Joshua and I gasped at the sight of his back. It was covered with welts from being whipped by a wide belt.

"Robert, do you see what I see?"

"I sure do," Joshua gulped. "He must be a slave from down south. It looks like this poor man has been whipped many a time. What kind of brutal bastard would do that to another man?"

"I've heard stories of men like him that come from the South," I said. "Some of the landowners buy men like him and work them like horses, if not worse. They whip them if they run away or do something wrong."

"I got this gut feeling that this man has run away and finally made it this far north," Joshua stated. "He damn sure almost died here. But what is a Negro doing with a white woman way up here?"

"Hell, I don't know, Joshua," I answered. "There is so much running through my head right now that I can't even think straight. Let's get them up to the wagons and build a fire. We sure as hell ain't going any further now, so let's get them back to health and maybe we'll find out what their story is."

Another hour passed before we got the woman and the Negro back to the wagons. We found a spot under some trees where we started a large fire and made a lean-to to keep the water from dripping on us. We were cooking up some beef broth and beef when the Negro sat up. He was scared to death when he saw us.

"Where is Miss Walker?" he exclaimed. "What have you done with her?"

"Easy there, friend," I said. "She's right behind you. She's lucky you were around. If it weren't for you holding her out of the water down there, she would be dead now. Take it easy. We brought you up here to warm up. We are not going to hurt you or her, so just relax and drink this."

The Negro took a sip of the hot broth. Every once in a while, he looked over his shoulder to see if Miss Walker was awake. He was more worried about her than he was about Joshua and me. After about ten minutes, we heard the woman groan and move around.

"Miss Walker, Miss Walker, it's me, Adam," the Negro called out. "Are you all right?"

Miss Walker sat up and saw Joshua. She grabbed

Adam's massive arms and said, "Where are we, Adam? Who are these men?"

"It's all right, Miss Walker," Adam assured her. "These two men pulled us from the river and saved our lives."

The woman didn't say another word for a minute or two, and then she regained her thoughts.

"Who are you?" she demanded to know. "Where did you come from?"

"Joshua and I are taking these two wagons of supplies to Station Point," I told her, "but the storm has made the river unsafe to cross. Our wolf found you two in the river by a tree that was torn from its roots. We pulled you from the river and brought you up here."

"You two sure came at the right time," she said, sounding relieved. "All I remember was crossing the stream when a huge wall of water hit the side of the wagon and threw us into the water. Where are the horses and the wagon?"

"I'm afraid the horses drowned, ma'am," Joshua told her, "and the wagon is in pieces along the riverbanks."

She let out a scream. "What are we going to do now, Adam?" she gasped. "Everything we own was in that wagon. What about the gold I had in the trunk and all my clothes?"

"I don't rightly know, Miss Walker," Adam answered. "I guess we'll have to head back to Virginia."

"You know damn well we can't go back there!" she retorted. "They are looking for us there and in North Carolina."

Joshua and I looked at each other, but didn't say a word.

We sat back and let them give us the information we needed to know.

"Where are you two going again?" she asked.

"We have to take these supplies to Station Point," I explained. "From there we were thinking of heading south into Virginia."

For a long time not a soul said another word. We all were thinking of what she had said to Adam. Then Miss Walker regained her breath. "How much would it cost me if we were to go back into Virginia with you?" she asked.

"Not a darn cent," said Joshua.

I looked at Joshua and nodded with him. "You two hear me out," I said. "Joshua and I must know the whole story, and it had better be the truth or we'll let Halfmoon over there have his way with both of you. Do you both understand me?"

Adam saw Halfmoon, and we knew he was scared of him. Miss Walker looked at him also and said, "All right, the truth and from the beginning."

"We have all night and all day tomorrow to hear the truth," I pointed out. "It'll be a full day before any of us can cross that stream. Let's get some food, dry ourselves out, and get some sleep. We will all start fresh in the morning."

"That is a very good idea," she agreed. "But what are your names?"

"My name is Robert Flint, and my friend here is Joshua Wells," I introduced. "We grew up together in the Mohawk Valley. This wolf is our friend also. His name is Halfmoon. Now Joshua and I sleep very well, and old Halfmoon sleeps with one eye open, so if I were you, I would not try to run away or do anything. I guarantee he will be at your throat before you can start anything."

Adam and Miss Walker both looked at Halfmoon, and he let out a low growl. Joshua and I almost laughed, but we managed to hold it in.

"Don't worry about us moving one inch all night," said Adam.

Joshua and I went to our wagons and crawled underneath like we always did. We started our own fire and got comfortable.

"Well, Joshua," I said, "what do ya think about those two?"

"They'll still be there in the morning," he stated. "They will tell us the whole truth. They seem awful scared of us and of any other man for that matter. It'll be very interesting to hear their story."

"I sure as hell agree with you on that," I responded. "We'll hear them out, and then decide if we'll leave them here or take them with us to Station Point. I got this gut instinct that the four of us are going to be getting into something later on. I just wish I knew what it was."

"Well, like we said in the beginning, Robert, all kinds of trouble and good luck will be waiting for us. I'm sure hoping this is good luck. She is a beautiful woman, that's for sure," Joshua pointed out.

"I noticed that first thing, Joshua," I said with a laugh. "She sure isn't a poor, uneducated woman either. I can tell she was brought up with schooling, and a hell of a lot more than we ever got, that's for darn sure."

We both laughed and kept looking over at Adam and

Miss Walker. Halfmoon was keeping his eyes on them as well. We decided to get some sleep. Tomorrow would be another interesting day.

I awoke and lay still for a minute, thinking of what had taken place already and all that might happen in the hours and days ahead. Joshua was already up and making breakfast while he petted and talked to Halfmoon.

"You're a good boy, Halfmoon," he said. "You did a good job last night. I see that our new guests didn't run off."

I stood up and walked over to them.

"Well, Robert," Joshua greeted, "let's get over to those two and see what story we'll hear this morning."

"Yeah, I guess we'd better get to the bottom of this and decide what in hell we should do next."

We brought Adam and Miss Walker some breakfast. Adam looked up and said, "I'm sure hungry this morning. I slept real well too."

Miss Walker took the plate of food we offered and said, "I look like a mess, don't I?"

Joshua answered, "No, you don't. Hell, what do ya expect after being half-drowned and beaten by that raging river?"

"My clothes are ripped to threads and I'm almost naked," she complained. "I need to get some better clothes before I freeze to death."

"Robert, Adam, and I will look down river," Joshua offered. "Maybe we can find that trunk you were talking about last night."

"I would be truly in your debt if you could find it," she

replied. "There is almost a thousand dollars in gold in that trunk, and that is everything I have."

While we were all eating, I noticed the river had gone down almost three feet from where it had been the day before. That was a good sign for us. Hopefully in a day or so we could make it across the water and get back on course.

When we were done eating and got the fires going again, Miss Walker turned to Joshua and me and said, "That hit the spot. I was starving and now I feel much better."

"That makes two of us, Miss Walker," Adam said.

Miss Walker took a deep breath and said, "Now I'll tell you how we both got here."

Joshua and I sat down and waited to hear the truth and nothing else.

"My name is Lily Walker," she began. "I'm from North Carolina, close to the border of South Carolina. My father had a small plantation where he raised tobacco and some cotton. We had almost one thousand acres there. About five years ago, during the American Revolution, the British were all over the county. My father never liked them, but he had to give them food and whatever else they wanted. It was during that time that my father took me to South Carolina where he was going to do some business. I was only fifteen years old. My mother had died when I was eleven while giving birth to my brother, and a few days later he died also. My father had maybe ten Negroes who helped on the farm. He was never mean to any of them; as a matter of fact, people around the county always said my father was too nice to the Negroes. He treated them all as hard-working people, and he always took good care of them. My father never had so-called real friends because of this."

The more Lily spoke, the more Joshua and I held onto her every word. Adam remained quiet while she was talking.

"My father knew the farm was in safe hands when he and I both left for the day," she continued. "We went just across the state line to a small town near a very large plantation. When we arrived in town, the place was filled with British soldiers and their officers. We were there only for an hour or so when some men told my father that the man he was to see was out at Live Oaks Plantation on the edge of town. We took the horse and buggy and drove to the plantation to find this man. As we drove near the cabins in the fields, the worst thing I had ever seen happened before our eyes. They were beating three Negroes that were tied up to a post. Two were old men and the other was this man here, Adam."

Joshua and I looked at each other, not knowing what to say. I started to say something, but Lily held up her hand. "Please," she said, "let me finish."

I sat back and waited.

"They were whipping these poor men so hard that blood was running down their backs," she went on. "They were yelling for mercy. The more they screamed with pain, the harder the overseer whipped them. My father ran over and yelled, 'What in hell are you doing to these poor souls?'

"The man my father was supposed to see about some business was the one doing the whipping, and the damn British were watching and laughing. My father asked them to stop, but they didn't. Then this man, whose name was Frank, finally stopped. He turned toward my father and said, "This is what we do with niggers that run away, and if I had my way, I'd kill all three of them now."

"My father said to Frank, 'I came here to do business with you, but after seeing how you treat these people, you can go to hell." Frank looked square into my father's eyes and said, "Well, buy these poor souls then." My father asked, "How much for all three?' and Frank said, 'Five hundred dollars and they're all yours."

Lily took a deep breath to collect her thoughts and then continued.

"My father didn't ask for a lower price. He just reached into his pocket and paid the money. He didn't say another word. Some men cut the Negroes loose and threw them on the back of the buggy. As we drove away, Frank yelled to my father, "Y'all go back north, nigger lover, but you better watch your farm. There is a war on, and you never know what might happen."

Joshua and I had never heard of such cruelty before.

Then Joshua spoke, "What happen after you left, Lily?"

"We headed out of there in a hurry," she answered. "We wanted to get as far away as we could before nightfall. We went off the main road and back into the thick woods about ten miles from that town and plantation. We were scared to death they would come after us and kill us. We never even had a fire for the night. We took the three men off the buggy. They were covered with dried blood and were so thirsty. We laid them on the ground and tried to treat the wounds on their backs. Adam here was the only one who could move and help us. The other two men died during the night. They were so old and weak that they couldn't handle the trip.

"In the morning, Adam dug two graves and buried them out in the woods. We didn't even mark the graves. We were afraid someone might dig them up or do something worse. We stayed in those woods for another day and then headed back home. My father took all the old trails and kept away from the main roads. Then as we got closer to our farm, we saw large columns of smoke coming from the house. We stayed at the edge of the woods and saw the British burning down the house and all the barns, killing what they couldn't take with them."

"What happened to the hired hands?" I asked.

"This bastard Frank took them," she scowled. "We saw him and his men leading them by ropes down the road heading back to South Carolina."

We looked over at Adam. He held his head in his hands, crying like a baby. Lily put her arms around him and cried as well. Joshua and I just sat there, sad for their loss.

I had to walk away and so did Joshua. We headed toward the riverbank and stared at the water.

"I know what you're thinking, Robert," Joshua said. "I feel the same damn way. I now believe I know what our mission truly is. These past twenty minutes have shown me what we have to do after Station Point."

"We fought the damn British and won," I stated. "Now it is like Grandpa Robert said to my father years ago. He told my father and yours and all the Flints that the next war would be about freeing these Negroes. He had this dream, and damn it he was right. I believe that you and I are going to help these people get free and travel to the north. After the war, everybody who had slaves up north set them free, but them people down south didn't."

Joshua put his arm around my shoulder. "This is our calling, Robert," he said. "We now know what we have to do."

When we turned around, Adam and Lily were standing there. They had heard everything we had said

"You two can't do it alone," Lily said, "but Adam and I can help you."

Adam had a look on his face like I had never seen in any man. He said, "I will die for you two men, just like I would die to protect Lily here. She saved my life back then, and you two have saved both our lives now. From this day forward, I'll be with you and the four of us will free many of my people in the South."

"Why were you calling her Miss Lily here a while back?" I asked.

"I talked to her like that every time we meet strangers," Adam explained. "That way they think I'm her slave. When we are alone, I call her Lily."

"How do you know you can trust us?" Joshua asked. "You hardly know us."

"Anybody who would risk their own lives next to a raging river to rescue a white women and a Negro man must be a mighty good person," Lily answered. "We met many men on the road who wanted to kill Adam and rape me. They think I'm no good because I travel with a Negro."

At that moment the four of us—a former slave, a beautiful woman, Joshua and me—made a pact to do what we could to free as many Negroes as possible. We put our hands together, and the power that came from our four souls was like nothing I had ever felt before. We looked at each other and smiled. Then old Halfmoon crawled underneath us and let out the loudest damn howl we'd ever heard. We all laughed, and at that moment we knew we would never part again.

We all walked back to the campfire and sat down.

"My father had a sister who lived not far from our farm," Lily told us. "She and her husband didn't have much of a farm, but they were honest people. My father, Adam, and I went to their home and stayed there for nearly two years. My father knew who burned his place, and he found out that all the Negroes he had working there were sold all over the South. He tried to get enough money to rebuild the farm, but no one, not even the banks, would give him the money. My father finally found out that this Frank controlled the banks and half of the people in town. It was almost a year ago when the bank that owned part of the farm came to my father and told him that he was four years behind on taxes. We didn't have the money to pay them, so within a month Frank foreclosed on the farm."

"What happened to your father, Lily?" I asked.

"He was heartbroken," she sobbed. "We finally realized that Frank was behind the burning of the farm and every damn thing that had happened to us. Then one day my father went into the woods and killed himself."

Joshua and I couldn't believe what we had just heard.

"After Adam and I buried him," Lily continued, "my

aunt and her husband just up and moved to Station Point because they heard there was land to be built on. That was the last we heard from them. In the meantime, Adam and I weren't safe in that county. We knew that sooner or later Frank would come for us. But before my father killed himself, he told me where he buried the gold, the gold I had with me. The day before he died, Adam, my father, and I dug it up, and he gave it to me. Adam and I left right after we buried my father. Everything we owned was in the wagon that is now at the bottom of the river."

"It was almost dark when we tried to cross the river," Adam added. "I knew the water would get higher during the night, so I gave it a try anyway. We were almost across when a high wall of water hit the side of the wagon, and that is all I can remember until we woke up here by the fire."

I drew in a deep breath. "That is a hell of a story," I said. "I know how you feel, and now here you are with nothing. But let me tell you both this: Joshua and I will take these supplies to Station Point and get paid. Then the four of us will try to find your aunt. But for now let's search the riverbanks and see what we can find."

We all agreed, split up, and headed for the river. We hadn't gone too far when Joshua yelled, "Hey, Robert, I found the trunk hung up on this tree down here, but I'll need you or Adam to help me get it."

Adam heard Joshua and ran downstream to where the trunk was lodged against a fallen tree. By the time I got there, they had already dragged it up the bank and pried it open.

"It's all here, Lily," Adam announced, "your clothes and even the gold in that old wooden box."

I heard her squeal with delight. She ran so fast that she slipped on the muddy bank and fell headfirst into the river. The water was only knee deep, and when she stood up she was covered with mud. The three of us laughed like crazy at her. She was about to walk out of the river when Halfmoon charged into the water and knocked her over again. By then, the three of us were bent over in wild laughter.

Again, she stood up, but this time she was laughing with us. She sat back down in the water and played with Halfmoon. Old Halfmoon was having a heck of a time with her. By the time the two of them were done playing, they were both covered with mud.

Joshua yelled out, "Come here, Halfmoon, and let the poor girl back on dry land."

Halfmoon ran from the river and started to shake the water off his thick coat. He sprayed water and mud all over the three of us as well.

Then without a word, Lily casually ripped off all her clothes. She stood knee-deep in the water and said, "To heck with these old wet rags. And I'll tell you all this now; this isn't the last time you all will see me naked. There are a lot of miles from here to where we're going, and I'll be darned if I'll start being shy of taking a dip in the water naked in front of you three. The sooner you all get used to it the better."

She walked out of the river, naked to the world, shuffled over to her old trunk, and searched for something dry to put on. The three of us didn't say another word. We walked back up the river, carrying her chest of belongings, and left her alone to get dressed.

As we got near the top of the bank, Joshua smiled and said, "I tell you what, fellas. That Lily is one hell of a woman. I swear, no matter what comes along in the years ahead, that woman will have an answer for it."

"I feel sorry for any man who tries to get in her way," I added. "She is as tough as they come."

"Now you two see what I have been putting up with for nearly five years with her," Adam said with a laugh. "She is smart and beautiful, but she can be mean as hell if she wants to be."

We set the trunk on the ground next to the fire and waited for Lily to join us. Within a few minutes she came up over the hill, looking absolutely beautiful with the sunlight shining down on her. She walked over to us, sat down, and said, "So, what do we do now?"

"We have been thinking that by morning we should be able to get across the river," I told her. "I hope we can be at Station Point in two more days if the weather holds out."

"I want to tell both of you that Adam and I are so very grateful for all that you have done for us," Lily said. "I know now that this river has brought the four of us together for a reason. I know deep down that we have the ability to free many slaves."

"Joshua and I think so too," I replied. "Like I said last night, our grandfathers told us many years ago that the next war will be among ourselves, and that the men who fight it will die for the freeing the slaves in the South. We know now that they were right, and we are the ones, along with you, who will get it all started."

"We'll set up a system," Joshua declared. "It'll be called the Underground Railroad."

"There you go again, Joshua," I scoffed. "You do come up with the wildest names for things, just like you named Halfmoon. Then so be it. From this day forward, we four will call our system of freedom the Underground Railroad. When we speak to people about freeing slaves, that's what we will call it. Maybe someday others will help us."

Adam thought for a moment. "You know, Joshua, that is a good name for it," he stated. "And now I'll tell all of you something. I never knew my father or mother, but my grandmother once told me when I was about ten or so that she had come over from across the ocean where they captured her and put her in chains. She said she was taken to a place in Virginia where she was sold as a slave. The man who bought her had a big plantation in South Carolina. My grandmother was fourteen when she was taken there. She gave birth to my father when she was sixteen years old. None of us really know how old we are, but my grandmother was a smart woman. She worked in the big house where the owner had her cooking and cleaning. There she learned a little at a time how the master ran the plantation. They always thought that she was ignorant and never paid her any mind, but my grandmother did learn a lot. She never could really read or write, but she knew some.

"She told me that when my mother had borne me, they sold her to another plantation. My father begged to go with her, but they said no. Well, one night a month or so later, my father ran away to find my mother. He didn't get far.

The master's men tracked him down with some dogs and hung him on the spot. My grandmother told me that they never cut him down from that tree. They told all the slaves that he would hang there until the buzzards picked his bones as a warning for any slave who had any ideas about running away."

Again, Joshua and I sat there and listened to this horror. We had never even heard of such things, although we knew that the Indians had done some horrible things to the settlers in the Mohawk Valley during the French and Indian War. This, on the other hand, was something beyond our understanding.

"This is why I ran away from my master, and I was almost to Virginia when they caught up with me," Adam continued. "They say there is a place in Virginia called the Dismal Swamp where runaway slaves go. They say there is some good land in the middle of this deadly swamp and many people live there. That's where I was running to before they caught me and dragged me back. That's when Miss Walker and her father bought me and saved my life."

"Now listen to me, Adam," Lily spoke up, "and you listen well. You have got to quit calling me Miss Walker in front of strangers like we have been doing. I don't care what people think of me. You just call me Lily in front of anybody. Since the four of us are about to do what we must and we'll be going who-knows-where, you can't call me Miss Walker anymore. If you say that around strange people, they might think you are a runaway slave. I want them to think you were born in New York, not the Carolinas, and that you are free. You must always remember this, Adam.

All of our lives will be on the line all the time, so you must always call me Lily."

"Whatever you say, Lily," he agreed. "I'll do just that from now on."

"The other thing we must do is keep teaching you how to read and write," Lily continued. "You can do a little, but we need to work extra hard at this. You never know when you'll be asked to prove that you are a free man from New York."

"Lily, maybe you can teach Robert and me some too," Joshua said. "We went to school some, but most of the time we ran and played in the woods or went hunting."

"Well, I'll be," she gasped. "I thought I only had Adam here to worry about, but it looks like now I got two more to teach."

We all laughed and kidded each other about this schooling. Even old Halfmoon joined in by barking. He knew we were all a big family from now on.

For the rest of the day, we sat near the fire and talked until the late-night hours. We all had our own stories to tell. Adam and Lily were interested in hearing about our grandfathers and all their adventures. They couldn't believe what the war was like for us in the Mohawk Valley. We, in turn, were amazed by their stories of the South. We all knew that from that day forward we would be a family, and there was nothing we wouldn't do for each other. We all had one goal, and that was to rescue as many slaves as we could and get them north to freedom.

The morning came with the warmth of the first week of October. We had been lucky so far with the weather. Usually in the fall the mornings were cold, and the winds would come from the north.

By the time we ate and had the horses hooked up to the wagons, it was nearly nine o'clock. Adam sat with me, and Lily rode with Joshua. Halfmoon wanted to walk in front of the wagons.

I yelled back to Joshua and Lily, "Let's hope that the bottom of this river is hard enough for the wagons to cross."

"There won't be any problems, Robert," Joshua assured me. "The force of the river during the storm took all the mud from the bottom, and there is nothing left but hard rocks."

As we eased the horses and wagons across the river and up the other hill, we all let a cry of joy.

"You were right, Joshua!" I cheered. "It was harder on the bottom. Now let's get away from here and never look back."

For the next ten miles, things went very well. The road was starting to dry up. There were signs of strong wind damage all along the way. Many trees were pulled from their roots, and many pines had just snapped in half.

I said to Adam, "We were real lucky the other night. Look at all this damage. All we had was some torn canvas from that strong wind."

"Lily and I were lucky too until I tried to cross that river," Adam replied. "If it wasn't for you and Joshua, we would have never made it."

"Well, I'm like my grandfather," I told him. "He would always say there is a reason for everything, and now I believe he was right."

"I sure would like to have known him," Adam said. "He must have been one brave and thoughtful man."

"He sure was," I stated. "I think about him every day, and I know he and Joshua's grandfather are watching over us all the time."

It was almost five o'clock when we decided to find a place to camp and rest the horses for the night. We found a small field just off the road, and we pulled the wagons under some tall oaks for the night.

Joshua walked over to me and said, "I tell ya what, Robert, it sure don't take long to get set up for camp now. Lily works harder than both of us put together."

We laughed as we watched Adam taking care of the horses. The man had a way with animals that was certain. Lily had the campfire going, and whatever she was cooking smelled mighty good.

We all sat down and ate like we had gone without food for days.

"Damn, Lily!" Joshua exclaimed. "Do you always cook like this?"

"She sure does, Joshua," Adam confirmed. "She can cook better than any woman in the South. That's why I'm so strong. She sure can feed a hungry man."

"I did most of the cooking after my mother died," Lily told us. "We had a Negro woman who taught me how. I just loved her. I miss her a lot. I hope someday I can find her."

After supper, I explained to Adam and Lily how Joshua and I camped for the night and how we protected ourselves under the wagon where the muskets were.

"Lily, have you ever shot a musket?" I asked.

"Only a few times with my father when we were hunting," she answered.

Adam let out a laugh. "Lily, you are the best shooter I ever saw," he said. "This woman can kill a rabbit on a dead run. She's done it many a time."

"Oh, Adam, don't say such things," Lily scoffed. "But I can shoot better then most."

"Did you here that, Joshua?" I said. "Tomorrow we'll show Adam and Lily our firepower and where we keep everything."

"That will be fun," Joshua agreed. "I only saw my grandmother shoot the musket once. She was really good."

"You two should show Adam how to shoot," Lily encouraged. "He is not too bad, but you should see him with a long knife. He can hit a mark twenty feet away."

"I throw the knife better than I shoot," he said with a smirk. "I never had much practice on shooting, being a slave and all. They kind of frowned on any slave carrying a musket."

"Well, that makes sense," I said with a laugh. "I guess if you're a slave they don't want you going around with a damn musket."

We all laughed.

"Tomorrow morning I want to give you a long knife, Adam," I then said. "We have a few different knives in our supplies. I also want to take time to show you both where we keep all the muskets and powder. You never know who we may meet on this road or anywhere."

The rest of the evening we talked about what we should do when we got to Station Point. We decided to look for Lilly's aunt and then ask her what she thought about our plans.

The next day, the wind had started to come from the north. Joshua was telling us that there was going to be heavy frost come nightfall. As always, I believed him, and I went on to tell Lily and Adam how he could predict the weather. Joshua's instincts were always right.

We had gone maybe ten miles when we saw a sign near the road telling us that Station Point was only ten miles away.

"Well, Robert, what do ya think?" Joshua asked.

"Let's camp here today and get there tomorrow," I suggested. "It's only noontime now, and I want to have Lily and Adam fire the muskets for a while."

"That sounds good to me," Joshua agreed. "I miss shooting. We haven't shot in a month or more."

"I know. The time sure has been going fast since we left home. The farm seems so far away, and I think about it all the time. But what lies ahead of us is going to be something, I'm sure."

We told Lily and Adam about our plans, and they agreed with us.

"I think it is best if we all go into Station Point early in the morning," Lily explained. "This way people can gossip about us all day. Can you imagine what they will say when they see a woman and a Negro and two men all dressed in buckskins? They will wonder for days who we are."

We all laughed.

Adam said, "I know one thing; they haven't ever seen a bunch like us before and probably never will again."

"Joshua, we'd better keep Halfmoon in the wagon with us tomorrow," I said. "You know, he ain't much on strangers. You remember what happened last time in Albany?"

"I sure do. I don't want to do that again."

Lily asked me, "What did he do?"

I told her and Adam how Halfmoon had grabbed that man by the throat before we got him off him.

"But Halfmoon looks so gentle."

"Don't let that fool ya, Lily," I warned. "He is fine with the four of us, but when strange people get too close, he can tell when they have friendly intentions or bad ones. He'll know before we do. He'll growl first and attack second, so always watch him. He'll let ya know."

We made camp and then showed Adam and Lily how we will protect ourselves if we are attacked on the road or at night. We showed them where everything was stored and took turns going through the drill. It had to be done. We all knew we had to be the best, considering what we were about to do. One small mistake and we would all be killed. We also showed them how to hide in the woods for hours without being seen or heard, and how to kill if we had to. We did this until dark, when we decided we'd better have supper and get settled in for the night.

"The things you two showed us today have never been done in the South," Adam said. "I would have never been caught if I had known all that. I tell you this: I'll never forget it."

Lily said, "That was something else. I hope I can remember it all."

"Don't worry, Lily," I said. "We'll do it over and over as the days go on. We will become better at it in time, but we need to do it like we breathe. Eventually, it will become second nature."

Joshua came back from the wagon carrying a small blanket. He sat down next to the fire and unrolled the cloth to reveal four beautiful long knives.

"Adam, this is our gift to you," he told him. "Robert and I want you to have these four knives. You are a better knife thrower than we are, so please take them."

Adam's eyes opened up real wide, and he grabbed each knife with his huge hands. As he looked at them, we saw tears streaming down his cheeks. He looked at Joshua and me and could hardly speak. When he did, he said, "Nobody ever gave me a gift like this. They are beautiful and so well balanced. The oak handles are amazing. I will make a leather sheath for each of them. I'll have one for the back of my neck, and one for around my waist, and the other on my leg."

"The back of your neck?" I asked.

Adam stood up. "Think of this knife in a sheath just over my shoulder," he said.

We all watched as Adam reached behind his massive shoulder, and in an instant he grabbed the knife and threw it into a tree twenty feet away.

"Well, I'll be damned!" Joshua exclaimed. "Robert, did ya see how fast he did that? Hell, I have never seen a man throw a knife that fast and hard in my life."

"I know one damn thing," I replied. "I feel sorry for the

person who is standing in front of him. A man wouldn't have time to blink before he was stuck in his heart with that knife."

Lily smiled. "I told you two there isn't a man alive who can throw a knife like that," she reminded us.

"I may not be able to shoot them black powders," Adam added, "but I can throw a knife. Again, I want to thank you two for giving these to me. I will cherish them forever."

"Wait," Joshua said. "I have something for Lily also." He went back to the wagon and returned with another blanket, a larger one this time. When he laid it on the ground and unrolled it before Lily, she let out a small scream.

"You have buckskins for me!" she exclaimed. "Where did you get them?"

"We have very close friends who are Mohawk Indians," he told her. "They made them for us before we left. They told Robert and me that if we ever found a woman who would look good in them, we should give them to her. Well, Robert and I talked about this last night, and we decided you are that woman. Wear these and you'll blend in with the woods. They are a lot more comfortable than your dresses."

Lily also had tears running down her cheeks. It was the first time any of us ever heard her being so quiet. She grabbed the buckskins and ran behind the wagons. The three of us laughed. When she finally reappeared, none of us could say a word. She walked in front of us with the buckskins on. The firelight bounced off of them and her face. The beaded work on the neck and arms of the shirt were beautiful.

"Damn, Joshua, we are in trouble now," I moaned.

"Why is that?" Lily wondered.

"With you looking so beautiful in them buckskins, the three of us will be fighting all the men off you all the way to the Carolinas," I announced.

"You three men quit teasing me," she scoffed. "You know darn well I don't want any man. You three are all I want. Maybe someday I will get married, but it'll be a long time before that happens. Then again, living with you three for the years ahead may cure me of ever getting married."

We all laughed, and I knew she was telling the truth. Still, I was sure someday Lily would find a man to love and have children with, but he would have to be something special. No ordinary man would ever make her happy.

Lily rummaged through her clothes and then handed Joshua a leather pouch.

"Here. I want you two to have this. It is the thousand dollars my father gave to Adam and me. We want you to take care of it."

"We can't accept this money, Lily," I said. "This belongs to you."

"Now it is all our money," she insisted. "We are a family and we should keep it that way."

Joshua took the money. "If that's what you two want then it will be. We have some money also, and we will be getting paid after we give the men the supplies tomorrow. What we'll do is put it in with what we have in a steel box hidden inside the wagon. If any of us want to spend it, then we all must agree to it."

Lily and Adam both nodded.

The air was getting very cold. We kept the fire going all night. The wind started to blow and a few snowflakes were falling. The four of us slept together under the wagon out of the wind. Even old Halfmoon was curled up next to us. We had plenty of wool blankets, and we were all very warm throughout the night.

Morning came with a cold wind. During the night it had snowed almost three inches. We were all surprised by the early snowfall. None of us really wanted to get up and get going again, but we all knew we would find warm shelter in Station Point.

The cold wind came from the north, but this time it was bringing heavier snowfall along with it. There were times when we could hardly see down the road because of the blowing snow.

Adam was all bundled up with wool blankets. "Damn, Robert," he growled, "is it always like this?"

"No, it gets worse as the winter months come along."

"I sure ain't liking it one minute."

"I guess this is the first snow you have ever seen."

"Hell, yes. And I don't like it. I don't know what is worse—trying to keep warm or running from the master's hunting dogs."

I let out a laugh. "Well, in another hour we should be in Station Point. We'll find a place to stay until this storm blows through."

It was just about noontime when we guided the horses and wagons down a small hill. There straight ahead was the trading post. I yelled back to Joshua, "We are finally here! Let's tie the horses up in the back of the trading post. I see there is a good-size barn back there, so we'll get the horses inside first."

"I'm right behind ya Robert. The sooner the better. My legs are getting pretty cold now."

We drove the horses and wagons into the barn and finally out of the heavy snow. A man came out of the trading post and was walking into the barn when he called out, "Hello there. My name is Henry Simmons. I'm part owner of this here trading post. My partner is Luke Roberts. He's inside adding more wood to the fire. It sure is a damn cold day, isn't it?"

I shook the snow off my jacket. "My name is Robert Flint," I introduced, "and my partner here is Joshua Wells. We have brought your supplies from Patrick O'Reilley up in Albany. Sorry we're late, but the river back some twenty miles was too high to cross after that storm that came through."

"Don't worry about it," Henry replied. "You're here with all the supplies and that's the main thing. Get the horses fed and put them in the stalls over there and then come into the trading post."

Henry turned and went back inside. We all helped getting the horses fed, watered, and put into the stalls.

"I don't know about you three, but I'm damn near frozen to death," I said. "Let's get inside and warm up. We'll check on the horses and supplies later."

By the time we walked to the back of the trading post, the snow was a foot deep and coming down harder than before.

"We sure made it here in time, Robert," Joshua commented. "All of us would've froze to death another night out there, that's for sure."

Adam spoke up, "I don't know about you, Lily, but I can't even feel my toes no more."

We all entered the trading post and Joshua closed the back door. Henry greeted us again and introduced his partner, Luke.

"Glad ya all made it," Luke said. "We were almost out of everything here. Now we can re-open the store with new supplies. It'll be great news for the new settlers that have been coming here all summer."

Henry said, "You all come on over here near the fireplace and get warm. I'll get some hot rum for all of us."

We pulled up chairs and took off all our blankets and heavy coats. The fire was roaring, and it sure felt good. We sat there drinking hot rum and started to feel a lot warmer

Henry and Luke pulled up chairs, and I told them all about our trip and how we came upon Lily and Adam in the river.

"I got one question to ask you, Robert," Henry said. "Is that wolf you have with you friendly?"

I looked at Halfmoon lying on the floor, asleep or pretending to be.

"Yes, old Halfmoon here is a special wolf," I told him. "He is our protector and companion. He lets us know if he doesn't like someone. I know he likes you and Luke here because he hardly ever sleeps around strangers. Don't worry. You're both safe, and I know he is liking this fireplace."

Luke then said, "I know it isn't our business and all, but

I ain't never seen a bunch like you four before. Now that you have delivered the supplies, what are your plans?"

Joshua said, "The four of us are planning to head south into Virginia and maybe North Carolina."

"They have slaves down there," Henry pointed out, "so why in hell are you going there with Adam? You know damn well they will be looking for any Negro who ain't got papers saying he is a free man."

"I am a free man," Adam insisted. "And there ain't no plantation owner going to whip my back side again."

"I didn't mean that, Adam," Henry insisted. "It's just any Southern man who sees two white men, a woman, a Negro, and a wolf is gonna ask questions."

Lily had been quiet until then, but she felt the need to speak up. "I see it like this. We may be a strange bunch, but they sure are going to find out who we are in time. We all would die for each other. What we went through back on the road and next to that river has changed all our lives."

Henry looked at Lily and then at us and said, "Well, none of you has to worry about us giving you any trouble. Matter of fact, we really like all of you, even Halfmoon. Anybody that has come through all the tough times you four have been through and delivered supplies to us is all right in our book. There are some very bad men who would have run off with them supplies, raped Lily, killed the rest of you, and resold Adam. We want you to be our guests here for as long as you want. We have a nice cabin out back that we don't use. It is warm and will keep the cold out."

We decided we would do just that.

After a few more hot rums, Henry and Luke finally accepted the idea of us paying them for the use of the cabin. They also wanted to talk more to us about work in the morning. We told them that we would listen to anything they had to say and would think about it.

The rest of the day, we stayed with them and talked. I told them about Joshua and me and about our families. By the end of the day, we all were very close friends, and we all trusted each other very much.

The snow didn't let up by the time we went into the cabin out back. It was almost two feet deep, and the wind was still blowing from the northeast. This meant a bad storm was here to stay.

When we finally got inside the cabin and got a fire going, we were warmed up and little drunk. It was good to relax and just laugh and enjoy ourselves. The cabin had plenty of chairs and even a nice big oak table. It was all set up for cooking. The beds were all on one side of the cabin.

We decided we would talk to Henry and Luke in the morning and listen to what they had on their minds. We wouldn't just jump into any old thing. We would think and talk about it before we gave them a decision.

During supper, the four of us sat around the table talking about everything.

Lily said, "Can we first try to find my aunt? I need to know if she and my uncle made it here."

"Good idea, Lily," I said. "We'll find her if she is close by. I know she would love to see you and Adam again."

We all agreed that this was the first thing we would do as soon as the snowstorm blew through. Then we all agreed to listen to Luke and Henry about their plans for us, if they had any. We had a good feeling about them and knew it might be a good way to make more money for the trip south.

It was almost midnight when we finally stopped talking. I could hear the wind blowing and could see the snow sticking to the two cabin windows. The fire was doing fine, and none of us had to worry about keeping it going throughout the night. It was so good to finally sleep in a warm bed. My mind didn't wander like it usually did at night; I just took a breath and fell into a deep sleep.

Someone pounding on the cabin door around eight o'clock in the morning awakened me. Halfmoon started to bark.

Joshua was the first to get up, and he walked over to the window and looked out. He turned to me and said, "Robert, it's Luke and Henry."

"Well, let them in, Joshua."

Joshua opened the cabin door, and the two men walked in carrying two large cast iron pots steaming from the cold outside.

"This is a lazy bunch, Henry," Luke remarked. "It's after eight in the morning, and they are all still half asleep."

They both laughed and Henry said, "We brought you some hot breakfast, so let's get eating before it gets too damn cold."

We all gathered around the table and started to eat. It really hit the spot. It had been a long time since any of us had eaten a hot breakfast.

I asked Henry, "How's the storm out there doing?"

"It is starting to clear up now," he informed me. "We

should be getting some warm weather before nightfall. I'll tell ya this: we have been living here for nearly four years, and I have never seen the snow come so damn early. I'm just glad that we have the supplies we bought a few months back. Now we'll be able to survive through the winter here."

"Have you two ever met my Aunt Kate or my Uncle John Jackson?" Lily asked.

Henry and Luke scratched their unshaven chins.

"That name does ring a bell with me," Henry answered. "It seems that they were the ones who bought that last piece of land from us about last fall."

Luke then said, "Yeah, I remember them. They were real nice people. They bought a lot of supplies from us and some land that nobody wanted. It's a good day's ride northwest of here. They said the further from the South they moved the better. Henry and I never asked them what they meant by that, but we thought it was odd."

Lily said, "Well, they have their reasons, just like we do, but that is another story to tell later. Can you give us a map or tell us how to get there?"

"Sure thing," Henry obliged. "I'll get the map and show you the best way to get there. There's some wild country out that way. There were Indians there a long time ago, but they all moved further west."

While Henry went back to get the maps, Luke said, "Henry and I wanted to know if you four would like to stay here for the winter. The reason being is we want to start another trading post way west at a place called the Great Kauhawa River. It feeds into the Ohio River. It isn't too far from North Carolina. It is in the lower part of Virginia."

The four of us looked at each other and started to get excited about this new trading post idea.

"Do you or Henry have a map of where this river is located?" Lily asked.

"We sure as hell do. They just got it surveyed here last year. We went out there and saw it would be a great location, being near those two large rivers. There are a lot of people taking the Ohio westward, so there isn't very much out there now but in a few years there will be."

Henry came in with the map. Lily brought all of us more coffee and sat down at the table. I could tell her mind was already focused on this map.

Henry said, "Now, here is what Luke and I have been thinking about since you all came here. We would like to go out there within a week and set up a trading post, but we can't leave this place unattended. So we would let you live here and work it while we are gone. You'll have to deliver supplies to different folks scattered all over these hills. We would leave one of the wagons you brought here and take the other with us with supplies to get started out there."

The more they both talked about this idea, the better it sounded to all of us.

Henry continued, "Now this is the other part of this idea. When spring gets here, we would come back here and take over this trading post again, but we would like the four of you to run the trading post out there. We would give you the place to run with hardly any cost to you."

The four of us looked at each other, and then one by one we nodded in agreement without saying a word.

Finally I stood up and said, "Well, my friends, looks like you got a deal."

Henry and Luke stood up and smiled.

"We know we can trust all of you," Henry confirmed.

They shook all our hands and Luke said, "Well, the two of us had better get started and decide what we'll need to take on our trip. It may be a rough early winter around here and maybe a hard trip to the Great Kauhawa River."

Joshua then said, "Can we have this map to look at while you two are gone?"

"Hell, yes," Henry answered. "We have a few more that we can take with us."

Henry and Luke left and started to unload the supplies we had brought.

"Damn it."

"What is the matter, Robert?" Adam said.

"I never took the strong box out of the wagon last night. Now they'll find it."

Adam smiled and walked across the floor. "Is this what you are looking for, Robert?"

"When did you get it?"

"Me and Halfmoon went out before dawn and brought it in."

"Well, I'm glad somebody is thinking ahead. I must be getting too relaxed these days."

Joshua laughed and said, "Well, Robert, we'd better get the muskets and our powder. Henry and Luke will think it is theirs and sell it."

Joshua and I went out to the barn and got the muskets and all our supplies that we had brought from Albany. By the time we got back to the cabin, Lily and Adam were already looking at the map.

"I know some of the places on this map," Lily said. "Adam and I also know a lot of places where we can get in and out of Virginia and North Carolina without being seen. There are a few ways that a man could get through those mountains and lose anybody who is chasing them."

Lily and Adam had drawn a few lines through the mountains and along rivers that were not even marked.

I asked Lilly, "Are you thinking what I'm thinking?"

"You bet your life I am. With the new trading post located in this spot and the ways we can get in and out of the South, everything will be perfect for us. No one will ever find us once we get to these mountains here. Then we can take the people we free across to where we are now. I know very well that my aunt and uncle will hide them. Then when it is safe, we'll send them up into New York this way."

We all agreed that this was a blessing from God. We had a place to bring all the slaves we could break free and a route to follow, and the most important thing was that we had a cover—the trading post at the river. If it got really hard, we could go up the Ohio River and disappear for a long time.

After an hour or more, we had gone over every aspect of the map. We had to hide it in a place that would never be found by anyone else.

Lily gave Joshua the map and took a large stone from the fireplace next to the floor on the right side, away from view. He put the map inside a leather pouch and placed it behind the stone. He replaced the stone so that no one would ever notice it had been disturbed.

That evening Henry and Luke brought in some supper. We all ate together and really enjoyed each other's company. Henry asked, "What are your plans for tomorrow?"

"I want to go and see my aunt and uncle," Lily declared. "Then after we spend time with them, we'll come back here for the night if there is enough daylight left."

"The reason I'm asking is that the day after tomorrow the two of us want to get started for the new trading post," he explained. "The weather this time of year has never been normal. We don't want to get caught in another blizzard."

I said, "We'll be all set up and ready to run things here until spring. The trading post is full now, and we should be all set until you get back."

"Well then, that's what we'll do," Henry announced. "We'll head out the day after tomorrow, and God willing, we'll have good weather all the way."

The Meeting

The day had finally come. This was the day that we had all talked about for the last week. Would Lilly's aunt and uncle accept us and our plans for freeing slaves?

We said good-bye to Henry and Luke and told them that we might be back that night but not to be alarmed if we weren't back until the next day. The four of us and Halfmoon started up the narrow road, which soon became a narrow path. The woods were very thick and the sun's light—what little there was—never even touched our backs. Halfmoon was ahead of us by twenty feet. Every once in a while he would stop, look all over, and listen; when he was satisfied, he continued along the path. There was something bothering me as we went up and down the hills and across small streams. I couldn't put my finger on what it was, but something told me this trip wouldn't be so damn easy.

We got to the next rise and I said, "Let's stop here for a bit. I've got this damn gut feeling that something ain't right."

"I've been having the same feeling, Robert," said Joshua.

"Lilly, Adam, stay here with the horses," I instructed. "Joshua, Halfmoon, and I are going on foot for a little ways. By this map, your aunt and uncle's house should be down around that hill. We want to make sure all is normal there."

"What do you think is wrong, Robert?" Lily asked.

"I can't say yet, but, damn it, when I get these feelings, I take it real easy until I see for myself."

"We'll stay here," she said. "If you need us in a hurry, just fire your musket and we'll be there right away."

Joshua and I started to walk slowly over the next hill. Halfmoon went ahead of us. Suddenly, he stopped dead in his tracks.

"Robert, look at Halfmoon," Joshua said. "He sees something, and he doesn't seem to like it."

Joshua and I crawled on our stomachs to some brush that would give us a good view of the cabin. From there we saw four men walking around the cabin. They had horses outside, and it looked like they had been there for a few days. We didn't see any sign of Lily's aunt, but thought that maybe she was inside.

"What do ya think, Joshua?" I asked.

"I don't know for sure, but let's just sit tight for a minute and see who else may be there."

Within a few minutes, we saw two men carrying some furniture out of the cabin. Then a man came from around the back with a horse and wagon. They started to load furniture and other items in the wagon.

The Meeting

"I don't like the looks of this, Joshua," I said. "Something tells me this ain't normal."

"I agree with ya there, Robert. Now what in hell do we do?"

"Let's get back with Lily and Adam. We'll tell them what is going on there, and then we'll decide."

"I know they aren't moving again," Lily said when we returned. "Something is wrong. We'd better get down there quick."

"Easy, Lily," Adam said. "Let Robert and Joshua figure out a plan first."

I took a deep breath and said, "We'll do like our grandfathers used to do during the wars. We'll surround them and be very quiet and careful. We don't want to warn them of us being nearby, so leave the horses here, take your muskets, and slowly move closer to the cabin. When we are all set, I'll yell out to those men first. We'll see what their reaction is. If I'm right, they'll start to fire at me. When they do that, you'd better aim damn good and fire back. Wound them or kill them, makes no damn difference to me, but you'd better hit them. I believe there are no more then four men there, maybe one inside or close by."

We all got into position, and then I yelled to the men by the cabin. "Hey there! What are you doing?"

One of the men looked toward me but couldn't see me. He yelled out, "Show your face, man." He reached for the pistol in his belt.

I yelled, "Don't draw that damn pistol, Mister, unless you plan on using it."

By then the three men were standing facing me, but none

119

of them had a clear sight of me. Then the other man yelled toward me, "What in hell do you want?'

"I want to see the woman and the man who live here come outside."

The three men just looked at each other, and I knew something was wrong. One of the men was very tall. He was dressed in torn old clothes. He yelled up to me, "You get down here and we'll show ya."

Then I heard a scream from inside the cabin. That was all I needed to hear. I took careful aim at the tall man and pulled the trigger of my musket. The silence of the woods was broken by loud musket fire from around the cabin. He fell backward and landed in the mud and snow. The other two men also fell where they were.

We all ran toward the cabin. By the time we reached the old front porch, two more men had come through the door. One had his pistol drawn, and the other had a musket. As they stepped off the porch, I saw Adam throw his long knife and it found its mark. He hit the man with the pistol dead center in his chest. He grabbed the knife and just looked at Adam. Then he took two more steps and fell to the ground. The other man started to raise his musket toward Adam, but Adam was already a move ahead of him. His second knife was already thrown, and it too went deep into the man's stomach.

"You black son-of-Satan," the man yelled as he fell backward into the cabin.

Another scream came from inside. We ran inside the cabin and there was Lilly's aunt—naked from the waist down. She was cut pretty badly. Her husband was tied up in the corner. His face was red from the blood where he had been beaten.

Lily screamed, "Aunt Kate!" and ran to her. She held her in her arms and cried. Adam ran over to Lily's uncle, untied him, laid him on the floor, and tended to his wounds.

Joshua and I ran out of the cabin to see if anyone was still alive outside. We heard a man yell. When we turned around, we saw he was about to attack us with a knife. Out the corner of our eyes, we saw Halfmoon run and jump onto the man's back. He sank his massive jaws into the back of the man's neck. The man and Halfmoon fell forward into the snow. The man yelled with pain. Finally, we told Halfmoon to let him go, but he remained standing over him.

We turned him over, and I asked, "Who the hell are you? And what in hell are you doing here?"

The man looked at us and said, "Go to hell."

"You had better answer me, or I'll have our wolf finish you off."

Halfmoon had his teeth showing and was waiting for us to tell him to finish this miserable, foul-smelling man. As soon as he saw Halfmoon, he yelled, "All right, get that damn wolf off of me."

"No, you son-of-a gun," I snarled. "You tell us now while he is standing over you."

"My boys and me were stealing from these people."

"That ain't all that you did, you bastard."

"Well, we took turns with the woman, that's all."

"Where in hell are you from?"

"We are up from Virginia. We needed supplies and

money."

By then Lily had walked out the door over to this low-life. She said to us, "Are the others dead?"

"Yes, they are all dead except this one."

As soon as I said that, Lily took out her pistol and shot the man point blank in the head.

"Now he can join his other bastard friends. They all deserved worse, but I don't have the damn time to do it. All these miserable scum have raped my poor aunt in there. My poor uncle may not see tomorrow. They cut him up real bad."

Joshua said, "Adam told us no man had better ever piss her off. He sure as hell was telling the truth."

"No lie, Joshua," I agreed. "We'll never have to worry about protecting her. I'm just glad she loves us. I'd hate to have her running me down."

Joshua and I went to each man and tried to learn as much as we could about him. Of the six dead men, only two had any papers on them. One man had a folded up poster that read:

WANTED
REWARD FOR RUNAWAY SLAVES
WILL PAY $500.
DELIVER TO CHARLESTON, SOUTH
CAROLINA
TRADER: ANDREW PICKINS

"Well, I'll be a damned," I said. "These low-life bastards are looking for runaway slaves. Looks to me like they would steal and kill for a handful of gold."

"Now I know we did the right thing by laying them out," Joshua replied. "They deserved to die or be hung."

After we searched the men, we took their guns and whatever else we could use and went back inside the cabin.

Adam had stoked up the fire and was giving Lily's uncle some hot coffee to drink. He had cleaned the poor man's face from the blood that had been running out of the cuts. Lily had put her aunt in bed and had taken two wool blankets to cover her. The poor woman was in shock.

Lily looked up at us and said, "I'm sorry I killed that man like I did, but I was so damn mad that I didn't think."

"Don't worry about it," I replied. "One of us would have slit his throat by now anyway."

I handed her the old worn-out poster that we found on one of the men. She called Adam over, and they both read it.

Adam just looked at Lily and said, "You did the right thing, Lily, blowing his brains out. I would have made him suffer for a while first."

Lily's Aunt Kate and Uncle John were finally asleep. We made some supper, but we were all a little shaken up by what we had seen. Halfmoon lay by the door, where he would stay until we left. He did this whenever he was worried about us.

Adam said, "Your uncle will be all right, Lily. He is a tough man. He has stopped bleeding now, and he'll be fine come morning. "

"I won't be going back to the trading post with you tomorrow," Lily said. "I have to stay here and make sure my aunt and uncle will be fine. It may be a month or so, but they need me now."

"Well, that's what we were thinking also," I said. "Why don't you two stay here? Joshua and I will go back tomorrow and tell Henry and Luke what happened out here. We can handle the trading post until you are ready to come back."

"I sure ain't going to leave you out here by yourself, Lily," Adam maintained. "I'll stay with you. There is work to be done around here, and I can do it until your uncle is up to it."

Lily took Adam's hand and said, "Adam, I don't know what I would do without you taking care of me. You have been so good to me and have protected me for so long."

"I told you long ago, Lily, that I would never leave you alone. And I ain't about to start now."

Joshua stood up and said, "Well, I guess we'd better dig a hole for those dead men out there. The wolves will be on their bones before dawn, so let's get rid of them now."

Adam and I walked out the door with Joshua and found some shovels in the shed out back. We dragged the bodies far from the house and dug the graves. No final words were said, and no marker of any kind was placed over them. The devil would take these so-called men soon enough.

We took the wagon and the horses and put them in the barn. We bedded them down and fed them for the night. By the time we got back inside the cabin, it was cold and dark outside. We stoked the fire and found some ale in a jug on the top shelf. We passed it around until it was gone. We all felt a little better, but we knew this would not be the last time we would have to kill some low-life scum.

What we all had to do that day would forever change our lives. There was no turning back for any of us. We saved two poor innocent people's lives, but by doing this, we had to take six men's lives.

We talked about this until late at night. We knew there was no other way to have stopped them from killing Lily's aunt and uncle. I knew they would have killed us if we gave them a chance. From that moment on, the four of us would always be on guard for any stranger.

After the sun was up for nearly an hour, I noticed Lily's uncle was starting to sit up in his bed. He looked around and remembered what had happen the day before.

"Kate! Kate!" he yelled. "Where are you?"

Lily ran over to her uncle, kneeled in front of him, and took his hand. "It's me, Lily, Uncle," she said. "I'm here and Aunt Kate is fine."

Uncle John grabbed Lily and hugged her.

"What in hell are you doing here, Lily?"

"It's a long story. I'll tell you soon enough, but first come with me and see your wife."

She took her uncle's hand and slowly walked him over to where her aunt was sitting up in bed. He looked at her and then said, "I'm so sorry, Kate. I tried to stop them bastards, but there were too many for me to handle."

"I'm not mad at you, John," Kate told him. "You did the best you could against them. I'll be fine in a few days. The important thing is that we are still alive, thanks to Lily and her friends. If they hadn't shown up when they did, we

125

would have been dead. I heard one of them tell the other man to burn the house down after they took everything they wanted."

By then Lily had both their hands in hers. "We are all here now," she said, "and no one will ever do that to you two again."

"Tell me how you came here with your brave friends," Kate said.

Lily explained how she and Adam met Joshua and me. She also told her of the plans that the four of us had and where we would be until spring.

Lilly's aunt and uncle didn't say a word while she was talking. Then her aunt said, "I can tell you all right here and now that John and I are behind you all the way. We will do whatever it takes to help you with this so-called Underground Railroad to help the slaves. From here we can take them even farther north where no men like that will ever hurt them again or take them back south."

Lily smiled and said, "I knew you two would help us. I know it is the right thing to do. And we know there will be hard times for us, but we'll do whatever it takes to do this. Now that we know you will help us, we can go ahead with our plans of getting back down in the South or wherever we can free those poor souls."

"Well, Joshua and I had better get back to the trading post and let Henry and Luke know what happened here," I said. "I know by now they are starting to wonder where in hell we are. You and Adam stay here as long as you need. We can manage the trading post until you come back."

We said our good-byes to Lily's aunt and uncle and told

them we would help them in any way possible. Joshua and I then got our horses and headed back. Halfmoon once again took point.

By the time we got back to the trading post and explained all that had happened, it was nearly dark.

"Well, you boys did the right thing by killing them bounty hunters," Henry told us. "We're surprised they didn't try and rob us. Maybe they had seen you four here and decided not to."

Luke said, "I wish to hell they would have tried to rob us here first. I would have enjoyed killing them. All them bounty hunters are the same. They'll cheat, lie, steal, or do whatever it takes to make a damn gold piece. Well, now they can rot in hell. I'll tell you two something else: there are hundreds of them out there, so you be damn careful and don't trust one of them. The day you do is the day you'll pay with your life."

"Luke is right," Henry confirmed. "We grew up together like you two. Many years ago, when we were about your age, we left home looking for our own life. We headed out to St. Louis and from there we went west. Back then there were only a few white men who ever went that far west. Well, there were some French trappers, but I tell you, it was tough living. We made enough the first few years, so we came back East and sold our furs and pelts. We had plenty of money and every man knew it. It wasn't long afterward that we were attacked by a handful of these thieves. All hell broke loose. Old Henry and I were pretty shot up, but we survived. We killed them all and just let them stay where they fell. We figured the wolves and buzzards would take care of them. From that day on, we haven't said a word about it to no man. You are the first men we've told, because we trust you."

Luke said, "So, my friends, now you know about us, and that's why we are letting you two run this place and the new trading post next spring. I know that you four have kept something from us, but that's all right. Still, we sure as hell would like to know what it is. Maybe we can help."

Joshua looked at me and smiled. "Why not, Robert?" he asked. "Let's tell them about our plans. I know Adam and Lily won't mind now."

"The four of us have decided to stay here until spring, as you both wish for us to," I began. "Then we'll go to your new trading post in Virginia. We would like to use the trading post as a cover for a stopping place on this Underground Railroad. We will buy or rent the business from you. No one will know that you are owners or part owners of this trading post. What we want to do is get so-called conductors set up on certain routes from the South to Ohio and finally into Canada."

Henry and Luke looked at each other and smiled.

"Well, I'll be," Luke said. "Old Henry and I thought that you four had something up your sleeves, but damn, we didn't expect this."

Joshua started to get uneasy and said, "We won't say another word about it to you. We don't want you two thinking we are crazy."

"Hell, no," said Luke.

"We are behind you all the way," Henry assured us. "I know damn well it would work by having the trading post as a cover. This so-called Underground Railroad—where would you even start finding help in the South? Every rich person has slaves working the cotton and tobacco crops down there. And if they ain't rich, they are hunting down runaways. How in hell can you even find one person to help you down there?"

"That will be a big problem, I know," I said. "But there has got to be somebody living there among all the slave owners who could start them on their way north."

Luke scratched his chin and said, "There is a man we know who lives in South Carolina right plumb in the middle of some of the largest plantations around."

"Who is this man?"

"He is my brother Victor Roberts. Hell, he has been there since the British were marching all over down there and along the East Coast. He is a blacksmith, one of the best there is. He has a big shop there. All the rich plantation owners come to him for ironwork. The last I heard from him was almost two years ago. He said in his letter that he had three men working for him."

Joshua then asked, "How do you know he would help us?"

"He told me in his letter that he hated those rich plantation owners, but he loved their money," Luke answered. "He said that one time he had to go to one of them fancy plantations to fix some wagons. When he got there, they had two slaves hanging from a tree, and this overseer was whipping the hide off them both at once. My brother didn't say a word. He just did the work on the wagons and left. But he said he was shaken up for days by what he had seen.

From that day on, he has hated them and how they mistreat them poor black folks. That's how I know he'll help you once you get there."

"Where could we meet him, Luke?" I asked.

"I'll give ya the town's name and where it is. But you'd better not take Adam with you. If ya do, you're going to get more damn trouble than you can handle. They aren't too kindly on two men and a woman riding around the countryside, and they sure as hell aren't going to let a Negro roam free with you."

"We know there is a lot to think about before we start this," I stated, "but we will figure it out in time."

Henry said, "You'll need some type of cover going into those areas. Maybe you could go as traders. That is common all over this land. You could take one of the big wagons and have supplies to sell from town to town. That way no one will even think of you as strangers. If you can get a certain route established from town to town, you'll be able to have this conductor help you out. But you'll need to have at least some safe houses all the way from here to Georgia. You sure won't be able to have all the slaves in the damn wagon going up the road. There will be bounty hunters just like the ones you killed on the roads checking for runaways or just trying to rob you."

Joshua and I thought about this for a while, and then we told Henry and Luke that we'd think about doing it that way. We had a lot to think about until spring, but we knew we would come up with a good plan before we started to go south.

"It's getting late, and I know you two are all ready to

start out in the morning," I said. "Let's all get some sleep and say our good-byes in the morning."

Henry and Luke agreed. They were facing a long trip, and they hoped the weather would be kind to them.

The next day Joshua and I got up early and stood on the porch of the old cabin. The early morning October sun was setting the oak and maple leaves afire with color. The frost had come early that year, and we were glad that we were there for the fall. Joshua said he had the feeling it would be a tough, hard winter. We were both glad we were not the ones heading into the hills of Virginia. We heard Henry and Luke cussing as they brought the horse and wagon around to the front of the store.

"Well, my good friends," said Luke, "I guess we are ready to go."

I said, "We'll be fine here. Don't worry about the store. We'll protect it like it is ours."

Joshua smiled and said, "Old Halfmoon here will keep an eye on it during the night. There ain't anybody going to bother it or us."

Henry laughed and said, "That's for damn sure. That Halfmoon is a great wolf to have as a friend."

Halfmoon must have sensed they were leaving. He ran off the porch and sat between Luke and Henry. They reached down, patted his head, and gave him some food they had leftover from breakfast. I called Halfmoon back to the porch, and as Henry and Luke started to pull away, he barked and we waved good-bye.

"We'll see you back here in the spring," I said. "Have a

safe trip. Good luck."

As we watched them disappear around the corner and over the steep hill, we knew we would see them around April. They were two tough characters, and they could handle almost anything.

Joshua said, "Well, Robert, let's go open the trading post. Maybe we'll get some business today."

"I sure hope so," I replied. "It'll be a long day if we just stand around dusting off the supplies."

We laughed and went into the store. We knew just about where everything was, so we could handle any orders the people would need.

It was just about noon when a man and a woman came in with their two young boys. They asked where Henry and Luke were, and we told them all the latest. They said they would tell their neighbors about us so everyone would know that we were running things until April.

The next few weeks were very busy. People wanted to stock up for the winter because they didn't want to come five miles in the snow and cold to get supplies.

We figured that we had almost two hundred people come into the store from mid October to the end of November. That was just about all the people who lived nearby and out a few miles. They were a tough bunch. Many were Germans, and some were from Ireland. They were all great people, friendly and willing to do anything for us if we asked them. They reminded me a lot of the folks back in Sprout Brook. They too were strong. Joshua and I talked a lot about home, and it seemed so long ago that we had left. But we weren't sorry for leaving. We had our own lives now, and soon we would be doing something that no man had ever tried. We knew we had to try to free the Negro slaves. We couldn't change their owners' views or even free very many, but we sure as hell would get as many as we could to Ohio and Canada.

It was the first week of December when Lily and Adam came to the store with her aunt and uncle. It was so good to see them all again. John and Kate looked like new people after all the rest and care they had gotten.

We had a big dinner together that first night. It was sure good to see them laughing and happy again.

John said, "I never really had time to thank you both for what you did for us. We are fine now and back to normal, and it has been so damn good to see Lily and Adam again."

"What my husband says is the truth," Kate added. "I'm fine now. Once in a while I think about what happened, but life goes on and we are alive and all together like a big family. You two men are our family also, and always will be."

Joshua and I thanked them for their kind words.

As the night went on, we talked about the latest gossip from the trading post. We told them about all the people who lived in the area. We also assured them that no one knew what had happened at their cabin and no one ever would.

John said, "Kate and I have listened to Lily and Adam's idea of this Underground Railroad. We have been talking, and now that we are all together, I want to tell you what we have decided. We are behind you on this, and we will do whatever it takes to hide these poor slaves here. I have a brother who lives in Ohio who will take them from here to his home on the Allegheny River in a place called Cypress Swamp. He lives on the banks of Lake Erie where he can take care of them until we can get them into Canada. There isn't a hell of lot out there, but there's some very good farmland. A man could do just fine there with some hard work and all."

Joshua asked, "What does your brother do?"

"He used to be a captain on a whaling ship out of New England," John told us. "He made plenty of money whaling for oil. Then he hurt his leg at sea and couldn't get around very well while bouncing on the water. So he sold his boat and went out there on the lake. He loves the water and just fishes all day."

"How do you know he will help?" I wondered.

"There's one thing about my brother and me," he replied. "When we need each other, we do whatever it takes. When I see him in the spring, I'll tell him all about this Underground Railroad. He had a few free blacks on his ship, and he always told me how hard they worked and what good men they were. I know he will do this."

"Everything is coming together for us," Lily declared. "We have stations from Lake Erie to the hills of Virginia already. That sure is a load off my mind, but the damn hard part is from Virginia south."

Then Joshua and I told them what Luke had said about his brother in Georgia, near Atlanta. We also told them what Henry and Luke had told us about the trading post in Virginia and how we could use it as a front.

Lily and Adam were very excited about this news.

John and Kate spent the night in the cabin with Lily and Adam. Joshua and I had moved into the trading post upstairs until spring. It had an open loft that overlooked the whole store. It was quite large, and we both had plenty of room. Halfmoon loved it there; he slept at the top of the stairs and kept watch all day and night. People would see him sitting there and say, "He is a damn big wolf, or whatever he is." They never wanted to pet him, and we were glad of that.

John and Kate loaded up supplies and went back to their home the next morning. Lily and Adam helped us at the trading post. Once in a while we had to take supplies out to some families, but very seldom. Most of the time we sat around the wood stove and made plans for our upcoming journeys south. We talked about how and when we would get into the South and the plantations and what would we do then. We all had different ideas about how to bring slaves away safely, but we didn't know how we could keep them concealed on the road, or anyplace else for that matter.

One day Joshua said, "I have an idea that just might work."

"I knew you would come up with something," I remarked. "You always do."

"Do you remember how our grandpas used to build wagons and how big they were?" he asked.

"I sure do. They were the best around."

"Now hear me out all of you, and let me finish before you laugh at me."

Lily said, "We won't laugh at you, Joshua; not much anyway."

We all laughed, even Joshua.

Joshua said, "What if we build a big wagon like our grandfathers did, but this time we make it higher off the ground? If we do this, we could build a false floor in it, maybe big enough so two to four people could lie down in there."

We all tried to picture this. I said, "Well, I'll be damned. That just might work, Joshua. Go on and tell us more."

"If we get into some bad areas where there may be slave trackers looking for runaways," he continued, "they can crawl into this false bottom and not be seen. We would have loose boards over them, built so they lie on cleats and not directly on top of the slaves. We could still have all the supplies in the wagon. Nobody's gonna look under the damn supplies for people. They may look in the wagon, but they won't see anything except supplies. We could have holes drilled into the side for air, but small enough so nobody can see in. Plus, we'll have water barrels and other supplies hanging on the sides so there ain't no way anyone will know there is a false floor."

"You are a smart man, Joshua," I exclaimed. "You're the spiting image of your grandfather, Ben Wells."

Lily said, "You are a *very* smart man, Joshua. That is the greatest idea any man could've had."

Adam smiled and said, "It is perfect. They'll see a big wagon and think we need it for all the heavy supplies we carry to sell."

Joshua went on to say, "I know it will be hard lying in

there, but with some blankets down it might not be too bad."

Adam said, "They won't care. They have been through much worse pain than that. I know. I was whipped like a mule, even worse. Lying on their backs for a few miles ain't gonna hurt them. And I tell ya one thing: they won't make a sound. They know if they do, we'll all be killed or hung on the spot."

"They will never hang any of us," I insisted. "We'll die fighting before any man whips or tries to hang any of us."

We all agreed to that. We knew none of us would be taken alive. This was our oath, and we knew sure as hell that we would take as many as we could with us if we were to die.

The next day was very cold and the snow was starting to fall again. It soon covered everything like a wool blanket. Seeing snow had always made Joshua and me feel more relaxed. We went about our daily tasks of keeping the trading post clean and organized. It was after lunch when Adam and Lily came by the trading post. Adam walked over to where Joshua, Halfmoon, and I were sitting around the wood stove.

"I have been thinking about this wagon," Adam said. "We had better start reworking the big one you two brought here from Albany."

Joshua jumped up and said, "That's it, Robert. We can rebuild the wagon we brought here. It is bigger than most wagons. We can easily redo it any way we want."

Adam smiled and said, "I knew I could think of something to help."

As we were running out to the barn, Lily tried to get in the back door. She yelled, "What in blazes are you three up to now?"

We told to her about Adam's idea of redoing the old wagon in the barn. She thought it was a great plan.

"I'll stay in the store with Halfmoon in case we get any customers," she offered.

Joshua, Adam, and I opened the barn door and searched for any lumber we could use. Henry and Luke had everything we needed. Adam started up the fire pit and got the blacksmith tools ready for any ironwork that would be needed. Joshua and I started to take the wagon apart from the axles up.

For the next month, we toiled over this wagon. It was hard work, and we spent many hours trying different things. Finally, near the end of March, we had just what we wanted. It was one of a kind, that's for darn sure. We had added the secret bottom to it. We knew no one would notice it. All any man would see was an unusually large wagon. We had plenty of air vents cut into the sides, and we could position supplies to cover them up from anyone's eyes. Inside we added another foot to the original sides and more heavy cleats for the canvas. Under the front seat we built a hidden compartment for pistols and powder. There was only one way to open it, and we practiced opening it for many hours until it became second nature for us.

With the extra weight and height, we knew we needed three teams of strong, well-trained horses to pull it. That wasn't a problem, as we already had two teams that came with us when we delivered the supplies to Henry and Luke. John and Kate had an extra set of strong horses that they had given us, so during the days when the weather was warmer, we had all three teams working together. They started to work well together, and they sure had the power to run when needed.

The winter was cold and snowy, but we were so busy working on the wagons that the time went by quickly. By the time we had the horses and wagon all set to go it was the middle of April. The trading post would be quiet for a week at a time, but once the weather got warmer, the local settlers would come all at once. It would take all four of us to supply the people with what they needed for the coming spring.

It was near the end of April when we saw four riders come up to the trading post. They were strangers to us and to the local men who bought supplies from us and chatted about the winter and upcoming spring.

Joshua watched as they came up the road and said, "Look, Robert, they are a rough-looking bunch."

Adam walked out onto the porch and stood with Joshua and me. Halfmoon was lying in the warm sun. He suddenly jumped on all fours and started to growl.

"Joshua, go in and get Lily," I said. "You two get the muskets ready. Tell her to stay inside and to be ready for anything."

Joshua walked inside and then reappeared with a musket. As the four men rode up to the store and dismounted, they didn't say a word. They stood side by side, and the man who must have been the leader said, "We are passing through and need some supplies."

I answered, "Well, we may be able to help, but it has been a long winter here and we are running out of everything."

One of the other men, who was dressed in ragged clothes, said, "I see you have enough to feed that nigger there."

Adam started to move.

"Don't do anything, Adam," I said. "Not yet anyway."

Joshua said, "It is none of your damn business about our friend here. We'll sell you what you need and then you get down the road. We ain't looking for trouble."

The leader said, "We are looking for some men who were maybe out this way last fall. Have you ever seen them?"

"I can't say that we have," I answered. "Why do you ask?"

"One of them is our brother; the others are just friends. They were hunting up this way."

They were hunting all right, I said to myself, for slaves or anything they could steal.

"They probably never came this far north," I stated. "We have been here since last fall, and no one has come through that we didn't know."

One of the men looked around said, "Well, that sure looks like their horse back there. Where did ya get that horse back by the barn?"

Joshua raised his voice, "I really don't remember. Maybe some passerby traded us for some supplies he needed. We get a lot of people passing through here."

Then the one man who had said nothing all this time spoke up, "How is it that you got a nigger here with you?"

I was getting mighty angry at these men, but I held myself back. "Are you talking about our friend Adam? He is a free man, born in New York. Joshua and I hired him almost two years ago—best man we ever had. If I were you, I would treat him as a good man."

"So you two are nigger lovers, are ya? Where we come from, we treat our horses better than those slaves."

The time for kind words had ended.

Joshua said loudly, "You men had better leave now. And we ain't selling you as much as a handful of flour. Get on down the road and don't come back here."

The four men were getting nervous and slowly reaching for their side arms. Lily walked out the door. She had a bead on the leader and said to him, "You heard Joshua! Now get out of here!"

One of the men laughed and said, "Well, look at that, boys. We got a white bitch and a nigger with two dumb Yankees. They must all have fun together at night."

There was a pause for a second, and then the sound of Lily's musket exploded. The smoke flared as one man was hit within twenty feet of where she was standing. Suddenly all hell broke loose. The other three men grabbed their pistols, but before they had them out two more lay dead on the ground. The last man reached for his knife, but before he could use it, Halfmoon jumped from the porch right onto his chest. The man reached for his knife and was about to come down on Halfmoon. Adam leaped off the porch, grabbed the man by his hair, and slit his throat.

While all this was happening, Henry and Luke were almost to the trading post.

Henry yelled, "What in hell has happened here? This is a hell of a thing to come home to."

Luke stopped the wagon and ran over to us. "Are you all right? Is there any more of this trash around?"

Joshua stepped off the porch and said, "If there was, it sure as hell headed the other way, hopefully back south."

Halfmoon finally realized who had come on the wagon. Once he heard Henry's and Luke's voices, he ran over and greeted them.

"We're damn glad to be back home," Henry said, "but we sure never thought this would be the first thing we would see. Damn, what a mess! We'd better look through their pockets and see who they were and where they were from."

Joshua and I joined Henry and Luke and went through their personal belongings. The only thing we found was another poster like the one we had found on the dead men at John and Kate's house. I showed it to Lily and Adam.

"See what we are going to run into down south?" Lily said with a disgusted look on her face. "If these four have come all the way north to hunt down black people, they will be like ticks on a dog down there."

Adam looked down at the blood on his hands and said, "It ain't been five months and I have already killed two men. I don't want to kill anybody, but it always seems like I ain't got no choice."

Luke put his arm around Adam's big shoulders and said, "You did what you had to do, Adam. There ain't no good

142

time to kill any man, but when the scum of the earth comes a-calling on you and will kill you in a minute, you ain't got no choice but to kill him first."

All we found in the men's saddlebags was ten dollars. There was also a paper saying they were slave trackers.

Henry looked at it and said, "Them bounty hunters think they can go anywhere and bring back Negroes. They don't care if they are free or not. All they care about is the five hundred dollar reward. I bet they would burn any paper that they found on a poor black man and tell them back in Charleston that he's a runaway."

Henry said, "Let's get them out into the woods and bury their bodies. I'm glad there was no one here watching. There ain't nobody going to come looking for poor white trash like this."

It took two hours to bury them on the property. No marker was placed, and no sermon was said. They too will go to hell with the devil.

That afternoon Henry and Luke got settled back into their own place above the store, and Joshua and I moved back into the cabin with Lily and Adam. Lily had a big pot of stew slowly cooking over the fire, and it sure smelled good. Henry and Luke closed up the store and came into the cabin. During supper we all talked about the winter and what the latest news was in the area.

Henry told us about their journey to Virginia and their new trading post on the Great Kauhawa River.

"The road, or should I say 'trail,' there was really tough in some areas," he said. "There were streams to cross, and we even had to cut a few downed trees out of the way. We didn't meet one person on our way there. I thought for sure we would at least meet some trappers. It was the last day of November when we finally got to where our land is located on a hill overlooking the river. It sure is a nice piece of land. There were some local families trying to get their farms started. They were a hard bunch, but they were so good to us. We hired some of the men to build the trading post on a small bluff overlooking the river. There is a path that leads from the river to the trading post, so it isn't hard to get to. And what a view we have looking up and down the river. We finally got it closed in when the bad weather came. Those men sure built a strong building. Those Germans and Scots are damn good carpenters. That building will stand for a hundred years with a good roof on it."

"It sure sounds like my kind of place," I stated.

"I know it sure would be my kind of place to live in," said Joshua.

"When do you want us to go there?" I wondered.

"Well, we were thinking about that on the way back here," Henry answered. "We figured in another week or two. There is some work to do there before we can open it up to the settlers passing that way. We want to get you all there before something happens to the place. We don't want to have somebody come in and homestead the land, so the sooner the better for all of us."

"While you two were gone, we rebuilt the old wagon," Adam said. "It is something like you have never seen."

"These three men worked so hard and long on it, and I think you'll be impressed with it," Lily said.

I explained what we had come up with for moving supplies and slaves that we could free. I told them that we'd pay for the wagon and supplies that we planned to take with us to the new trading post.

"There is no way in hell you four are paying us for the wagon or supplies," Henry scoffed. "You have stayed here, run this store, and made money for us. Don't even think of paying us. We are partners, and we'll help each other as long as we can. Now we don't want to hear another word about this matter again."

The rest of the evening we talked about the new trading post, and what supplies we should take to stock it. We were low on supplies, but we had enough to get started. Henry and Luke had a man going back to Albany to reorder supplies from Patrick. They expected them to arrive in about a month.

We told Henry and Luke how we planned to set up different stations from the new trading post to John and Kate's place, and how John would take Negroes up to his brother's land on Lake Erie. Henry and Luke were surprised that we had already done so much planning.

The next morning we showed Henry and Luke the wagon in the barn. They smiled and Luke said, "Well, I'll say this for you, men. You sure as hell can build a strong wagon. I can tell you had some good teaching from your grandfathers. They were very good carpenters and black-smiths. Hell, this will last a long time, and the way you have that false floor in it is perfect. I wouldn't have known about it if you hadn't showed it to me."

The rest of the day we added water and feed barrels to the sides. Then we loaded hundreds of pounds of supplies.

The wagon still had room for more, but we didn't want to fill it up completely. We needed room for all of us to be comfortable during the long journey.

The Great Kauhawa River

The day had finally come that we had talked about for almost a year. It was May 5, 1794. The warm spring weather was finally upon us. The smell of apple blossoms filled the air and all the woods around us had come alive. Green grass shot up in the meadows, and the spring rains had given new life to the small streams. We were ready to begin our second journey to Virginia.

Henry and Luke said we should be there in two months. It could take longer with the large wagon and the heavy load of supplies. We were in no hurry; we just wanted a safe trip and hoped we wouldn't come across any men like the ones we had killed. If we met any on our way, we would know how to handle them, but killing was the last thing we wanted to do.

When it was time to say good-bye to Henry and Luke, John and Kate came to see us off. It was a sad day for all of us; we had become a very close family. But we all knew what we had to do, and we wanted to help Henry and Luke get their new trading post up and running.

Halfmoon jumped up on the wagon, barked, and wagged his tail in delight. We told each other we would keep in contact somehow.

As we started the three teams of horses down the road, we all became quiet. Each of us thought about what might lie ahead and how we would handle this new adventure.

We must have been a sight to anybody we passed. We were in a most unusual wagon, one that no man had ever seen before. Then there was Halfmoon, a wolf close to a hundred and twenty-five pounds. If that wasn't enough to see, there were two white men, a woman in buckskins, and a black man. We all laughed and made jokes about it.

It was so good to be moving again and seeing things we had never seen before. The country was beautiful; we could see the hills behind us and some open land ahead. Far off in the distance we could see the Great Allegheny foothills that climbed high into the sky. That was where we were to go. The map that Henry and Luke had given us included great detail. It had every stream and small trail drawn on it. They were very smart men, and I understood why they were so successful in whatever they did. I just hoped time would make me just as wise.

It was almost the end of the third week on the road when Joshua looked at the map. He said, "We should be coming to the Ohio River tomorrow, and then we will meet the Great Kauhawa River. We have to follow the Kauhawa River south. That's where the Shenandoah Valley is, and by what Henry and Luke drew on this map, that's where we'll come to the main route into North Carolina."

"This is supposed to be the easiest way through the mountains," Adam said. "I heard this from a few slaves who had tried to escape but were caught and brought back."

It was late in the afternoon when we decided to stop for the night. We found a great area to rest and take care of the horses. There was a small stream that flowed so slowly and plenty of green grass for the horses to graze on all night.

As always, we had a great supper. Lily proved herself to be the best cook around. She could take any type of meat and make it into a feast.

While we were sitting around the fire, I looked at Lily for a few minutes. She noticed me and said, "What are you looking at, Robert?"

"I was just thinking that we had better get you a dress or something before too long."

"Why do you want me in a dress?"

"Well, ya just can't keep wearing them buckskins all the time. When we get down further south, you're gonna have to wear a dress and kind of blend in with other women."

"I'm not wearing a frilly dress at the trading post, Robert."

"As much as you like those buckskins, Lily, ya gotta get into the part of a sweet Southern belle," Joshua reminded her.

"To heck with the sweet Southern belles," she scoffed. "I hate dresses and the way those women act. They make me sick."

We all laughed. Lily was really getting mad at the idea of dresses and all. I then said, "Well, we'll just have to cut some of your hair so you'll look more like a man."

Joshua burst out laughing. "That ain't gonna work either, Robert. Lily has a figure like an hourglass. You're sure can't hide that."

"All right, you guys," Lily scolded. "I know I have a large chest and can't hide that, so I guess you win one on me wearing dresses. But I'm not getting in one until I have to." She smiled and said, "There is no way I can win with you three. It just isn't fair, three against one."

Adam laughed and said, "You got that wrong, Lily. You are as equal as we are. You can out-shoot, out-swear, and out-do any man at just about everything."

Joshua brought out some ale, and we sat there enjoying one another's company and drinking. Even Halfmoon was having a good time. He lay next to fire and watched us, wagging his tail.

The following day was an easy one for the horses. We started to cross the low rolling hills into Virginia. On each side of us the hills turned into larger hills that were covered with deep hardwood and pines. The road followed a slow-moving stream that cut into the lush green land ahead.

Within three days we had come to the Ohio River, a wide and strong river heading west. We stopped the wagon, rested the horses, and stretched our legs. The area was beautiful. Off in the distance we saw the mountains disappear into the skyline to the west, and there on our left was the Great Kauhawa River coming from the southern range called the Allegheny Mountains. This was where we would start the last leg of our journey. We were to follow the river and the road that crossed the mountains. Then at the top we would go southwest as the river flowed between the Allegheny Mountains and the Laurel Mountains. It was here that the river was formed between these two beautiful mountain ranges. The valley was almost as beautiful as the one we had been through. There at the mouth of the river was where the new trading post was located. Henry and Luke told us that settlers could raft the river and that the land along the banks was rich. It was a farmer's dream to have such fine rich earth.

We decided we would camp there for the night. The next day we would start the slow ride to our new home. It was not even three in the afternoon when we saw some riders on horses and a wagon off in the distance coming our way. We started to get nervous about seeing strangers.

"Now let's just relax," I said. "Not everybody we meet will be bad."

Three men on horses rode in front of a wagon. On the wagon were a man, a woman, and three small children. When they got closer, we saw that the one man was wearing buckskins and carrying a beautiful musket. He had beaded work all over his buckskins and some beautiful knives tied at his waistband. He also had two powder horns that were even bigger than our grandfathers'. They were covered with drawings that this unusual man must have carved with one of his knives.

"Hello there," he greeted. "Can we come into your camp?"

"Yes," Joshua answered, "please come in and have some coffee."

The men dismounted, walked toward the fire, and sat down. The one man, who was tall and well built, sat down and said, "Where are you folks headin'?"

"We are going southwest to the mouth of the Great Kau-hawa River," I told him. "We are opening a new trading post there."

"That is mighty pretty country down there," he replied. "I have been through there a few times coming from the Carolinas. Why did you all stop here for the night?"

"We wanted to rest the horses and start fresh in the morning," I answered. "We need to follow the river into those mountains."

"I guess you didn't know that there is a small settlement just over those hills there," the man said.

"No, we didn't. Our map never said anything about a settlement out here."

"Not many people know about it," he stated. "I founded it in 1775. It was originally a fort, but now it's a small settlement called Boonsboro. My name is Daniel Boone."

Joshua and I looked at each other.

"Joshua and I have heard your name spoken by our grandfathers and fathers," I said. "My name is Robert Flint and this here is Joshua Wells. We are from the Mohawk Valley in New York. These are our friends Adam and Lily. We are all going to work at the trading post together."

"It is sure nice meeting you folks," Mr. Boone replied. "I heard of the Mohawk Valley when I was a Wagoner for General Edward Braddock when we were cutting roads to Fort Duquesne in 1755. They changed the name of that area to Fort Pitt. I heard that the French and Indian War was mighty hard on all you folks up there."

"It sure as hell was," I answered. "Our grandfathers

fought in both them wars. They had some stories to tell us over the years growing up. Now they are both dead, and our fathers are still back there farming."

"I know the feeling," Daniel said with a nod. "I tried a little farming with my father in North Carolina, but I hated it. I could never stay home long enough, so I became a captain in the militia. I was defending some settlements from the Indians. The Shawnees captured my brother and me, but we were lucky and escaped."

"So what do you do now?" I asked.

"I had some land out West, but I lost it all," he answered. "I ain't a good businessman, I guess. So now I help guide young families like I have here to Boonsboro to settle or go west. But I'm fixin' to go west and live off the land in this place called Femme Osage Valley. It's the most beautiful place I have ever seen. I'll just hunt and enjoy my remaining years with my wife and family."

For the rest of the afternoon and late into the evening, we talked to Daniel. He reminded Joshua and me of our grandfathers and fathers. We told him about our lives in the Mohawk Valley and all about our grandfathers. Daniel was so laid back and pleasant to talk with. He told us about the wilderness he had seen and all that he had done.

"You folks are real nice," he said, "but I gotta ask you something. I don't want you to get mad at me, and I know it ain't my business, but seeing that big wagon there, I'm a-wondering if you have other plans besides running a trading post."

Lily said, "Yes, we do. Go ahead, Robert. Tell Daniel what we are going to do."

I looked at her and the others and said, "All right, I will."

I told Daniel what we planned to do for the slaves in the South and how the Underground Railroad would work.

After another hour and many cups of coffee, Daniel said, "Well, I have been down in the South a few times and I know one thing: they sure as hell think differently than us. I saw some slave-trading going on and thought it would just die out, but as I hear more and more about it and how these plantations are getting bigger and bigger, it's no doubt that they want cheap labor. They say there are more and more slaves coming in all the time from Savannah, Georgia, and different ports in the South. Tobacco farming is all there is in Virginia. They are growing cotton from North Carolina down the Mississippi and even sugar cane. There is a big demand for cotton up north, and the English are buying all that they can. The other thing I heard about a month ago is that this man called Eli Whitney has invented this cotton gin machine. They say it can pick more cotton than thirty slaves."

Joshua said, "No wonder the farms are getting bigger. Now they can grow a hundred acres of cotton and get it to market quicker. No wonder they are bringing in more slave labor."

Daniel leaned back and said, "I can see what will come in the years ahead. There is gonna be a damn war among ourselves over this slavery issue. I know that I'll be dead and this will be a fight like no other in this country. We fought the French, the British, and even the Indians, but this will be a bloody one. In a way, I'll be glad to be dead when it comes."

Everyone around the fire agreed.

"You're saying the same things our grandfathers told us a long time ago," I said. "They said that it would be like no other battle any of us had ever fought, that it might even be brother against brother. Hell, I can't imagine fighting against Joshua. He is closer than my brother ever was to me."

Daniel continued, "I tell other men this back East or wherever I go, and they all think I have been in the damn wilderness too long. But you four remember what I say here tonight. I'm sure you or your kin will be fighting in that war someday. I just hope you can free as many people as you can before hell comes down around us all in this country."

"We will do our damnedest, Daniel," I promised. "We'll be very careful and we'll not just jump into the hornet's nest. We have a lot to do, and God willing, we will free some of these poor people."

Daniel Boone and the others bedded down with us that night. All night long I said to Joshua, "I wish our grandfathers could have met this great man."

"Don't worry, Robert," Joshua replied. "They are looking down at us this very night. Just look at the sky above us. You see how clear it is?"

"I sure do."

We lay there for a minute or so and then Joshua yelled, "Look at that, Robert! Look at those two falling stars over toward the west."

We both looked and, sure enough, we saw two falling

stars sailing over the horizon. At that same moment, Half-moon let out a howl that could've wakened the dead.

Daniel came over to us and said, "There is your answer, my friends. Your grandfathers have heard you, and they are telling you and your friends that you are about to do the right thing."

"How do you know that?" Joshua asked.

"When you've lived out in this wilderness as long as I have and lived with Indians, you know a sign when you see it. This is a sign from your forefathers," Daniel stated. "They're letting you know that they are with you now, and that they agree with your journey. They're also saying that the wolf Halfmoon is truly the spirit of that man Coppernol that you two told me about. That wolf knows more than all of us put together, so make darn sure you never doubt his actions when you come upon strangers. He'll let you know if they are good or evil."

"We have said that before," I said, "but we were never sure it was so."

"Well, I'm telling you now, it is true," Daniel insisted. "He is something special. I have only seen one other animal like him in all my life. There was this Indian who lived across the Mississippi that I met a few years ago. He had special power, and he also had a wolf like yours. Those two were well known and well treated by many different tribes all along the Mississippi River. They say he and his wolf are both over one hundred years old. They live all over the wilderness and nothing can hurt them. They say he is the spirit of many Indians—not one tribe, but many. They say he can make it rain and thunder whenever he wants. I would like to meet him someday before I die. They tell me that no one knows when or where he may appear."

Daniel then left us and went to sleep.

Joshua, Halfmoon, and I sat there most of the night looking at the sky full of stars and wondering what the next day or year might bring us.

Early the next morning, we all had a big breakfast and then it was time to go our separate ways. Daniel shook our hands and said, "You four go with God. Be very careful. I know that someday before I die, I'll hear about you four and even Halfmoon there. I have this feeling that some of the Negroes that you free will be out my way. There is no law there or men to come after them. They will be well accepted by the Indians. They have a certain bond with the black man, so I know that they will be safe. I have enjoyed myself very much with your kindness. You people are always welcome in Boonsboro. I'll tell them about you and that someday I hope we'll meet again, if not in this lifetime, then in another. Until then, I'll say my last good-bye."

Just as quickly as they all came into the camp they were gone. As they disappeared over the hill, I knew we would see Daniel Boone again.

It was eight o'clock in the morning. The sun was getting warmer each day. We knew that a hard ride with the wagon lay ahead, but we were excited about finally arriving at our new home.

It took nearly a month for us to get through the mountain pass and down into the low lands of Virginia. On July 10, we finally arrived at the trading post. It was exactly like Henry and Luke had described. It stood on a bluff overlooking the Great Kauhawa River. It was there in between the Laurel Mountains and the Great North Carolina Piedmont Mountains that this river was born. The view was so beautiful. We could see nearly twenty miles in all directions. All along the riverbanks, we saw new farms being built and farmers plowing the land for the first time. The fertile black earth revealed all her riches. Such land was hard to find anywhere else.

When we reached the trading post, two German farmers were standing on the long wooden porch. They both smiled when we walked toward them. The one German, who had a long graybeard and the bluest eyes that I had ever seen before, was the first to speak.

"I see that our new storekeepers are finally here. It is good to see all of you with such a big wagon filled with supplies, which we need badly. My name is Karl Klockman. This man here with me is Hans Klingman. We came from Germany maybe fifteen years ago. We met Henry and Luke a long time ago. They are good men, and we have watched this post for them since they've gone. Now that you have arrived, we will let you take over this fine store. We helped build it, and we know it is a good building, very strong. It can take the winds on this hill here. Now we must go and tend to our planting."

I thanked them very much and asked what they were growing.

"We grow some tobacco," he answered, "and maybe we'll have a big apple orchard. We might raise some cows for milk and butter, but whatever we plant in this fine earth will grow very well."

Lily smiled and asked, "What is this place called?"

They both laughed.

"We don't rightly know," Karl answered. "Henry and Luke never said what it is called, but they told us that the four of you would come up with a name for it before too many settlers come here."

I said, "Well, that sounds like them two. They send us way out here into the wilderness to a place with no name. You wait 'til I see them again. I'll give them hell."

We all laughed and sat on the porch, gazing down at the green valley floor below.

Joshua smiled, stood up, and said, "I got it. We'll call it Round Knob. We are high on a hill here, and there isn't too much around us. And without walking all around here it sure looks round to me."

The three of us stood up and walked behind the trading post and came back onto the porch. Then Adam said, "It sure looks round to me too."

I laughed and said, "Then it is settled. From now on, this place will be called Round Knob."

We all let out a cheer. Joshua went to the wagon and brought back a jug of brandy. "Now before we get damn drunk," he said, "let's get these great horses unhitched and put them in the barn out back in the corral. We'll drive the wagon close to the back door so in the morning we can unload the supplies."

Adam was the first to get the horses unhitched and walk them back to the corral. I went with him, and he and I found a great spring that flowed from the high rocks behind the barn.

I said, "This place is perfect. We've got fresh water close by and even a nice meadow for the horses to graze in. I tell you, Adam, living here may be hard to leave when it comes time for us to go south."

Adam smiled and said, "This is what I have always dreamed of all my life. And here I'm with great friends and a new life. God does work in funny ways, don't he, Robert?"

"He sure does, Adam. He sure does."

In the middle of the afternoon the four of us wandered around the trading post and barn. The land was perfect for our needs, as well as the horses. Fresh spring water flowing into a small stream found its way down the hill and into the river. There were many streams all over the area that fed a never-ending supply of water to the river. There was a large meadow big enough for the horses to feed on. Just like Henry had said, there was a good easy road that led to the bottom of the hill. It was the perfect place for a trading post and station for the people we would free. There was a good view in all directions. Another good thing was that there was only one way to get there by horse or wagon. If more men than we could handle ever attacked us, we could move into the large boulders behind the barn and work our way down into the rocky face that surrounded the trading post. From there we could easily lose any man looking for us.

It was late in the day by the time we had explored the land around the trading post. We had a good view and understood how it laid. We wanted to get inside and see what we had to do with the store.

When we opened the door, we all stood there with our

mouths wide open. The interior was beautiful. We could sure tell by the great woodworking that these Germans knew how to build. There were huge oak timbers, straight as arrows, supporting the log rafters and roof. There was no lack of logs in this building. I had never seen anything so well put together. All the logs were mortised and pegged with large dowels. The stone fireplace was a work of art. Every stone was laid with care, and not one looked out of place. They had even put in a Dutch oven alongside the firebox.

Lily ran toward the back into another room. She yelled out to us, and we all came running. She was sitting on a large oak chair, and around a large table were five more chairs. The table was long and shiny, as if the sun was reflecting off it.

We went from room to room, and in each area the wood and furniture were beautiful. In all, there were four large rooms on the first floor and an open staircase to a large loft. The loft was a place where we could store supplies or even have many people sleep.

We finally went into the kitchen and sat around the huge table. We couldn't help but laugh and smile. This was heaven, and we knew there could never be another place like this for us in the entire South. It was built just as we dreamed it would be. There was not one little thing we would change. We sat there drinking the rum, relaxing, and having a good time. It had been so long since any of us had a chance to just let go, be happy, and not worry about any sound we might hear. We talked about how we would stock the shelves and where we could keep this and that. There was a lot of work to be done before we could open up for business, but we knew it would happen in a week or sooner.

The next few days were non-stop action for us. We worked long hours to get the supplies in order and priced out. Finally, the day arrived when we placed the sign on the front door that read:

OPEN
THE ROUND KNOB
TRADING POST AND DELIVERY SERVICE

Adam made a doorbell. It rang each time someone entered the store through the front door. It sure did look and sound good. Lily baked some pies and biscuits for the new customers. Joshua and I took care of the supplies people needed. The two old German farmers who had met us when we first got there came to visit. They were so happy to see us, especially since we had everything that they needed. We told them how we loved the place and that they were master carpenters. We also told them that we would have them build us more things as time went on. They were such good men and fun to be around.

Karl said, "Where do you get more supplies from?"

"We hope that Henry and Luke will start sending supplies when we need them," I told him, "but it is hard to get word to them; we have been wondering how it will work out ourselves."

"There is a place called Williamsburg about a day's ride west from here," Karl said. "They have a trading post there, but the people around here cannot just leave for a day or so and get supplies. What if you and Joshua went there yourself? Maybe you could get some things from them. They get plenty of supplies from the Carolinas and all over. It is much easier than waiting for things to come from Henry and Luke. They are far away, and you never know what may happen on the road these days."

"We sure as hell know about that," I agreed. "Maybe that would be a good idea for us. We might do better business by buying from them, but I think we'd better get word to Henry and Luke first."

"That is the other thing I wanted to tell you," Karl said. "I have a son who is going back that way in a day or so. He has this girlfriend back East, and he wants to bring her here so they can get married. Write a letter to Henry and Luke, and I'll have him take it to them. He has to go right by their place anyway."

"Karl, you are a great man," I said. "I'll write and tell them what we want to do here. Thank you so much for this great news."

"Well, you are welcome. You are nice people and everybody here likes you. I'll send my son here tomorrow to get the letter. He will be there in two or maybe three weeks. He can ride a horse like the devil is at his heels."

The first day we opened was very busy with all the local settlers coming in to buy supplies. Karl told us that there were almost four hundred people in the area and more were coming every week. I wrote a letter to Henry and Luke, telling them all the news. I asked them if we could start buying local so that maybe we could make more money.

Getting another route for supplies was a good idea. We needed to find out more about the area and what the latest news was in the Carolinas. We had to get into the areas where the slaves were being held and go see Henry's brother. First of all, we needed to get ourselves known, spread the word about our trading post, and start up different routes deeper into the south.

That night we talked about how and when we could get further south and start making contacts with the right people. The only way to do that was to get a firm hold on the area near the trading post. Then maybe later we could hire someone to run the store while we all went deeper into the South. There was so much planning to do, and we knew we had to take it slow and easy for a while.

It was the last week of August when Karl's son returned with his girlfriend. His father came to the store as soon as he got back. We were all sitting on the porch enjoying the weather and the view, when Karl brought us the letter.

"My son did as you said," he announced. "He delivered the letter to Henry. Then Henry told him to stop in on his way back with his girlfriend and bring you a letter. So here it is. I must get back home now. I have a wedding to get ready for."

We said good-bye to Karl, and then I opened the letter and read it aloud:

Dear All:
I received your letter and was so happy to hear from you. I'm glad all is going well for you there. I'm sorry to tell you that Luke has died. He died almost a

week after we got back. The trip was just too much for him. He caught a bad cold and just couldn't get rid of it. He said to me on the day he died, "Henry, I want our family to have my share of the trading post here as well as the new one. They are the only family we will ever have. They will do fine there. They have the guts and dreams to do well in the store and in the other business."

I agree with my old friend Luke. I too want you four to have the store free and clear. I'm old and have not been doing so well since Luke died. I have no desire to run both places. I have this one and it is plenty for me to handle. I will try to come out next year to see you all, but God will let me know whether of not I should. I know you four will do the right thing and will work damn hard at the store and at the other business.

Lily, your aunt and uncle have moved into the cabin in the back of the store here. I needed them here to help run this place with me. They sold their cabin to a young couple that are working hard making a farm. They are too old to kill themselves out there. They are very happy here, and they give their love to all of you. They said that the railroad is ready and the conductor is waiting for passengers. I'm sure you all know what she means.

The paper that comes with this letter shows that I have given you the trading post and all the land that comes with it. There is almost twenty acres there. Luke and I have loved you all like a family, and I know this is the right thing to do.

I dearly miss all of your laughter and spunk. I hope your life will be full like mine is and Luke's was.

Sincerely, Henry

Not a word was spoken after I finished reading the letter. All we could hear was our own crying. We all grabbed each other and held on tight. Halfmoon howled for nearly five minutes.

Joshua broke the silence. "Listen to old Halfmoon. He knows Luke is dead. He is crying just like we are."

"I need a damn drink now," I muttered.

Joshua said, "I'll have one with you."

We walked into the kitchen. I reached for the rum and set it on the table. Lily and Adam joined us. We each poured ourselves a large mug of rum and then I said, "Here is to Luke and Henry. We sure will miss them both."

I knew somehow that we would never see Henry again either. Even so, he would live on, just as Luke did by being in the trading post that they had built together.

Lily was getting drunk and she said, "I just realized that this place is all ours. He even wrote all our names down as the owners."

Adam looked up and said, "What in hell did you just say, Lily?"

"I said all our names are on this paper saying we own this place together."

Adam looked at the paper and saw his name there right alongside ours. "Well, I'll be damned," he exclaimed. "He did put my name down there too. Don't he remember that I'm black and a runaway slave?"

Joshua jumped up and said, "You ain't a damn slave anymore. You have papers saying you're free, and now you own property just like the three of us do. There ain't a damn man alive who can take it from you, Adam."

Adam looked up at Joshua and cried like a baby for close to a minute. He then stood up and said, "It is true. I'm a free man, and now I own property. And if it weren't for you three I would be dead or in the fields picking some plantation owner's cotton and thinking of how I could run away again."

"This is what it is all about," I declared. "We are going to the South to free as many people as we can until they find us dead up here on the porch."

The rest of the night we sat around and got drunk as a bunch of skunks. We had lost a dear friend, but we had gained our own place. We knew what we had to do next.

The First Step

The next month Joshua and I made plans to meet the owners of the trading post in nearby Williamsburg. We wanted to see if we could do business with them. We also wanted to find out who they were getting supplies from and where. We had to be careful from this point on out. No one could know of our real plans. To them, we would just be some young men wanting to start a good business in trading supplies.

One morning a rider came up the hill. We had never seen him before at the trading post. He got off his horse and said, "Can I post something on your store for all the people to see?"

"Yes, you sure can," I answered. "What is it anyway?"

"Well, it is hard to explain, but you people are now living in the new state of Kentucky," he said. "Just down the road heading south is now called Tennessee."

I said, "What in hell do you mean?"

"Listen, Mister, I ain't got time to explain it to you," he

griped. "Just read the paper, if ya can read."

"Don't worry, I can read."

The rider got back on his horse and took off down the hill.

I was still holding the large paper he'd handed me when I yelled for Joshua and the others to come to the front porch'.

"What's the matter, Robert?"

"I ain't rightly sure, but a rider came by and said to nail this to the store so all the people can read it."

"Well, read it Robert." Lily said.

NOTICE

This land that was once claimed by Virginia is now a new state called Kentucky, as of 1792. The land south of here, which was once claimed by North Carolina, will be the new state of Tennessee in 1796.

"Well, I'll be damned," I said. "All this time I thought we were in Virginia and now it is Kentucky. And I guess south of Williamsburg will be Tennessee. Hell, I'm all mixed up now."

"That makes all three of us, Robert," Joshua said. "It took them two long years to get here and to let us and the people know. Now what in hell do we do?"

"I guess nothing has changed," I said. "Let's go into the kitchen and get that old map Henry and Luke had and see where we are now."

We got the map out and laid it on the table. It was dated 1787.

"You see how all the original colonies were," I said. "There were thirteen, but it looks like each one has claimed more land that leads to the Mississippi River. You see how Virginia, North Carolina, South Carolina, and even Georgia have claimed this land. Now it looks like this."

I drew in the new boundaries the way I thought it might look. I even figured Georgia would become a state and showed how it might look.

We looked at the map and then Lily said, "We are a lot further from the South than I thought. It'll be harder to get there to free slaves than I thought."

"Nothing has really changed in distance," I maintained, "but now the states will have their own laws. They'll be different from state to state. We'll have to know which state we're in and what its laws are. Before, there was no state or laws. We could do almost anything and get away with it, but now who in hell knows."

Joshua said, "We ain't selling this place. We still have a straight shot to Atlanta. This is still way out in the wilderness, and we will be safe here for many years to come."

"I agree with you, Joshua," I said. "We are staying put. When I get to Williamsburg, I'll ask how far it is to Atlanta and how long it takes to get there by wagon."

Within a week, just about all the people who had traded with us had read the poster on the porch. They were happy, but many didn't want to be living in a new state. They were very independent and were concerned that they would soon be taxed. They were right. Before too long, they had to start paying taxes on almost everything.

It was early October, and I had to get to Williamsburg quickly. I knew we might get some snow and cold weather, so I needed to get supplies in before winter. I asked Lily to go with me. She smiled and said, "Yes, I want to go with you. We can pretend we are husband and wife."

"That is a great idea," I approved, "but we'd better get you a ring and put you in a nice dress."

"I knew that dress would come back at me," she muttered. "I'll do it, but the first chance I get, I'm taking it off."

We all laughed at her and then Joshua said, "You sure would look funny, Lily, leaving town naked."

"What do you mean, Joshua?"

"Well, you ain't taking anything with you besides that dress you'll be wearing."

"Then I'll ride back here naked as a jaybird."

"It is getting too cool out for that, Lily."

"You know, you men are impossible to live with," she complained. "All right then, I'll wear that damn dress there and back home. But once I get halfway up this hill, I'm tearing it off and going naked."

We all laughed.

That morning, I was on the wagon and Joshua and Adam were standing there talking to me about the trip to Williamsburg. Lily walked out the front door wearing a plain but pretty dress. Her hair was put up and held under a nice hat. The three of us had never seen her look so beautiful. She smiled and turned around a couple of times for us.

"Well, which one of you fine gentleman will escort me to my wagon?" she asked daintily.

The First Step

We all tripped and almost fell trying to reach her hand. She burst out laughing and said, "My, I must teach you fine handsome men some manners when I get back."

The three of us looked at each other and laughed.

"You sure had us going didn't you, Lily?" I remarked.

"You see?" she said. "I can become a flirt and a Southern belle when I want to. But you three need some learning on how to act around fine women like me."

"You're darn right, Lily," I agreed. "When you get back, I believe you had better teach Joshua and me some manners. We don't know how to act around fancy women."

"I will teach you how," she said. "And I'll teach Adam how to be a coachman like they have in the South. We'll need a job for him so they don't get suspicious of any of us. There will be times when we'll have to act rich, like we're from good blood. If we are to succeed, we will have to become them and go to their fancy balls and all. If we get caught, we'll be killed, so we better spend all winter learning this. Maybe by next year we can be good enough to go into the deep South and meet these plantation owners."

What Lily said was the truth. She knew exactly how we had to act when we got there. Thank God she was brought up with them. She sure could sweet-talk any man there. She could also turn into a mean bobcat and fight like one when she had to.

We finally got Lily onto the wagon. She had a hard time climbing the tall wagon with her dress on. She was cussing like hell all the way there because she had to wear it and act the part.

When we pulled into Williamsburg, we were amazed at

how big the place was. There were many stores on both sides of the road into town. There were all types of people in wagons and on horseback.

Lily said, "Well, here we are, my dear husband."

I looked at her and almost started to laugh. She took her elbow, hit me in my ribs, and said, "Don't you laugh at me, Robert. Start acting like we're married and we'll be fine."

We saw the trading post up ahead and eased the horses and wagon in front of the store.

Lily whispered, "Don't forget to help me down. I may fall with this damn dress on, and I don't want to be laughed at."

"Yes, dear," I remarked.

She gave me a dirty look and then smiled. I helped her down, and we walked into the store together. The owner saw us pull in and met us at the door.

"Welcome," he greeted. "Is this your first time here?"

"Yes, it is. My name is Robert Flint, and this is my lovely wife, Lily. We own the trading post over in Round Knob."

"Well, it sure is a pleasure to meet you," he said. "Your wife is a very beautiful lady."

"Well, thank you, kind sir," Lily replied. "And what is your name, may I ask?"

"Oh, it is George Wilcox. I own this store."

"It is sure a fine store you have here," I said. "I was wondering if you and I could talk in private."

"Why, yes. Let's go in the back."

Lily and I followed him into the back of the store. He offered us a chair.

"Would you like a glass of ale?"

"That would be nice," I answered, "but my wife isn't allowed to drink the devil's water. She did once and was sick for a week."

George laughed, turned his back, and went to get the ale. Lily gave me a look that would kill, kicked me in the ankle, and smiled.

I almost laughed, but I managed to hold it back.

George and I drank the ale. "Now," he said, "what can I do for you?"

"I have been thinking of expanding my trading post business, but I need a smart man like you to sell me more supplies. I would like to have you do this for me. You see, my wife and I travel a lot back south to see her cousins, and I can't be at my place all the time. I would hire a man to run my store if I knew I could get supplies from you or wherever you buy them from."

"That's a very good idea," he stated. "I get supplies from Knoxville and Atlanta every month. I would like to sell you all the supplies that you need."

"Well, it all depends on how much they will cost me from, let's say, you or me picking them up myself down south."

George looked at me and thought real hard about it. I knew he would sell the supplies to me cheap. He knew that I would get them myself and make more money on them.

"I'll tell what I'll do for you, Robert," he then said. "I'll sell them to you for an extra twenty cents per dollar."

"That's a little more then I wanted to pay," I replied. "Let's say ten cents on the dollar, and I'll pick them up here from you. You won't have to bother delivering them to me."

"Sounds fair to me," he agreed. "That wagon you have is quite different that any I have ever seen."

"Yes, it is," I said with a nod. "I built it with my friend. It can carry twice as much as any wagon around."

"I can see that it can," he said. "Is there anything else I can do for you?"

"There is one more thing I need to know," I added. "How long does it take to go from here to Atlanta?"

"Now let's see," he said, thinking. "It takes about twenty days by wagon to Atlanta and five days to Knoxville. Why do you ask?"

"My wife was just wondering how long it would take to go see her cousins in Atlanta."

"Do your cousins own a plantation in the South?"

"No, they have a small farm," Lily answered, "but it's so hard to get good help there."

"I have some close friends who own about twenty slaves," George told me. "They have a good-sized place outside of Atlanta. They are growing cotton, and with that new cotton gin they are buying more land and slaves. I think everybody should have at least a few slaves. They are cheap to own, and it costs very little to feed and house them."

I was starting to get real mad at this man, so I jumped up and said, "We must be going. It is a long ride back home. Now you go ahead and order those supplies. Here is five hundred dollars. This should cover about all the supplies and expenses."

George grabbed the money and said, "It sure will, and I'll send word to you when they get here."

I shook his hand, and then Lily and I got the out of there quickly. We were about to lose our false front with this man.

We got on the wagon and didn't even turn around to wave to him. We had to get out of town, away from this man and his ideas.

When we finally got out of view, Lily hiked up her dress above her knees and said, "Damn, I'm hot from wearing this stupid dress. And that man back there was getting me madder than blazes by all his talking about slavery and how good it is. I wanted to shoot him right between his eyes."

"I know the feeling," I said. "That's why I said we had to get going now. At least we got him thinking we are married and believing all the other lies we told him. The main thing is we can get supplies up here and not waste too much of our time going all over the country for them. Now we can do what we've been talking about for two years."

When we got back home, Lily was happy to finally get out of her dress. We sat down and told Adam and Joshua all that was said.

Joshua said, "Well, it sounds like we'd better be careful around this George Wilcox. He could be trouble if we get too friendly with him."

"You don't have to worry about that," said Lily. "I'm never going back to see him unless it is very important to us. A man like that will tell everybody around who we are."

"I'm sure they know by now," I said, "but all they know and all they will ever know is that we are married and that

Lily has cousins near Atlanta who own a small farm. That's all they will get out of us, that's for damn sure. But we did get what we wanted. I gave him money, so now he thinks we are wealthy and that we go south a lot."

Lily added, "Did you see how he came down on his price after we told him we would get the supplies ourselves? He knew darn well that we would. He sure doesn't want to lose any money to be made off of us."

Adam said, "It sounds like all the pieces are about in the puzzle now."

"It is beginning to look like it," Lily agreed. "I've got to start teaching you three how to act and what to wear if and when we get down where the rich plantation owners are."

"We have all winter, Lily," I pointed out. "I sure hope we can act somewhat civilized."

"Don't you worry. I'll have you all acting the part real soon."

Joshua said, "What if we all traveled in the wagon like we have planned, but we look like we just came from the wilderness. I mean, we all would wear our buckskins. Adam could wear them too. We could say he has lived with the Indians or has just been living off the land for a long time."

I agreed with Joshua. "We could look like we had been in the mountains for a while and tell them that Adam is free and that he had just come to live with us. Then, as we get closer to Atlanta or the rich counties, we could get all fancied up and say we're from up north and that we're investing in land, or we could tell them we're traders. Hell, I don't know which way to go. I just feel damn uneasy trying to be a Southern gentleman and all."

Joshua then added, "He's right, Lily. I think we'd better do what we do best; maybe not you, because you have lived that way for a while. Robert and I are just plain men from the hills in New York. I know damn well we would be caught trying to be what we ain't."

Adam laughed and said, "They are right, Lily. I say we go just as we are here. It'll be hard enough as it is trying to free my people and keep away from them trackers. We'll have to be as sharp as my long knives all the time just to stay alive. If we get in with them fancy masters and all, they'll accept us as we are. They will really think they are smarter than we are. So let the fools think that. It'll be better for us."

"You're right, Adam," Lily answered. "Let them think we are just poor folks trading goods all over the South. We won't threaten them. They will think we are poor and stupid. That way we can look around and no one will pay us any heed. And the best part about this whole crazy idea is that I won't have to wear a damn dress."

We all laughed, and I said; "Now you are even talking like us."

Lily screamed out, "Oh my God! You're right. You three are teaching me bad manners, and if this keeps up, I'll forget how to be a lady."

Joshua said, "You will always be a lady to us, Lily. And by the way, how come you didn't come back up the hill naked like you said you would before you left?"

Lily rolled her eyes and ignored that remark. "You guys can go and do what you have to do," she said. "I'm going to the stream to take a bath. I'm covered with dirt from that ride to town. My poor skin couldn't breathe with all those darn clothes on."

On a rainy November day, our supplies were finally delivered to our trading post. The man who delivered them said, "George wanted me to deliver the supplies to you instead of you coming to his store and getting them."

"Well, that was very kind of him," I replied, "but why?"

The man paused for a minute and then said, "Oh, that's the way he is, that's all."

I could tell by his voice and the time that it took him to think of an answer that he was lying. He had been sent to see and hear what he could and then go back and tell George Wilcox.

Joshua walked out from around the trading post and came toward me.

"This is my best friend, Joshua Wells," I introduced. "We run the trading post together."

Then around the other corner of the house came Adam. I didn't know what to say to him. It didn't take long for Adam to figure it out.

"Master Robert, I is all done with feeding thems chickens," he said. "Nows what can I dos?"

I was tempted to laugh, but I knew I'd better not.

"You go inside and sweep them floors, boy."

"Yes, sir, Master Robert."

Adam went inside the house. The deliveryman said to Joshua and me, "I see that you got a good nigger slave there. It's hard to find any up this far that ain't free or have run away. I knew some men down near Knoxville who hunted down runaways. Come to think of it, they ain't been around for a few years. Last time I heard, they were in Pennsylvania. I wonder what ever happened to them."

"Well, let's get my supplies off this wagon so you can get back before dark," I said.

Within an hour Joshua and I had unloaded the wagon and sent the man on his way. We didn't say another word to him or even offer him any water to drink. The sooner he got the hell out of there the better. We all knew he would tell old George Wilcox about everything he'd seen, especially Adam.

I called everyone into the kitchen after the man was at the bottom of the hill.

"Did you hear what he said, Lily?"

"Every darn word of it," she growled. "Adam, you are a true actor. That was the best performance you have ever given."

"You have done that before, Adam?" Joshua asked.

"I sure have," Adam told him, "but it has been a long time since I had to do it with Lily here."

"Well, I'll be damned," I said. "I thought you just thought it up on the spot."

"No, Robert, but I did have to think quickly. I heard him talking to you, and I figured he was just nosing around to see what he could find out. I decided I'd give him a good show. Maybe now they won't come back here. They may really think you are my master."

We all laughed.

I said, "You know, we are a strange bunch. What is so damn funny is that we can get into character within a second when we have to—and we sure have got them believing we are normal like them."

Lily said, "It is so good to be able to think and do what we have to when we need to. This is what will keep us alive. There will be many times when we'll have to do something different to get by the trackers and whoever else gets in our way. By the way it sounds so far, we'll do just fine."

"I wonder what that deliveryman will say to George," I said. "I wish I was there listening to him talk."

"They won't be back this winter," said Joshua.

"I told the driver that we wouldn't need anything more until February," I confirmed. "I don't want them coming for a visit either. The less we see them, the better it is for us. In the meantime, Lily, you'd better start teaching Adam how to talk."

Lily and Adam looked at me strangely, and then they realized I was joking with them and they laughed.

We had plenty of supplies to last all winter. Most of the farmers along the river had already bought all that they were going need. Many had grown some wheat, and they had strong cows that gave good milk for churning into butter. Karl brought us milk, and we traded it for some cloth. His wife wanted to sew a new dress for her new daughter-in-law.

The people in the area knew that Adam was a free man, but we didn't tell George or anybody else. They would all know soon enough. The only thing we could do at the moment was plan a route into the south. We had everything in place from the north. The real test would come in the spring and summer. We were as ready as we could get. It could be years before the plantation owners figured out how the slaves were getting free, but then again, there was the chance we would be caught on the first try. That didn't matter. We had to give it a shot.

Southern Road to Atlanta

In the new year of 1795, we were ready to set our plan in motion. In March, Joshua and I went to Williamsburg to pick up our supplies in Atlanta. George had sent word by a young man telling us that they had come in.

When we arrived in town, people were driving their wagons with supplies and coming and going out of the stores. There seemed to be more people than when Lily and I were there the previous fall. That may have been because we were pretty much alone all winter and we hardly saw anyone around. This place seemed way too busy for Joshua and me.

I said, "You wait until we get further south and near Atlanta. There are thousands of people living there. I can't imagine that many people in one town."

When we pulled the wagon around the back of George's trading post, we saw George standing there with the man who had delivered the supplies to us the previous fall.

"How are you, George?" I greeted.

"Well, I'm doing just fine," he replied. "How is your wife doing?"

"She is fine and busy with the store."

George said, "Tom here says you've got a nigger slave up at your place working for you."

I took a deep breath and said, "George, he isn't my slave. He is a free man. He has papers saying he is. I brought him with us from New York. He was born up there just like Joshua and me. After the war, he was freed like a hundred others were at that time."

Tom, who had no teeth, said, "Well, he sure talked like a dumb nigger slave, and he called you master and all."

At that instant I was about to kill this idiot, but Joshua stood up and stopped me.

"He was just kidding around," Joshua stated. "He does that to everybody he sees. The man can speak better English than you can. He was taught at home just like we were. He is very smart, so the next time you see him, you'd better call him by his name—Adam. And there's another thing you'd better watch out for."

"What's that?" Tom asked cautiously.

"Adam can throw his knife faster than you can say 'Mississippi.' So if I were you, I'd be very careful around him and watch what you say."

"And there's one more thing you'd better be careful of," I added.

"What's that?"

"Me," I snapped. "I like Adam, and he is a hard worker. I tend to lose my patience quicker than he does. I will kick your stinking butt or any other man's if they come on our

property and start calling him dirty names. Do you understand me now, ol' Tom?"

"I guess I do."

"Well, then," I said, "we have no other business to talk
to you about. Let's get our wagon loaded so we can get
home."

George never said another word, but when we were all
loaded, he said to Joshua, "I hope this will not hurt our
trading together."

"No, it won't, George," Joshua assured him. "We'll still
do business, but I don't want that idiot coming up to my
place ever again."

"I'll make sure he doesn't," George stated. "You both
are good men and I like doing business with you."

"We will as long as people just leave us alone," I said.
"All we want is to run a good trading post for all the good
settlers that live up near us. We don't care what other people do or say. As sure as Joshua and I are standing here, we
will make trouble for men like your Tom if they get on our
bad side."

"I understand, Robert. There will be no trouble from me
or others, I assure you."

Joshua and I didn't look back or stop at any other store.
We just got the horses to run some, and we sure stirred up
the dust as we left town. People were watching us as we
left them covered in dust. We laughed all the way home.
The horses even enjoyed the short run. It was good for their
big legs to loosen up some.

On the way home Joshua said, "I guess I opened my
mouth too soon again, Robert."

"Hell, no, you didn't," I replied. "You knew I was about to jump off that wagon and kick the rest of Tom's teeth out. You did the right thing. It is about damn time we stopped hiding the truth about Adam. The sooner they know he is free, the better. To hell with what they think. We have a long road to travel, and I sure as hell ain't gonna start worrying what people think about slavery. I want people to get used to the idea that we have no say on the matter. This way they'll never suspect us as being the type of people who would try to help the slaves escape."

"Good thing Halfmoon wasn't there," Joshua said. "He sure would have Tom's skin between his teeth by now."

When we arrived back at the trading post, Lily was very busy with some of the local farmers. They had come in for their spring supplies. I was glad that we had more supplies to sell to them. I sure didn't want them to go to Williamsburg and buy from George. In time, we hoped to build a larger trading post. I knew the area would soon grow, and the establishment of a new state would bring more people to this beautiful valley.

During the next month we were very busy selling supplies to the farmers and newcomers who were just arriving into the area.

On a Saturday morning in April, Karl and his son came into the store. It was odd for them to come together and so early in the morning. We were cleaning and restocking the shelves. Karl looked around the store and said, "Can we all talk? I just want to make sure there is no one else in the store."

We all stopped what we were doing and I said, "We are

all alone here. What do you want to talk about?"

"My son here, Hans, and I went into Williamsburg the other day," he began. "We just wanted to see the town and all. We had only been there once a long time ago. Well, anyway, we were in that trading post just looking around. We didn't buy anything from there. I'd seen this George Wilcox once before, but he doesn't know me at all or where I live. He was talking to a few men who sure looked like a tough bunch. They weren't from around here, though. Men like that don't farm. They had a Southern tone to their voices. I overheard them bring up your name. Then I really tried to listen."

"What did they say?" Joshua wanted to know.

"Well, George and this man named Tom who works for him were telling the men about you and your trading post," Karl told us. "I thought nothing of it until one said something about Adam being here."

"What did you hear, Karl?" I pressed.

"They asked Tom if he knew if the Negro was a free man or not. They also wanted to know all about you three. They were asking all kinds of questions about where you all came from and just being real nosey. Then they saw me standing there and didn't say another word. They slammed the door shut, so my son and I left."

Karl's son then added, "When I went to deliver the letter to Henry that you gave me, I saw these same men talking to Henry. I never thought much of it until we saw them at Wilcox's store talking to him. Then I realized that something was wrong. That's when I told my father that we'd better talk to you now."

Joshua asked, "What did Henry say to you about this?"

"Well, on the way back with my girlfriend," Hans said, "I got the letter that I gave you. Henry told me that these men were looking for some other men who went up into this area and were never seen again. They must have told them about the four of you and Henry's trading post here. I figured they put two and two together. That's why they came looking for you. Henry told me he told them nothing and that he didn't know where you all went."

A knot formed in my stomach. Joshua and I looked at Adam and Lily. They also were feeling very uneasy.

Karl said, "It isn't our business to know about this, but we like you all very much. We want to help you if you'll let us, but we need to know what is going on."

"Let's close the store and go in the kitchen," I said. "We had better talk now."

We closed the store, went into the kitchen, and sat down around the big table.

"I need a damn drink first," I muttered.

Karl smiled and said, "Bring me one too. I think I'll need it."

I took a swig of my drink and said, "What I'm about to tell you two must never leave this room. This may put you in danger for the rest of your lives. You can go now and forget that you told us anything or you can listen and take your chances."

Karl smiled and said, "My life has always been in danger. When I lived in Germany I was always in danger. I have been hunted there since I was my son's age. I was never a bad man, but I had my beliefs, and I was not going to have the government tell me what I could or could not do. I have killed many men there fighting for my beliefs. I finally had to leave quickly with my young wife and a few dollars, but I have never been afraid of a damn thing. Go ahead and tell me what you have done or what you all are planning to do."

For the next two hours we told Karl and Hans about what had happened up at Henry's and what we were planning to do in the future.

Karl smiled and said, "You have nothing to worry about. We are with you all the way. I have friends and a brother not far from Henry's trading post. They are Quakers, and they have already helped a few slaves to escape to freedom."

We all took a deep breath and smiled.

"We feel a great weight has been taken off our heads by telling you about this," I said. "Now I want to ask you and Hans if you could run the trading post once in a while. The reason being is that we four would like to get going on this plan, and we would be gone a few months at a time or longer. We need someone here who we can trust to help keep the trading post going. This is the only safe house we'll ever have. This place must never become suspicious to others or it will be over."

Hans stood up and said, "You have my word that I will run it, and that I will never tell anybody a damn thing about its purpose. If anyone asks, I'll just tell them you all have gone into the South to buy and sell goods, that's all."

"We will pay you for running the trading post while we are gone," I told them.

"I don't want any money from you good folks," Karl replied. "You pay my son and I'll do anything I can for nothing."

After Karl and Hans left, we talked about these men who were asking about us.

Joshua said, "We'd better be on guard from now on. I have this feeling that they will be coming here for a visit. We had better make plans for who-knows-what. Tomorrow, Adam, you take some muskets and whatever we'll need to the rocks near the spring. Find a good dry place for them. Then over on the west side, near the grove of tall pines, put two muskets out of sight, but in a place where they'll be easy to get at."

Adam said, "I'll do it at first light."

Lily then said, "I'll just be a happy wife cooking in the kitchen. I guess I'd better keep a simple dress hanging in there so I can get into it in a hurry so I'll look the part."

"Joshua and I will do like we always do," I said. "We'll be in the store, and Adam will work in the barn, moving supplies around. It may be a few days, but let's get them out of our lives once and for all. I won't leave this place with them still in the area. We'll get Hans here after all this is over. I don't want him to get hurt or involved in any fights."

A week went by and nobody out of the ordinary came to the trading post. Even so, none of us ever let our guard down.

Almost another week went by, and then about sunset we saw five men on horseback coming up the hill to the trading post. Adam was the first to see them. He ran into the back of the kitchen and told Lily. Lily stripped her clothes off then and there, put on her very plain dress, and went into the store. Joshua and I stayed in the store and Half-moon waited on the porch, sitting like he always did. We knew he'd be able to tell if they were friend or foe.

When they got to the front of the store, Halfmoon stood up and growled like hell. That was when we knew they were not friends from below. I walked out onto the porch, took one look at them, and knew they were trackers. Hell, I could smell them ten feet away. They were dirty and their clothes were pretty worn from all the trails they had been on.

"Hello there," I greeted. "Can I be of help to you?"

The meanest looking man said, "Maybe you can. We are looking for runaway slaves, and we hear you have one here."

"You must be mistaken," I answered. "I do have a Negro here, but he is a free man. I have known him for a long time. He has papers saying he is a free man."

"We want to see him and those papers you have."

"I don't have to show you a damn thing," I snarled. "You're not in Georgia or the Carolinas. You're on my damn property and I don't have to show you anything."

"I also know you have a fine-looking woman here too," the man said with a sneer. "You don't want something to happen to her, do you?"

"Listen, we don't want any trouble here," I said. "We are just traders trying to make a living."

"Well, I'll ask you again," the man pressed. "Where is that nigger and those papers?"

By that time Joshua had come out of the store holding his musket. Then Adam opened the loft window, and he too was holding his musket. Lily walked out onto the porch with Joshua. She was wearing her dress and holding her musket.

The man then said, "Well, I see you do have help here, don't you? I also see that fine wife of yours. I guess you hide behind her dress, huh?"

One of the other men yelled, "Get down here, nigger! I want to see your black back. I bet you are covered with welts from all those good whippings you got from running away."

Joshua spoke up. "I think you and your scum friends had best get back under whatever rock you all climbed out from. Get your horses turned around and ride down the hill before you end up being thrown off the mountain for the buzzards to pick at."

"Well, ain't you a brave man," the leader remarked. "I see you all are nigger lovers. You know what we do to nigger lovers, and especially fine white women who love niggers?"

Those were the last words that man ever spoke. Adam fired his musket and hit him in the throat. The blow knocked him backward onto the dirt. The other men were about to pull their weapons when a shot was fired from behind them. We didn't know who fired it, but another man was knocked to the ground. By then, Joshua had shot the other man on the horse. Lily then fired and killed the one man who had just gotten his pistol out and fired it. It had hit just before my foot on the porch. I could feel the wood splinter as the ball hit the wood. The last man started to turn and run for it on his horse, but he was killed before he knew what hit him.

After the smoke cleared from the firing, we saw Henry. He was on his horse carrying two pistols, one in each hand. They were still smoking from the powder burn. All of us just stood there looking at him. We couldn't believe our eyes.

I yelled, "Is that you, Henry?"

"Well, who in hell did ya think it was? Daniel Boone?"

Joshua ran to him and said, "Well, I'll be a son-of-a-gun. It is you. What in hell are you doing here?"

Henry got off his horse. Halfmoon recognized his voice and ran straight to him, barking like crazy.

Henry said, "I could smell trouble coming your way, so I figured what the hell. I might as well go and get in it with ya. Besides, I missed my old friend Halfmoon here."

Henry got down on his knees and hugged Halfmoon. He then stood up and said, "I can't leave you four alone for two years and ya go and kill five more men. Hell, don't ya ever have time to relax?"

Adam ran outside to greet Henry. We all hugged him, and I finally said, "So what are you really here for?"

"I missed you all," he said. "Hell, you're my family. I sold the trading post to your aunt and uncle, Lily. I didn't want the damn place anymore after Luke died. I was lonely and didn't want to stay there anymore, so I up and sold it and came to see you all."

Lily asked, "What are you going to do now?"

"Well, I thought that I would come and help you here if

ya want me to," Henry answered.

I said, "You bet your life you can, Henry. We would love having you here. From now on, this is your home too."

Henry looked at each of our faces and saw that we meant it. A few tears rolled down his cheek into his gray beard. He didn't need to say a word; we all knew how he felt about it.

After a minute, he wiped his nose and said, "Let's get these bushwhackers buried out back somewhere. Hell, we did it once; we can do it again."

Adam got the wagon and we put the bodies in the back. Henry told us of a place way in the back of the property that was easy digging. So off we went with the dead trackers. When we got to the spot, Henry said there were two more men buried back there also.

"I'll tell ya that story over ale later."

By the time we buried the men and got back to the store, it was almost dark. Lily had prepared a large supper for all of us. After supper, Joshua got the two jugs of ale and brandy, and we sat around the table and told Henry all that had happened since we'd taken over the trading post.

Finally, Henry said, "I've got something to give you all." He set his big bag on the oak table, opened it up, and emptied it. After he shook the last out of its contents onto the table, we saw a big pile of gold—nothing but gold. We were speechless.

"What the hell are ya looking at?" Henry asked. "Take it. It belongs to all of you."

"Where the devil did you get all this gold?" I finally asked.

Henry smiled and said, "It was Luke's and mine. It was what we made looking for gold in the West years ago. We took all the gold nuggets and gold dust we had found over ten years out there and put it into gold coins. No one knew where it came from except those two dead men out back that I told you about. They followed Luke and me for days and days waiting to steal it. Well, that is as far as they got back there. Old Luke and I were waiting for them in those rocks. We killed them and buried them back there."

None of us had ever seen that much money in our lives.

"It's yours now," Henry said. "All I want is to live here 'til I die. I want to help you all in any way I can."

We all hugged him and thanked him for the gold.

"Where in hell are we supposed to hide it?" I asked.

Henry laughed and said, "I guess none of you have found Luke's and my hiding place, have ya?"

Adam said, "Hiding place? What in God's name are you talking about, Henry?"

Henry stood up and walked over to the wall that separated the kitchen from the store. He reached behind the log support beam and unhooked a hidden latch. He turned and smiled at us, and then pulled a section of the wall out into the kitchen. There it was: a two-foot by two-foot section that swung out of the wall and into the kitchen.

"Here is your secret compartment," he announced.

We looked inside the hidden compartment and saw a small leather pouch. Henry brought it out and set it on the table. He opened the pouch and pulled out an old map that was made of leather. It showed a long mountain range and rivers. He pointed to one area on the map and said, "This is where the gold came from."

Joshua asked, "Where in hell is this place?"

Henry replied, "It is far north of the fort in Santa Fe in Mexico territory. There is a Spanish trail north of Santa Fe and across the Colorado River lies land unknown to most people from the east. There are many Indian tribes living up there. They are very deadly for most men going into that area, but they have seen many white trappers over the years, mostly French. They have accepted them because they have married into their tribes. But other white men have been killed there. They knew Luke and me, and we always traded with them and respected their lands. It took time for us to gain their trust; they are great proud people."

Adam said, "I bet ya they don't have slaves up there."

Henry replied, "They have never seen a black man before, but I'm sure they would accept you and be friends with you."

"Now," Henry continued, "if all your plans turn out badly and every Southern man is looking for you, and you have no damn place to hide, you take this map and go. No man will ever find you out there. Just understand that if you do go, your lives will never be the same. It will be many years before this country will go across the Mississippi River. It is vast and wild, and it would take any man a lifetime to see it all."

We sat back down at the table and looked at this map. We finally put the gold and map back into the hidden compartment and closed it.

I said, "Well, now we have money and a map to take us as far as any man has gone. I have this gut feeling that we'll be doing just that someday."

Henry smiled and said, "I also have that feeling, but I'll be too damn old to go with you. I'm sure between the four of you, you'll find your way there."

Over the next few days we had a great time having Henry with us. Karl's son Hans came to the trading post and asked when he would be needed. We told him he could start working there the following week.

We decided to start for Atlanta on the second day of May. Everything was in place at the trading post, and the weather would be warm. We knew the cotton would be growing and the Negroes would be hard at work in the fields. That was where we needed to go and figure out a plan for our first move.

Henry had given us Luke's brother's name: Victor Roberts. He had a blacksmith shop just outside of Atlanta. That was where we had to go first. We had to tell Victor about the death of his brother Luke. We hoped we could use Victor as a conductor and his place as a station on the Underground Railroad.

The day before we left, none of us had time to sit and talk. We were busy loading the wagon with supplies that we could sell and use as a front on our way south. We had four extra horses that we would ride if needed. We could always leave the wagon and run from anyone who might come after us. Henry and Hans were set to take care of the trading post and any supplies that came from Wilcox. We wanted things to stay the same with George Wilcox. If he ever brought up the subject of the five men we were forced to kill, Henry and Hans would just say that they had never seen them.

The day for us to leave was finally upon us. We were as ready as we could ever be. There was plenty of supplies, food, and firepower. Joshua and I mounted our horses, and Adam and Lily sat in the wagon.

Henry looked at each of us and said, "Take damn good care of each other, and don't forget that I love you all as my family. Now get going and see ya all before fall."

We yelled good-bye and started down the hill toward the river. From there we planned to bypass Williamsburg, head south along the Log Mountains into Tennessee, and keep going until we came into Knoxville. There was a road that led through the mountains that they called the New Found Gap, and from there we could head on to Atlanta.

It was sad to leave Henry and our home that we loved so much, but we knew we had to try to free some slaves. Maybe just a few or maybe hundreds. If we just got one headed north to freedom then we would be happy.

Three weeks passed, and we were on the south side of Knoxville when we came across a small hamlet. The people there watched us as we drove the wagon into town. The children ran behind us and the dogs barked at the sight of Halfmoon. Those dogs had probably never seen another dog as large as him.

We pulled in front of the local stable where a man was watering some horses. I asked him if we could pay for some water and grain for our horses.

The man looked up at me and said, "You sure can, Mister. Just help yourself."

"We sure do appreciate your kindness, sir."

While we fed the horses, a few men walked over to us. One of them asked, "Where you all from?"

Joshua answered, "Kentucky. We have a trading post up there, and we buy and sell trade goods all over."

"Well, you have come a long way to trade, ain't ya?"

"I guess so, but we're heading to Atlanta to see what we can trade there."

"I ain't never seen a wagon like the one you all got. Where in the devil did ya get it from?"

"The three of us built it a year or so ago," I answered.

They kept looking at Adam and Lily. They didn't know what to say, but we knew they would think of something sooner or later.

Then one of the men said, "Whose wife is this fine-looking woman?"

"That's my wife," Joshua told him. "We were all born up near Canada."

"Canada!" the man exclaimed, surprised. "Damn, that is a long ways from here, I reckon. That Negro was born up yonder too?"

Then I walked over to the man and said, "Yes, he was. My folks owned him and set him free with papers and all after the war with England. He's like family to all of us. You see, we all grew up in the same little settlement together. Our grandfathers used to trap in Canada."

"You don't say," he responded. "Well, nice talking to you." The men turned away and left.

I walked back over to Lily and smiled. "So you left me and got married to Joshua?"

Joshua and Lily laughed. Adam then said, "Now you

have me born in Canada. I tell you what, you guys are good."

We paid the man for the water and grain for the horses, thanked him, and continued on our way.

The road was finally getting better to travel. The mountain passes were hard on the horses. The rest of the journey looked to be much better once the trails flattened out.

The next three weeks went by with no problems. We were finally beginning to see signs pointing to several small towns. Finally, we saw a sign pointing to Atlanta. We would soon be there. The town where Victor lived was called Sandy Bottom. We had an idea that it was close to Atlanta.

We were a day away from Atlanta, and we started to see large plantations. The fields were larger then Joshua and I had ever seen. We knew we were in the Cotton Belt. There were miles and miles of fences, and behind every fence was a cotton field. There were times when we saw slaves working in the fields. Some of the older slaves drove teams of horses with other slaves on the back. There were water wagons, and every once in a while, we could see a man riding all over the fields with his shotgun ready.

Adam said, "That is the plantation foreman. He rides all day long watching people work. He also makes sure they work and don't try to run away or find a shady tree to rest under out of the sun. Most of them are mean and heartless."

While we were crossing a small bridge, we saw three men come riding toward us.

I said to everybody, "Just stay calm and remember we are only traders. We'll stick to the story that we gave them in Knoxville."

We all agreed and waited for them.

They had beautiful horses and were dressed in some fine clothes.

Adam whispered, "They always dress like that. One of them may be the owner of this plantation near here."

They rode up to us and we stopped the wagon. The one man who was dressed real fine said, "Hello there. What is your business on this road?"

I did all the talking. "We are traders from Kentucky. We have a trading post up there, and we are down this way looking for new supplies to take back and resell. It's hard to get certain goods up that way, so we are on our way to Atlanta."

"Well, I can see you are not from around here or the Carolinas," the man said. "We don't see many folks wearing buckskins down here."

"Well, sir, this is all we own, and we don't like all them fancy clothes and such."

The man smiled and laughed. "What do you sell?"

"We have many things that are well made, like shovels and farm tools, but we also carry skins and pelts from Canada."

The man looked at us for a minute then said, "Why don't you take that big wagon of yours and follow me to my home? Maybe we can do some trading."

"I sure would like that, sir."

We followed the three men across a nice bridge and down a long road. On each side of the road there was a

newly painted white rail fence. As we got around the corner, we saw a huge plantation house. It was bigger than any
barn I'd ever seen. It had white columns on the front and a
large porch. There were big pots with all types of flowers in
them.

Joshua laughed and said, "Those flower pots are bigger
than the tub we took baths in back home."

As we pulled in front of the house, there were house
slaves running all over the place. They came out and
looked at the wagon. When we stopped the wagon, a young
slave held onto the reins for us. The owner yelled at the
house slaves, "Get back to work in the kitchen."

They quickly ran behind the huge house. The owner
said, "Get off your wagon and stretch your legs a bit."

The three of us got down from the wagon, but Adam
stayed where he sat. I looked at him and said, "Come on
down, Adam."

Adam shook his head and said, "No, sir. I will stays in
this here wagon."

Then I knew what was going on. Adam didn't want to
speak like he was free, but as if he had once been a slave.

The owner looked at Adam and me and said, "My name
is Charles Franklin and I own eight hundred acres here.
This is one of the largest plantations in the area. I have one
hundred slaves working my place, mostly cotton now."

"My name is Robert Flint, and this man here is Joshua
Wells. This is his beautiful wife, Lily."

He shook Joshua's hand and then mine. He looked at
Lily and said, "It is sure nice to see a beautiful woman like
you, Miss Lily. Joshua, you are a lucky man." Charles then

asked me, "Where did you buy this Negro?"

"Charles, sir, Adam here is a free man. He was born near Canada, like the rest of us. After the war, my father freed him and gave him papers."

"Well, that is too bad," Charles, remarked. "I would have liked to buy him from you. He is a strong man and young. He sure could father a lot of strong children here."

We all felt anger, but we knew we would always hear things like this from this type of man. We all just stayed calm and laughed.

"Now then, let's see some of them pelts and whatever else you may have," Charles said. "I feel like spending money today. I want to buy my wife something special."

Adam opened up the back of the wagon and brought out several items that he thought she would like, including some beautiful wool blankets that we had brought down from Henry's store.

Charles really liked them. He turned to me and said, "I'll buy every one you have. I know they will all sell before you get to Atlanta. Name your price and I'll pay you."

I smiled and told him the price.

"That can't be right," he replied. "They are very well made. I'll pay you double for them."

I smiled and said, "It's a deal. I don't rightly know what to charge down here."

"I'll tell you a secret," Charles said. "Whatever you have for a price on anything, you have to double it. You will do very well down here, Robert."

"Well, we really do thank you for the information, Charles."

"I'm glad that I could help. And I'm very glad to have met all of you. If you are ever down this way again, I want you to stop in and see me."

"We sure will," I replied. "I've got a question to ask you, sir. Is there a blacksmith in these here parts that I can see about some work on my wagon?"

"Now let's see," Charles thought. "Yes, there is a man who is the best around; his name is Victor Roberts. He lives right down the road from here about three miles."

"That would be good for us," I said.

Charles then said, "I'm having a small get-together here in about two weeks. I would love to have you three attend. You are very different than most people around here. I think you would enjoy it. What do you say?"

"Well, sir," I answered, "we are just plain folk and all, and we ain't got any fancy clothes to wear. All we have is what we have on and some other buckskins. We ain't never been in real pants and Lily ain't never been in a dress before."

"Well, that is what I like about you three," Charles countered. "You are plain country folk from the mountains. Please come and wear what you want."

"I guess we could get back here for it," I said, "We may just drop in if we have time."

"We'll have a great meal, and the men like to have shooting contests," Charles added. "Do you two shoot well?"

Joshua smiled and said, "We do all right, I guess."

"Well, you bring that old musket or whatever you shoot rabbits with, and we'll see what you can do against these

Southern gentlemen."

That was all I needed to hear from this man.

"All right then," I agreed. "We'll be here and try to shoot like you all."

"That is good news," Charles approved. "You all have a fine trip to Atlanta, and I'll see you all in two weeks."

We thanked him, said our good-byes, and left his fancy plantation.

When we got back on the road again, Adam smiled and said, "You three just melted in his hands. He thinks you are nothing but dumb mountain people. He wants us to come back so we can amuse his rich friends."

"Well, that is just what we wanted to do, Adam," I assured him.

Lily laughed and said, "We are going to outshoot those fools. We'll sucker them in for some money or trade goods or something good. Then we'll shoot the eyes off them."

Joshua added, "We played that game perfect. He feels no threat from us at all."

"Exactly," Lily agreed. "We'll make them feel superior and then we'll be able to go here and there without them suspecting a thing. And when we get to know the others, they'll feel the same way. But we must be very careful about what we say and do from here on out. They are not stupid; they know this country very well. We'd better meet Victor and begin."

We drove the wagon down the dusty road and finally came upon a small town called Cross Road Junction. Up ahead was a sign saying "Victor's Blacksmith Shop and Livery Stable." We drove the team of horses up to the large barn. A man walked out who looked just like Luke.

"I'm looking for a Victor Roberts," I announced. "Is he here?"

"That would be me. What can I do for you?"

"We need to talk to you about Henry and your brother Luke."

Victor smiled and said," Come on in the house and we'll talk."

Victor yelled for one of his men to take care of the horses and the wagon. A huge Negro came out from the barn and started to take the horses.

Adam got off the wagon and said, "I'll help you."

The big man looked at Adam and said, "If you wants to help, then I guess it's okay."

Joshua, Lily, and I followed Victor into his warm-looking home. It had a white picket fence in front of it. It was well kept, and he even had flower boxes under the windows on the front porch. We walked into his house and he asked us to sit down and feel at home. After we were seated, Victor asked, "How do you know my brother?"

As always, I did most of the talking. I explained that we all had become friends with Luke and Henry; I also told him that Henry was living with us in Kentucky.

"Luke is dead, isn't he?" Victor asked quietly.

"Yes, he is, Victor," I answered. "We all are very sorry. We miss him very much."

"I had a feeling he had died when you said Henry was living with you," he said. "Those men were like two peas in a pod. They were like brothers. Well, I'm glad to know that he had good friends like you folks. You all seem very nice."

"Victor, here is a letter that Henry told us to give to you. We have not opened it or read it."

Victor put on his reading glasses and opened the letter. After a few minutes, he said, "Do you have any idea what Henry said in this letter?"

"No, we don't."

"It seems that Luke had wanted me to help you in the mission you all have planned. From living here almost all my life, I would agree with Luke on this. It is a strange thing that is coming to the South. I don't like it one damn bit. More and more slaves are being bought and made to work the plantations. It is all greed, just plain greed. The whole world wants this cotton, and people are paying a fortune for it. So now the farms need to bring in slaves to work the fields and take care of it. If I were younger, I would move back north, but I can't. I have everything here and no family anywhere else. My wife died here about a year ago, so I can't leave her here by herself. I just try to ignore all the meanness that comes when people buy these slaves. I feel so bad for the slaves. If I were to say something about it, they would burn me out or kill me, so I keep my mouth shut. What can I do to help in this Underground Railroad?"

Lily answered, "We just need a place for the freed slaves to stay for a night. I know you are not really secluded here, but I don't know what else we could do."

Victor thought for a minute then said, "Well, there is a place my wife and I own, but I haven't been there since she died. It was about ten miles from here. A couple was living there for a while, but they never took care of it. Anyway, they are gone and the place is not near anyone. I used to go hunting out there for a week or so at a time. Maybe you can fix it up, live there, or use it as a station. I'll make out a bill of sale for you in case someone asks questions about it, but you'll never see me out there. I just can't go there again without my wife."

We thought about it for a while and decided we would take a look at it and see what we could do with it.

"It may be the perfect place for us while we are here trying to trade," I said. "We'll get used to the area and then see where most of the people come and go. Sooner or later, they'll know us by sight as the traders from Kentucky."

Victor said, "I'll write you a bill of sale, and tomorrow you can go over and look at it. I'll have one of my men go with you. His name is Sam. He is a damn good blacksmith; he has been with me for about fifteen years now. The plantations around here don't bother him or me. They know we are the only blacksmiths around for nearly twenty miles, so they never get on our bad side."

We stayed another hour or two with Victor and told him about Charles, how we met him on the road, and what took place afterward.

"Now there is a man who can become a problem for you," Victor warned. "He is very rich, and he knows everybody around the county. If you can get him liking you, you'll be fine, but don't cross him. He has people and connections all the way up into Virginia. He controls his slaves and his hired men with an iron fist. I've heard them complain to me when they come here. Even his foremen are afraid of him. Be careful and go easy with that man."

"We will," I promised, "and thanks again for all the help and information. We will go just outside town tonight and make camp. I don't want people to start saying we are living here or that we've known each other for a long time. We need to keep some distance. We'll always come by with the wagon. They'll just think you are working on that big unusual thing for us."

When we got outside, Adam had the horses all ready to go again. He shook hands with Big Sam. He and Adam looked like they had become friends. We started the horses and wagon down the road, and on the other side of town we found a nice stream where we could make camp.

That evening we talked, making sure we didn't speak too loud. Halfmoon would sure let us know if somebody came close by. We discussed the idea of using the old house of Victor's as a place where we could store supplies and certain types of goods.

That night I lay awake for quite a while thinking of all that had happened that day. I tried not to worry, but I knew we would be in danger for the rest of the summer here. I thought about how we could make our first contact with anyone who could help. It would be a very slow process, and we had to be extremely careful.

Settling In

We awoke the next morning with the southern breeze brushing against out faces. It had been a warm, quiet night, probably the first night we had slept at ease. We had a good breakfast that Lily made for us. We were sitting around talking when Sam arrived on his horse to see us.

"Good morning, Sam," I greeted.

"Good morning to you. Victor sent me here to take you to the house and told me I should help you get settled in."

"We'll be ready in a while," Adam told him. "I'll get the horses hitched up to the wagon and then we'll be on our way."

"I'll give ya a hand, Adam," said Sam.

Within an hour we were on our way to our new home. It was another hour before we came to a small stream that was slowly flowing along. We crossed the stream, and on the other side we saw the house. It was really run down, and the roof had holes all over it, but it sat in a beautiful location. The stream we had crossed flowed into a pond.

There were large trees all around the pond with hanging branches touching the water. There was a barn behind the house that could be fixed up to keep the horses and wagon safe when the weather turned bad.

"What a mess!" Lily gasped. "Still, I think we can fix it up so we will be dry from the rain. It sure is out by itself. It'll be just what we'll need when the time comes."

Joshua and I studied every angle of the area. There was plenty of open ground so we could see anyone trying to approach the house. This was very important to us. With a few days hard work and some lumber, we could really fix the house up nicely.

Sam came to the porch. "Give me a list of materials you'll need."

I read the list we had made up, and he said he could get just about everything we needed. He told us he would come back the next day with a wagon and the supplies.

"I believe this will work real well for us for awhile," I stated.

Joshua said, "I think so, but we'll need to know who lives around here. Why don't you and Lily take the horses and ride through the area and see what is around us?"

"That is a good idea. Joshua. If they see us together maybe they'll start thinking we have bought the place and are living here."

"Adam and I will get started fixing what we can until Sam gets back with material," Joshua added.

Lily and I got the horses and took our muskets. Adam and Joshua got busy airing out the house and re-nailing- the old siding.

"It sure is pretty around here, isn't it, Robert?" Lily commented as we rode.

"It is all right," I replied. "I like Kentucky better. Look! There is a road up ahead. Let's ride down it for a ways and see what's there."

"Looks like it's well traveled," Lily said. "Maybe it goes to a farm or another house."

Lily and I rode down the dusty road for about a mile. Then off in the distance we could hear people singing.

"What in hell is that?" I wondered.

"It's the slaves in the fields working," Lily told me. "They always sing while they work. I don't know why, but they all do. I guess it keeps their minds at ease while they're working so hard in the sun all day."

"Should we go and see?"

"Why not? Maybe we'll see the foreman. We should try to remember what they look like."

We rode along a fence that separated the cotton fields from the road. We saw at least thirty men and women, and even some children working in the field. Once in a while, one would look up at us and then quickly look back to the ground.

"They know we are strangers, Robert," Lily explained. "They don't know if we are farmers or if we're just passing through."

"I bet they have never seen a woman in buckskins before," I laughed.

"I forgot I had them on," she said with a giggle. "I'm so used to wearing them."

We rode a little further and came upon a wagon carrying

slaves coming or going to the fields. Behind the wagon was a man riding with his shotgun, keeping an eye on them. As we approached the wagon, the foreman yelled to the driver to stop. He called to us, "Are you two lost or something?"

"No," I answered. "We are just riding around and seeing the countryside."

"Oh, I remember you two," he said. "You, another fellow, and a Negro came to my boss's house a few days ago."

"Yes, we did, but I don't remember seeing you there."

"I was just coming in from the fields and I saw you. So what are you doing around here now?"

"We bought an old house about five miles from here from Victor Roberts."

"Mr. Franklin told me that you were going to Atlanta to trade," he said. "What happened?"

"We're not much on living so close together," I told him. "We decided we'd live here and go into Atlanta once in a while to trade. We like being out by ourselves."

"Mr. Franklin said you were from the mountains and all," he responded. "I guess it makes sense to live out there where you're alone. Nobody goes out there. It is a spooky place."

"Why's that?" I asked.

"That's where a few slaves went when they ran away from us," he explained. "We had the hounds on them before dark. Mr. Franklin came to the place, and he was as mad as I have ever seen him. He had this look in his eyes like he was the devil or something."

"What happened?"

"Mr. Franklin hung all of them in those trees. I told him not to because they were hard workers, and they cost Mr. Franklin a lot of money to buy them in Savannah. The look on his face scared the hell out of me. He said, "I don't care about the money. I'll teach these niggers they can't run from me."

Lily let out a nervous sigh. I said, "What did he say to you?"

"That's what scared me," he went on. "He told me he would hang me if I didn't do as he said, so I hung them. I'm afraid of that man, and so are all the slaves and all the men who work for him."

I didn't say another word to him. Then he said, "Well, I've got to get going. I have to take these slaves to the fields. If you see him again, I hope you won't say anything about our talk here."

"Don't you worry," I assured him. "It is between us, and we'll keep it that way."

After they were far enough away, I said to Lily, "What do you think about that?"

"That foreman is a decent man," she stated. "He is just doing his job, but I could tell by the sound of his voice that he is just as scared of Mr. Franklin as those slaves in the wagon. He may become useful to us someday. I think he might help us if he was paid well enough or if he just gets fed up with Charles Franklin."

While Lily and I were riding along, looking at the fields of cotton, we talked about the new house and wondered how Henry and Hans were getting along.

We rode for another hour or so and then came upon the

road we had been on that morning that led to the new place. We followed it, and like Victor told us, there was nothing around except fields and wood lines.

By the time we got back to the house, Adam and Joshua were on the roof patching some of the larger holes. They saw us coming, and Joshua yelled, "Well, it's about time. We thought you two were lost."

They came off the roof, and we all took a break for a mug of ale. The sun was really hot at that time of day. We knew we had better get used to the heat. We had all summer to go through yet. We told Adam and Joshua about the man we had met on the road, and what he had told us about Charles Franklin.

"I told you all what it was like down here," Adam said solemnly. "You are just now hearing some of the horrors of it all. Can you imagine what it is like all over?"

Joshua said, "Adam and I found a storm shelter out back. I guess it was for storing food and serving as protection against the bad storms they get around here. It is in better shape than this old house and may become useful later, but we'll have to hide it better than it is now. I was thinking of digging up some brush and replanting it over or around the storm shelter. If we do it right, no one will know it's there."

Adam added, "The way this place is built and the way it sits on the stone foundation, it seems very shallow from the outside. But when I was fixing some floorboards, I could see it was much deeper. I was thinking maybe I could dig it out more under the front room floor and make a trap door. We would have to cover it with a large old rug we have in the wagon."

Lily and I thought about this and agreed it was a good idea. We would sure use it if we had to in a hurry.

As we made plans for our new home, we also talked about going to Atlanta in a few days. We wanted to see what this place looked liked and ask around about trading supplies.

The rest of the day Lily and Adam cleaned the old wood stove so we could use it. Joshua and I rebuilt the corral for the horses and made sure they could go to the stream to drink. The pasture was knee-deep in new spring grass, and the horses loved it. Halfmoon also walked around the place and smelled everything.

The next morning, Sam came to the house with a load of lumber and some food for us. He had found everything we'd put down on the list. He was humming and smiling as he pulled up to the house.

Adam asked, "Why are you so happy today, Sam?"

"I'm always happy," Sam replied. "I knows I ain't working in them cotton fields all day long. I ain't gots no mean boss man yelling at me. I just have Victor, and he is the best man I ever known."

We all smiled and agreed with Big Sam. He was a good, hard working man. We unloaded the wagon and started to work on the house. We had plenty to do before we left for Atlanta.

The next week went by quickly. We had the house all dried in and windows repaired with new glass. The barn and corral were also completed. Adam and Sam had the storm shelter all cleaned out and had replanted bushes all around it so they looked like natural growth. The trap door and all the dirt had been dug out and thrown into the pond near the house. We didn't want any signs showing what we had done. We told Sam to tell Victor that we were going to Atlanta the next day and that we would stop in to see him on the way back in about another week.

Sam said, "I sure will tell Victor. I'll come out once a day and make sure the place is all right. The people around here knows me, and theys knows Victor. We used to come out here all the time, so they won't thinks nothing of seeing me around here."

As Sam left with the wagon, Adam said, "That man will help us a lot. He knows many of the slaves around here. He told me that his brother and mother still live on Charles's plantation. His mother is very old, and she is taken care of there. His brother works as a carpenter on the plantation, so he is treated well. I know if Sam thought they were mistreated, he would have somehow gotten them out by now."

I said, "Next time ask him if he goes there a lot to see his mother and brother. If so, he may be able to find out if there are any slaves there who have been thinking of running away."

"That is a good idea, Robert. He'll never speak to any of them about it, but he sure will hear what any of them are saying. They all know they can trust Big Sam."

The day we were to leave for Atlanta the weather was warm and a slight breeze helped cool the heat. We were just leaving the road that led to the house when Charles Franklin and another man came riding up. We stopped the wagon and Charles said, "I thought I would come up and see you before you left. I heard you had bought this place from Victor. That is a good idea. You will be able to work out of this place with your trading business. I have always liked this place."

"Why is that?" I asked.

"Well, let's say it has good memories for me."

We all knew he was a bastard now. His only memories were when he had hung all those runaways. We worked hard to smile and play dumb.

"Sam, the man who works for Victor, said he would keep an eye on the area for us while we were gone to Atlanta," I said. "He is a good man, a very good worker."

"That he is," Charles agreed. "His mother and brother work for me. His mother has been with me for nearly twenty years now. His brother was born there, and he is a fine carpenter. They are smarter than most of my slaves, so they are treated well."

Joshua asked, "So what brings you here today?"

"I just wanted to tell you that the party at my home will be in ten days," he told us. "I still would like you all to attend. You can even bring Adam along. He can visit with the other Negroes there. Maybe he will find a woman he likes. You know, I would like to have Adam's offspring."

I could feel the tension rise within the four of us, but we had to grin and bear it.

"Well, we're all looking forward to coming, Charles," I said. "We will be there for sure. Again, we thank you for the invitation. We'll see you then, but now we must get going."

"Then it is a date. I'll see all of you when you get

back." He turned his horse around and galloped down the road.

Lily said, "I hate that son-of-a-devil. He reminds me of that miserable man that took our farm. Someday I'll kill him."

We all knew she meant it. She had that look in her eyes that would kill.

"Easy, Lily," I said. "His time will come, but we must stay focused on what we have to do now. It is coming together better than I had expected. We'll play his game and we'll win. It may take a while, but we *will* win."

Adam rolled his eyes and laughed. "Charles wants me to bed down with as many women as I can," he remarked. "He must think I'm really stupid. There ain't no way in hell that I'll bed down with any women he has there. They all think we are animals and don't have any feelings. Good thing I can laugh at this or I would have killed him myself. The man is a damn fool."

The next two days were real smooth for us. Folks in the small towns that we stopped in bought a lot of our supplies.

Atlanta was like another world. There were so many streets and so many stores. Joshua and I had never seen so many people in one place. They even had bricks on the streets and many big beautiful houses. People of all types were walking and riding in fancy buggies. Some were dressed in expensive clothes, and then there were the poor folks who were just begging in the streets.

Lilly said, "I came here twice before with my father. I know some of the places, but it sure has grown since I was last here."

As we made our way through the busy streets, many people stopped what they were doing and looked at us. They had never seen the likes of us before. We stopped in front of a building that said:

COTTON INN
ROOMS TO RENT
FOOD, SPIRTS

I said, "What do ya think? This looks like a good place to stay a day or two."

Lily laughed and said, "Robert, this place is expensive. They may not even let us in. I know damn well they won't let Adam in there."

Adam smiled and said, "Don't you worry about me. I'm staying with the wagon and horses. They will steal us blind in one hour around here. I know these people, and I know how to handle them. Halfmoon and I will be just fine in that stable across the street. You go on in and give them people a laugh. They may even let you stay there."

We got off the wagon and walked inside. The place was filled with fancy furniture, and the walls were covered with red wallpaper. All the woodwork was beautifully carved. As we walked up to the counter where two men were working, we could hear people whispering about us. The man at the desk looked up and said, "Can I help you?"

"You sure can," I replied. "Me and my brother and sister want the best damn room you got here in this place."

The man looked us up and down and said, "I'm sorry,

folks, but we are all full. And even if we weren't, you couldn't afford a room here."

Then Joshua really got into character. "Well, we have come all the way from Kentucky, trading all along the way. Tell me then, how much is a room here?"

The man said, "Fifteen dollars. All your food is extra."

By this time, some men and women were standing around us, watching and listening.

Lily unbuttoned her blouse and almost exposed herself. She reached inside her buckskins and pulled out a leather pouch. She emptied it onto the counter in front of the man. A pile of gold coins fell out worth at least four hundred dollars. "I believe there is enough gold here for us to stay a month," she announced. "So now do you have any rooms?"

The man gazed for a second at Lily and then at the gold and said, "Why yes, ma'am. There happens to be a room that has just become vacant. I'm sure you have enough to pay for it."

The men and women let out one big sigh when they saw Lily and the gold.

"You are such a kind man," Lily said sweetly. "I want to thank you so very much for the room. We want one room together. You see we all sleep in one room back home in our cabin in the mountains. And there's one more thing I want."

"Anything you say, Miss."

"I want a bathtub. And lots of hot water so I can just lie in that tub all day."

The women behind us started talking up a storm. The men were just smiling.

The man at the desk said, "You can have anything you want, Miss. Do you have any bags?"

Lily laughed and said, "All we got is what we are wearing. We have a big wagon out front, and we are going to have our Negro friend take it across the street to that stable for a few days."

"Just sign this book with you names, and I'll give you a key for the room," the man offered.

Lily smiled at us and said, "None of us can write much, but we can make an X where we have to."

The man behind the desk didn't know what in hell to say, so he shrugged. "That will be fine."

We all made an X in the book and walked outside. The people followed us out as we got onto the wagon and went across the street to the stable.

When we got to the stable, we all fell on the ground laughing our fool heads off. We told Adam what we did and he just looked at us and said, "I knew damn well you three would pull something like that. I would love to have been in there watching all them rich people. You three will be talked about for the next two days. The word will travel fast about the gold you had too, so be damn careful."

"We will," I promised. "We aren't going out at night. We'll eat at the inn and walk or take the wagon during the day."

Joshua finally quit laughing and said, "I bet they are wondering where in hell we got the gold from. This will keep them guessing for a while, that's for damn sure. It was a good idea not signing our real names. The less they know about us, the better."

We helped Adam with the wagon and horses. He and Halfmoon would just stay around this area. We knew no one would bother the wagon at night. We decided the four of us and Halfmoon would go look around some of the streets and stores. We wanted to see what we could buy and take back with us.

When we all appeared on the sidewalk, the people from the inn were watching us. They really started to talk when they saw Adam and Halfmoon. We had brought our muskets with us. We knew we didn't need them, but it was good to have them just in case.

We went into a large barn that had just about everything traders like us wanted. The owner approached us and said, "I have heard that you all are from the mountains of Kentucky. Is that right?"

"Yes, that is," I answered. "We have a trading post there, and we also do some trading a few days from here out of our house."

The old trader asked, "What have you to trade or sell here?"

We told him what we had left and that we were looking for cloth, kitchen pots and pans, and things most people would need.

"I'll tell what I'll do," he offered. "Tomorrow you come here with your wagon, and I'll buy some pelts and skins from you. The people here are always asking me for those things, but it is hard for me to get any down here."

"Well, I'll tell you what I can do for you," I responded. "Next year, I'll bring a whole wagon full of pelts and skins for you. I will trade them for some of that fine cloth you have here."

"That would be great. I'm sure we'll do good business together."

We left the store, knowing we had finally made the whole connection on trading. This would make going to Atlanta and back home worthwhile. We knew the people wouldn't forget us, and we knew we had the game in play. Now it was time to free some people.

It was late in the day, so we decided to go to the inn and see our room. Adam and Halfmoon would be very comfortable in the wagon. We found a place for Adam to eat where there would be no problem with anyone running him off. There were other Negroes there and many lived nearby, but they were far enough from the rich whites, so it was safe.

"You go on and enjoy yourselves," Adam encouraged. "Halfmoon and I will eat and get back to the wagon before dark. There won't be anyone to bother us."

"I don't like the idea of leaving you here, Adam," I said.

"I know you don't, but we have to play the game, remember? I'll be fine; I'll just talk like the other slaves if anyone tries to talk to me."

"We'll be here bright and early in the morning."

Adam smiled and told us just go and have a good time, and most of all to stay out of trouble.

When we entered the inn, the manager ran toward us and said, "Is there anything you folks need?"

Lily gave him a sweet smile and said, "I sure would like to get into a big tub of hot water, and maybe put on some fine perfume if you have any."

"Why yes, Miss Lily," the man replied. "I'll send some

up with one of my staff right away. She'll get your bath water ready and take care of anything else you may need."

"Well, I sure want to tell you and everybody in this here room how nice you are to your guests," she said coyly.

Joshua and I tried like hell not to laugh.

We finally got up to our room, and when we opened the door, we just stood there looking at all the finery. Large hand-carved beds and dressers were in the room. The curtains and bedspread were covered with fancy lace, and the walls were decorated with the latest wallpaper.

"I ain't never seen such fancy wallpaper as this, Robert, have you?" Joshua asked.

"Hell, no," I replied. "I tell ya both something. It sure feels good to have money and be able to stay in a place like this. Plus Lily is going to take a bath in a fancy tub and all."

"That's right," she declared. "You two should take one too. You are starting to stink some."

Within a few minutes, the maids knocked on the door, and we let them in. There was three maids carrying hot water, and they began to pour it into the claw-foot tub. Joshua and I sat there watching, shaking our heads at Lily.

Finally, the tub was full and Lily turned toward us and said, "Well now, go and find your own bathtub. I want to soak in here for an hour."

I said, "All right, Lily. We'll go down to the bar, have a few ales, and find our own bathtub."

Before we got out the door, Lily had stripped down naked as a jaybird and got into the tub. She let out a groan.

"Lily, are you okay?" I asked.

"Heck yes, I am," she answered. "It just feels so darn

228

good to be in this hot water. Now get out and I'll see you later."

Joshua and I closed and locked the heavy oak door behind us. We knew Lily would enjoy the next hour soaking in that tub.

We walked down the stairs and into the bar. They had a long oak bar with a long brass footrest at the bottom. The whole back wall was glass, and the shelves were covered with all these fancy bottles of whiskey. There were about twenty men sitting and standing at the bar dressed in their finest clothes. A few men were at the tables, playing cards.

Joshua and I sat at the bar.

"I tell ya, Robert," Joshua said. "I didn't know they had so many different kinds of whiskey."

"I bet ya they ain't got any like our grandfathers used to make," I said.

"I bet they don't either. That corn whiskey they used to make would knock your moccasins off your feet if you drank too much of it."

We both burst out laughing.

"What do you men want to drink?" the barkeeper asked.

"I guess we'll stick to some cold ale if ya have any," I replied.

"We sure do." The barkeeper brought us back two large pewter mugs filled with ale. It was colder then we'd ever had. It was some good-tasting ale too. We had about two more when one of the men at the bar walked over to us and said, "I can see you men are not from Atlanta, are you?"

"No, sir, we ain't," I answered. "We are now living in Kentucky, but we was really from the Mohawk Valley in

New York."

"This is a long ways from home, isn't it?"

Joshua said, "Wherever we hang our hats is home to us. We ain't much on staying put in one place too long. There is a whole new country out there just waiting for our eyes to see."

"My name is James Fuller," the man introduced. "I have been living in New Orleans for the past few years. There are rumors going around in Washington that President Jefferson wants to send some men out into the Spanish Louisiana Territory."

"What does he want to do that for?" I asked.

"Well, it seems that he might be interested in buying that vast unknown land for the United States. Spain now owns New Orleans and part of west Florida, but this Frenchmen named Napoleon may want to sell it. But who really knows what is going on these days? One year the land is called something, and then it changes to a state."

"We sure know about that," I griped. "That's what had happened where we are from in Kentucky. We thought it was Virginia, and then we read it is now Kentucky. The country is sure changing fast nowadays."

"I saw you four come into town today with that very unusual wagon full of supplies," James said. "I guess you are doing real well trading and all."

Joshua answered, "We are doing pretty well. It'll take time for us to get a good trading route set up, but we are quite happy so far."

"Is that Negro your slave?"

I looked at him and said quickly, "No, he ain't. He is a

free man. He came with us from New York. He was born up there and is a damn good friend to us. Why do you ask?"

"I didn't mean to get you riled up," James said, "but I'm for freeing those slaves. I was just wondering how you two felt about the issue, that's all."

I looked around and said, "Well, that has been on our minds lately."

James looked at both of us and said quietly, "Why don't you two come up to my room for a drink? I would like to talk to you."

Joshua looked at me and said, "Sure, why not?"

We started to pay for the ale we drank, but James said to the barkeeper, "Put their drinks on my bill."

The three of us walked up the stairs to James's room. He had a huge room, the best one in the inn. He told us to sit down and have a drink. Joshua and I did as he said, and then he took out a cigar and lit it. He looked at us and said, "Have you two ever thought of helping slaves escape to the north?"

Joshua and I looked at each other. We didn't know what to say to him.

James smiled and said, "I have been around a long time, and I can always tell what a man is thinking. I have made a fortune playing cards. I know every face and what it means when I'm playing poker. By looking at you two, I know that you have the same ideas I have, don't you?"

I looked at James and said, "Does it show that easily?"

"No, but I can tell. Not many men could. You have a strong face, so it'll be hard for many men to know that you're lying to them."

"Well, you are right then," I confessed. "We are on a mission to free slaves and send them north. We call it the Underground Railroad. We have contacts all the way to Lake Erie."

James smiled and took a long drink from his crystal glass. "Now this is a step in the right direction," he approved. "What I'm about to tell you must never be said to outsiders."

"Well, there is Lily," I pointed out. "She is with us and so is Adam."

"That's fine. Now listen to me very closely." James sat down in a fine leather chair and placed his drink on a marble top table. "In the last three years I have personally helped five Negro slaves escape from down by New Orleans," he told us. "But I cannot do it alone anymore. I believe that a few men down there have suspicions about me. That's why I moved to Atlanta. No one knows me here. They just know me as a rich gambler. As soon as I saw you two and Lily in the lobby this morning, I had a feeling you were up to something. That's why I was hoping I could get a chance to talk to you. I have three men in hiding right now that have gotten this far, and now I have no people to help them to go further north."

Joshua said, "We can do it, can't we, Robert?"

"We've never done it yet," I admitted, "but we sure gotta start sometime. I say we do it."

We were about to start talking again when we heard someone knocking at the door. James stood up and asked, "Who is it?"

We heard a women speak and knew right away it was Lily.

I said, "It's all right. It's Lily. Let her in."

James walked over to the door and let Lily in. She looked great. She had a pretty dress on, and she smelled like spring flowers. She twirled around and said, "Well, what do you think?"

Joshua and I just stared at her. We had never seen her look so beautiful.

"You sure can take a man's breath away, Lily," Joshua exclaimed.

Lily smiled and said, "Well, thank you both. But now I have a bone to pick with you two!"

"What did we do wrong this time, Lily?" I asked.

"First off, you two never went and found a bath tub. You still stink and in front a fine gentleman as this man here. Then I get all prettied up and went to the bar thinking you two would be there. As soon as I walked in, four men came over to me and wanted to buy me a drink and supper. Finally the bartender told me you left with a strange man to his room. I started to get worried. For a minute, I thought I would have to put my old buckskins back on, get Half-moon, and start looking for you."

Joshua and I apologized to Lily for five minutes and swore we would never do that again.

"Then I accept your apology," Lily stated. "Now who is this man?"

We introduced Lily to James. He took her hand, kissed it, and said, "Miss Lily, you are the most beautiful woman I have ever seen. There is no one prettier than you all the way to New Orleans."

Lily blushed and said, "Well, thank you, James. I bet you say that to all the women you meet."

"No, Miss Lily, I don't. And I sure as hell don't lie either."

Lily turned to Joshua and me and said, "Now what in blazes are you two doing up here with this fine gentleman?"

I said, "Sit down, have some sherry, and relax, Lily. You've got to hear this."

For the next hour we told Lily about what James had been doing and what we were about to do.

She sat quietly for a minute and then said, "It sounds like we have our first freight to take north."

James looked at Lily and said, "I like that word, 'freight.' It will work great for all of us."

Joshua smiled and said, "Why not call people that help and hide the slaves 'conductors'?"

I looked at both of them and said, "Well, I think now we all have our new words figured out. The route we send the slaves north on will be called the Underground Railroad, the people who help them on the way north will be called conductors, and the slaves themselves will be called 'cargo' or 'freight' from this day forward."

We all had some fine brandy to close the deal. We spent the rest of the evening talking about how and when we would take our first freight north. James said he could have the three men at the stable tomorrow late in the afternoon. We all agreed that a good time to leave would be just before dark. We could be out in the country where we could set up camp and be safe. Then we told James that we were supposed to go to a party at the nearby plantation when we got back.

"You three go to that party," James insisted. "I want to come with you. I need to know where you live and what the roads are like around there. We'll tell this rich plantation owner that I'm a rich man who may be interested in buying some land out that way. I became friends with you when you sold me everything you had in your wagon. I can handle this type of men. I have been dealing with them for years all the way to New Orleans. I can be just as charming as they are—and the meanest man alive when I'm pushed into a corner. I'm a marksman when it comes to pistols. There's a few dead men in the South who had thought differently during a duel."

I said, "That's good to know. We can always use a good man with a gun when the time comes."

James asked Lily, "What is this plantation owner's name anyway?"

"Charles Franklin," she replied.

James smiled. "This is perfect," he said. "I know his sister in New Orleans. She is quite the lady down there. She married a rich man named Henry L'Bell. He made a fortune in shipping, mostly bringing slaves in from the coast of Africa. They think the world is theirs and that all the decent people should look up to them."

Lily said, "It is a small world, isn't it? I can see now that we will get along nicely. We all have hate for some of these people. We will do what we can, and maybe we'll fight a few along our way."

"Why, Miss Lily!" James said. "You do have a mean streak in that beautiful body of yours, don't you?"

Joshua and I laughed.

"You haven't seen anything yet, James," I warned. "She has killed at least two men already."

"Tell me more," James pleaded. "I'd better get to know all about you four before we really get into this full steam."

We told James how we all met and everything we had done together since then.

"You all sure have been busy," he commented. "I know now that I can really trust all of you to the end. Now let me tell you about me. I was born near Savannah, Georgia. I'm twenty-seven years old. I also have killed a few men in my time. My father was captain of a ship that had made many voyages to England until the war started. He'd already had made his money, so he took it easy later in his life. When he and my mother died, they left me with plenty of money and a nice home there, but I was young and wanted to see some of this land. I sold everything, went to New Orleans, and bought some land and a nice home there. I finally sold it to that slave runner Henry L' Bell. I didn't know he wanted it for cotton or sugarcane. By the time I found out, it was too late. We closed the deal, and he started bringing in his slaves to plant and pick the cotton. He expanded the plantation two-fold, and since the cotton gin was invented, he's growing even more cotton and sending it to England. I made more money than I'll ever need by doing it. I hate the bastard for what he does to those poor black souls. That's why I decided to spend my last gold dollar freeing as many as I can."

The three of us listened to this man's dream of helping these Negroes get their freedom. We told him that we would make a good friendship that would last forever.

We told James that we had to sell some supplies tomorrow first and buy some goods to take back with us. He said that it would be fine with him, and that he would meet us at the livery stable tomorrow about four o'clock. We all agreed with him, said our goodnights, and went back to our room.

When the three of us were inside our room, Lily said, "I like James. He thinks like us. He'll be very useful."

"I just hope we are doing the right thing tomorrow when we try to get those three men out of Atlanta," I said.

Joshua smiled and said, "We have the wagon, and we all know what we have to do. Once we get out of town, we can relax some. We won't have any problem with people coming up to us on the road. We'll just tell them we are all sold out."

"The sooner we get back to our new place the better," I said. "Then we can get those men heading in the right direction. We took real good notes and have maps of a safe way to our trading post in Kentucky. Once they are there, we can send them to Lily's aunt and uncle's place."

Lily said, "We'll just have to keep an eye out for that Charles Franklin and his men. We'd better keep the men in the cabin during the day."

Joshua laughed and said, "Well, Robert, I guess we never got to that bath tonight, did we?"

"That's for damn sure. Maybe we'll find a stream tomorrow. I don't think Lily will mind us for one more night."

"You two men are something else," she scoffed. "Good thing I put on that pretty flower perfume tonight. Now I may be able to stand you."

The three of us laughed and decided to go to bed. Tomorrow would be another day, and we knew we had better be at our best until we got far from Atlanta.

The next morning we checked out of the inn. The manager was so nice to us, inviting us to come back and stay there again. We thanked him for his kindness.

We walked across the street, which was already busy with people going here and there. When we got behind the livery stable, Adam had the horses all hitched up. Halfmoon started to bark like crazy. He was so happy to see us all together again. We knew he was ready to leave this busy town.

Adam smiled and yelled to us, "I see that you all had a safe evening in that fancy inn."

"We sure did," I agreed. "Lily soaked in a hot bathtub for over an hour while Joshua and I were talking business."

"What business was that?"

"We'll tell you all about it now before we get busy with new cargo today."

"What are you talking about, Robert? New cargo?"

We sat Adam down and told him all the latest news. Adam felt real good about it and said, "That is music to my ears. The wagon is all set, and I know old Halfmoon is ready also."

We met the new trader we were going to exchange supplies with. He was very happy, and he sure wanted our business when we came back to Atlanta. We shook his hand and started back to the livery stable to pick up our new cargo. It was almost four o'clock in the afternoon by the time we got back. We knew that James would be coming along very soon.

Within the hour, James rode in on his beautiful horse. He sure had a fine horse and saddle. He also had his side bags with him and he was ready to go. "It sure is nice seeing you all again," he greeted. "And this must be Adam and your wolf, Halfmoon. He sure is a big fellow, isn't he?"

James got off his horse and walked toward Halfmoon very easily. Halfmoon took a liking to James right away. The man was all right in our books.

"The freight is just outside of town," James told us. "There is an old burned-out building all by itself near a small stream. I went by there early this morning. Everything is safe and ready for us."

"Lead the way, James," I said, "and we'll be right behind you."

We followed James through the busy streets. Just on the outside of town, we saw the burned-out building he had told us about. James went ahead to make sure there was no one around. He waved for us to follow. When we came close to the back of the building, three men came out. They looked to be in their early twenties. They were dirty from being in this place, and their clothes were all rags. They had no shoes, and we could see where the chains had been on their wrists. They were caked with dirt and dried blood. The poor men looked hungry and damn scared.

Adam instructed them to get into the secret area below the main floor of the wagon. We gave them water and some food to eat while they were lying there for the next three hours.

When we were all set to leave, we headed out of town. We had to go through a busy street, which we knew would be the biggest test of how well we could hide people beneath the wagon floor. People on the street looked at us and said hello, but nobody stopped us. There were bounty hunters all over the place. We knew who they were at first sight. They all had that certain attitude, but none of them gave us a second look.

Once we were out of Atlanta, we all breathed a sigh of relief. Now we had to get further away and find a good place to stop for the night.

Adam kept asking the slaves who were still lying down in the wagon, "Are you fellows doing all right?"

"Yes, sir, we is. But we sure would like to stretch our legs some."

"We'll be stopping very soon, so just relax."

I knew it had to be hard for them to lie there for nearly two hours, but they knew they had to stay hidden until it was safe. After another hour, we finally drove off the main road to an area under some tall trees. There we knew we would be safe for the night.

Adam unhitched the horses, and Joshua let the men out. They crawled out slowly until their bodies began to move around some. They were stiff and tired, for sure. Adam called them over near the wagon after they walked around some to limber up.

"You men come here and sit down under this tree. We'll make supper and then we all can eat and relax."

The three men sat down and Lily went to them. "Let me look at your wrists," she said. "I'll fix them up in no time."

Lily looked at each man's wrists, took some water, and cleaned the open wounds. She put some ointment on them and bandaged them. She was so gentle. I heard one of them say, "Youse sure is a kind woman, ma'am. Why is all of youse doing this for us niggers for?"

Lily said, "You aren't niggers! Quit saying that word. I hate it! You are human beings, just like we are. You three had better start thinking of yourselves as equal men. You will be free soon, and the sooner you act like it, the better off you'll be."

The three men said they were sorry if they upset her, and that they would start acting better about life and themselves.

James walked over to Joshua and I said, "She is one hell of a woman, isn't she?"

"She sure is. She'll tell you the way it is, and you had better listen to her or else."

James smiled and said, "She is so good with those poor men. She is kind and warm, and she never stops doing for any of us." He then turned to us and said, "We did really well today leaving Atlanta. None of those bounty hunters paid any attention to us. It was a real test for us. I feel like we will have no trouble when we go back there again."

Joshua said, "We were lucky, but there will come a time when we'll have to fight our way out of something. Sooner or later they will want to look at the wagon, and then all hell will break loose. But we'll be ready for them, I promise ya that."

The hot spring sun was finally setting in the west. There would be no moon for the next few days. We decided to take turns standing watch and staying close under the wagon. We knew that there would be many days when none of us would sleep a full night. Halfmoon stayed close by, always on alert. He heard anything way before we did. He sure would let us know if danger was coming.

The rest of the night went by quietly with no noise, just the warm southern breeze rushing through the giant tree branches and leaves. The new freight slept peacefully all night. Not one of them moved a muscle. I planned to wait until early morning to give them some new clothes and shoes. I finally went to sleep thinking of the days ahead and what may be waiting for us around the next turn or over the next hill. I didn't know if it would be too much for me to bear. I just had to stay positive about it all.

It seemed as if I had only closed my eyes for an hour before Adam shook me awake. "Robert! Robert! It is time to get up and get going."

"What time is it, Adam?"

"It is nearly seven-thirty. We gotta get on the road and away from Atlanta."

I finally got up and had some coffee.

The three men who just a few hours ago were wearing rags now had all new clothes on. I said to Adam, "I see that you fixed up these men with new clothes."

"I sure did, and they love them. They act like new men this morning. I fed them, and now they are ready to go."

"Adam, you're a hell of a man," I told him. "You're always two steps ahead of me, aren't you?"

"I guess I am. That is fine with me. You have enough to do without worrying about getting new clothes for these men."

"Well, I sure thank you for it. Where is James?"

"He rode off about an hour ago. He said he wanted to make sure there were no roadblocks with bounty hunters looking for runaways up ahead. He'll be back in a bit."

By the time we got the horses hitched to the wagon, James was coming back to camp. He got off his horse and said, "The road is empty so far. I rode about two miles and checked it out. We should be all right for a while."

The men sat in the back of the wagon this time. We had taken a lot of supplies and blocked the front and rear so no one could look in. They would be more comfortable there than lying on their stomachs all day.

We were on the road for almost five hours when just ahead we saw a bridge where some men were sitting on their horses.

"Get ready," Joshua warned. "I think I see trouble ahead."

We made sure that our weapons were ready to go. The men in the wagon lay down and didn't say a word. When we got within ten feet of the four men, one of them said to us, "Hold up there. We are looking for some runaway slaves. They took off last night about a mile from here. We're checking all wagons coming and going."

James rode up next to the men and said, "We haven't seen anything since early this morning. I hired these four traders here and bought all the supplies they have in the wagon. We are going to my new place. I thought I would get a farm going and raise some cotton like they all are now. You can bet I don't have any damn slaves with me. I do plan to buy some when I get to my place."

None of us said a word. We just waited.

"Well, you look like a rich farm owner to me," the man said. "But what about that Negro driving the team of horses?"

"Oh, you mean Adam there," James responded. "He's with those mountain folks there. He is a free man from the north."

Then one of the other men said, "We want to see his papers."

Joshua stood up on the wagon and said, "We ain't gotta show you nothing, Mister. This is free country, and this wagon and this man are with us. If you want trouble, then come and try to look in this wagon or look at his papers. I don't think you can read anyway."

The man got this look in his eyes, and we knew he was the hotheaded one.

The other man said to him, "Shut the hell up! These people seem fine with me. We ain't looking for trouble, so you all can pass on."

James said, "A wise decision. You know how testy these mountain folks can get. They like a good fight, and that damn wolf they got won't even let me close to that wagon."

The four men smiled and one said, "Yeah, we heard that those mountain folks like to fight. They say that they share their women too."

Lily sternly said, "That's right, I just don't know who to sleep with every night."

The leader laughed. "Well, we held you folks up long enough," he said. "Get on your way and a have safe ride."

We passed them and never looked back. It went better than we thought it would. We sure didn't have time to bury four more men.

No one said a word until we were a good ways away from them. Then Adam said, "Lily, you were great. You sure had them believing you. You turned their mean remarks into a joke. They were just hoping we'd start something."

Joshua and I laughed. Lily just smiled and said nothing.

James told Lily, "You sure can lay it on thick or when you need to."

I said, "We told you how she was. She is good, isn't she?"

"Miss Lily, you are a woman of many wonders," James declared. "I just love watching you in action."

Lily stood up in the wagon and took a bow.

We all laughed, even the men still lying in the wagon.

We traveled onward. Adam turned to our guests and asked, "By the way, what are your names?"

One of the older men said, "My name is Storyteller. This man here is Freeman, and the other mans is Jacob. We all's been named by our master. He could never says our real African names, so he gaves us these names."

I said, "Tonight we'll talk about how you came here. I would like to know."

Storyteller said, "We likes to tell youse. We sure miss our homes and families."

The more I looked at them and thought about what hell

they had gone through to get here, the more it made me think of my own home. I couldn't imagine what it would be like to be captured and taken from your family. I knew all of us were thinking the same thing.

Halfmoon jumped in the back of the wagon and lay down next to the men. They started to pet him and talk to him like we all did. I knew Halfmoon felt their pain, and he tried to make them forget about it for a while.

We found another safe place to camp for the night. I knew in another few days we would be home at our new place. It would be so damn good to get back there. The three men sat around the fire with us while James stood watch.

"So tell me how you got captured in your land," I said.

Storyteller replied, "I can speaks for al' of us. That's how I gots my name was by telling stories on the plantation. The three of us are all from the same village. We were outs hunting. When we got back to our village, many mens attack us. Theys had guns and whips. Theys threw fishing nets over me and the others. They put irons on our ankles and our hands. We couldn't run or anything. Theys had many mens and some womens. Theys took us in a small fishing boat to a big ship out in the water. Theys puts us in the bottom of this big boat and locked us in. It's been hot and the men and womens cried, and many were throwing up all over each other. We had no water or food for almost two days. It was many days before we comes to Savannah. Theys lets us out on deck each day, and many of my peoples I knews were dead. Theys just threw them over the side of the ship."

Storyteller started to cry like a baby.

I said, "You don't have to tell us any more, Storyteller. I know it was hell for you. I'll tell you all something right now you will never be put in damn chains again. The five of us will die before that happens again."

The three men all had tears in their eyes, and each one of them extended their callused hand to me. I took each one and held it tight.

Freeman said, "Youse all are so good to us. We can never pay youse back for your help."

"You just did," Joshua told them. "You are here and your handshake is all we'll ever want. We will get you north, and you will have a new free, happy life. There are other men and women there just like you. They have their own small village, and you will be there telling stories again to your people."

Lily went to each of them and rechecked their wounds. "You all are healing very fast and that's good. Soon you'll be like new again."

Storyteller said, "Miss Lily, it is all that fine cookin' you does for us. That's whys we heal so fast."

It was good to see them all smiling. They felt safe with us, and they knew we would help them all that we could.

Within a week we were back at our new home. Sam was so excited to see us again.

"Welcome back home, folks," he greeted. "It seems like such a long time since you left. How did it go? Oh, I see you have brought back three new faces?"

Adam got off the wagon and hugged Sam. "Come on, Sam," he said. "Help me get the horses in the stable. I'll tell ya the whole story."

Sam and Adam took the horses, and I told the men to come into the house. When we got inside, I told them that they had to stay inside during the day. They could go just around the house at night. I showed them the trap door and the root cellar in case we had to hide in there.

Sam and Adam came into the house. Sam had made some fine chicken and biscuits for supper. We sat around the table and planned what the next step would be.

I had been thinking about this since we'd picked the men up in Atlanta. I was about to say what was on my mind when Adam spoke up first.

"Now listen to this plan. I think it would be wise if I took these men to our place in Kentucky. I know the way as well as anybody here. Remember you three have to go to Charles Franklin's plantation in a few days. He won't miss me, but he'd notice if one of you didn't show up. We'll take four horses, travel light, and move at night when we get close to any town. Once we get further north, we can go during the day. Hell, there ain't anything but mountains a few days' ride from here. Then we can get to our home. I'll give them a good map showing how to get from the trading post to Lily's aunt and uncle's place. They'll be safe there."

We all had questions, but within an hour we all decided this would be best.

"Well then, Adam," I said, "it's up to you. We all know you can do it as good as anyone."

We decided that Adam would leave in two days and re-turn in a few weeks. The next plan was this plantation party and how to introduce James to Charles. We still had time to think of a good plan, and we knew we could come up with something. We always did.

The next two days went by without any problems. The men stayed inside the house, and nobody came to visit us. This gave us time to get ready for Adam to leave with the men. When the day arrived for them to leave, we were a bit saddened by the idea of not seeing Freeman, Storyteller, and Jacob again, but we had to get used to that. There would be many we would never see again, but we wanted them to be free. We shook their hands, and they had tears in their eyes. They had plenty of supplies, and we gave each man a nice bowie knife to protect himself if needed.

We spent the next four days before the plantation party thinking about how we would introduce James to Charles and the local plantation owners.

James finally came up with a good idea one evening while we were sitting around the table. "Listen to this and let me know what you think."

We all sat up straight in our chairs, waiting for this great idea.

"I'll tell Charles and whoever else is there that I have interest in starting a steamboat company from St. Louis to New Orleans," he suggested. "This will get a few of them interested. I'll really build up the whole story and tell them how it will be the new West someday. It'll be the first step of western expansion. I'll also tell them that I may hire you three to sell supplies to me from your trading post in Kentucky."

Joshua said, "That's a great idea. Maybe when we are about to be hunted down and caught, we can head to St. Louis."

Lily laughed and said; "Now that is very possible. I can picture myself on one of those big flat bottom boats going down the Mississippi. I have heard the river is a mile wide in some places. Someday I'll see that great river."

James picked up his mug of ale and said, "Well, let's make a toast to our new lie and hope to hell that it works."

We sat and talked until late that evening. We had three more days to get ready and put on our best performance yet.

Plantation Party

The day of the plantation party we had gone over just about every detail of the plan. We decided to wear our best buckskins instead of the regular clothes most people would be wearing. We wanted to have them take one look at us and come to the conclusion that we really were mountain folks. James had put on his best clothes, the latest style he had bought in Atlanta. He also wore his beautiful side pistol in a hand-tooled leather holster. He sure looked like a gentleman from New Orleans. They would surely be asking him all kind of questions.

Sam said he would stay at the house and take care of some work that needed to get done. Since Adam and the new freight had gone, there were things that needed to be tended. Joshua and I brought our muskets, and even Lily had hers.

When we got on the wagon, I said, "Well, let's go and enjoy ourselves. We'll be the talk of the day, that's for sure."

When we started down the long dirt road that led to Charles Franklin's plantation, we didn't see any slaves in the fields. We thought that this might be a good chance for us to look at where they lived and maybe make some contacts. We knew it would take time for the people to accept us, and we were sure we would be watched by one of the overseers.

At the main house, many of the guests stared as we came into view with our big unusual wagon.

Lily said, "Well, here we go. I guess I'll put on my smile and try not to forget where in hell I am."

"Take it easy, Lily," I said. "Just relax, be yourself, and have fun. We'll mess with their heads all day."

"You're right, Robert. Let's have fun and not think too much about why we hate this man."

Joshua and I laughed.

"You three just make small talk for a while," James instructed. "I'll lay it on heavy in due time."

A young Negro boy came and held the horses as we climbed off the wagon. Charles walked down the steps from the porch and said, "I see you all got back in one piece from Atlanta. I also see that you have company with you."

James got off his horse, approached Charles, and said, "My name, sir, is James Fuller. You must be Charles Franklin."

Charles shook his hand and said, "Yes, sir."

"Well, Joshua, Robert, and dear Miss Lily have told me all about you. They say you have been very kind to them since they moved here from Kentucky."

"That's real nice to hear," Charles replied. "They are sure a different type of people than we are used to seeing around this county. They do fascinate me in many ways. I'm so glad they could make it, and I'm glad you have joined them. But what is a fine gentleman like you doing with these fine mountain folks?"

"I met them in Atlanta," James explained. "I bought just about all their supplies. We started to talk and found we have the same interest."

"What can that be?" Charles asked.

"I'm looking at starting a trade route from St. Louis to New Orleans along the Mississippi River," James explained. "They say St. Louis is the beginning of the new West. These fine folks may be useful to me for sending supplies there."

"That is a very risky business," Charles warned. "It would cost a lot of money to get such a route started."

I whispered to Joshua and Lily, "Here it comes. He's gonna give him the bait."

James smiled and said, "Well, I'm a very wealthy man. I don't worry about money."

Charles replied, "Maybe we can talk business later. I may be interested in becoming a partner with you." Charles then turned to us and said, "Make yourselves at home. There is plenty of food and drink in the house. Just go and help yourselves. I have to see some of my guests, but I'll see you all later."

Charles walked over to his other guests, and James walked to us and smiled.

Lily said, "Well, James, you sure laid it on thick as

honey back there. He bought every word of it."

"Didn't I tell you, Lily?" James said with a grin. "I know what these rich folks like to hear. Now he'll be telling all the men about the new business deal he may have with me. He doesn't know I'll take his money little by little. This so-called business deal will have me spending a lot of time with him. I'll get to know all about him and the others who have slaves here in this county. I'll work from the inside, and in time he'll never suspect me or you three as conductors. It is all coming together nicely."

I said, "I believe you're right. Just be damn careful, James. Charles isn't stupid, and he will do some checking on this business deal, I'm sure."

"Oh, that he will," James agreed, but he doesn't know I have very close friends in St. Louis who, should I say, are not the gentlemen type."

We went inside the house. It was beautiful. Charles had at least ten Negro housemaids, all dressed in white, serving food and drinks to all of his guests.

Joshua said, "Look at all this food. There is enough here to feed Cherry Valley back home, Robert."

"I'm going to eat as much as I can," I said with a smile. "There is food here I ain't never seen before. I'll try it all."

Joshua and I headed for the food while James and Lily took their time walking around and talking to the other guests. While we were filling our fancy china dishes with all the different food, people were watching us and whispering to each other. We knew they were talking about us and how we looked, but we didn't care what they thought. We at times spoke up louder than we should have and acted more like men from the wilderness than we usually did.

While we were walking and eating on Charles's front veranda, we came across some men sipping their brandy. Finally, one of them was brave enough to approach us.

"I see that you men are enjoying all this great food," he commented.

Joshua swallowed and said, "It ain't raccoon or rabbit, but I guess it's all right."

The other men heard Joshua's remark and walked over where this man was standing.

"You remember when we had to eat that damn skunk in Kentucky, Joshua?" I asked.

"I sure do," he replied. "Hell, we hadn't eaten in three days and that was all we could shoot. But he did taste good, didn't he, Robert?"

"He sure as hell did."

The men didn't know what to think of us, but then one said, "What did you shoot him with?"

"We have muskets that our grandfathers had during the French and Indian Wars and when we licked the British in New York," I told him.

"Well, maybe we can have a competition to see who can shoot the best," he suggested. "Charles has a wonderful shooting range out behind the slaves' cabins."

Joshua smiled and said, "Maybe we can do that. We ain't that good, but we do all right."

"Then it is settled," the man stated. "We'll meet you there in an hour. We'll go tell Charles what we are going to do. I'm sure he would like to shoot also. He is the best shooter in the county, so you'd better expect to be beaten."

The men walked away, shaking their heads and laughing at us.

Joshua said, "We hooked them, didn't we, Robert? Now we'll really show them something on their shooting range."

"Maybe we can get a little wager going on this," I suggested. "I would love to take their dirty money, wouldn't you?"

"Hell, yes. I'll fill my side pouch with their money."

Before we were to go to the shooting range, we saw James and Lily drinking some brandy. We told them about our upcoming sporting event.

James smiled and said, "I guess I'll have to get in on that with you both."

Lily added, "I'll just watch, but if they send a woman up to fire I'll be right behind her."

The four of us walked down the short dirt road and came upon the slaves' quarters. There were maybe twenty cabins and all the slaves were walking and sitting around. The women had a large fire going and were doing some washing. There were many half-naked children running all over the place. Some of the children ran toward us and touched our buckskins. We were sure that they had never seen clothes like these before. We both had leather pouches on our sides, and we gave all the children candy we had brought from Atlanta. Their folks smiled at us and nodded. We knew that they knew we were different. Lily really took a liking to the little ones. She got down on her knees and played with them. Some of the guests just shook their heads, probably thinking we were damn stupid.

Lily yelled, "You guys go on. I'll stay here and visit these people."

We knew what she was doing. She wanted to get the feelings of these people, find out what they thought, and learn who could be trusted.

We walked down a path to an open field and saw a number of metal targets about sixty feet away.

I said to Joshua, "Hell, this is going to be easy. They don't know that our muskets can shoot dead on at a hundred feet."

Charles stood there with his bright, shiny musket. We all gathered around him.

"Now, gentlemen," he began, "we are going to shoot at the first metal target on the left and work toward the right. Each man who hits his target will wait his turn until the last man has fired. Then we'll go to the next. Any questions?"

James said, "Is this a betting match, Charles?"

Charles smiled and said, "It sure is, and the bet is a ten dollar gold piece for each hit. Is that too much for you, Robert and Joshua?"

I reached into my other leather sack, pulled out five hundred dollars in gold and said, "I believe this will go for a while."

All the men let out a sigh.

"You must do real well trading in Atlanta," Charles remarked.

Joshua smiled and said, "Let's quit talking and get to firing."

The first three men up hit their target, and then Joshua and I hit ours. James also hit his, as did Charles. The first three men missed the next target, but the four of us hit ours. For the next six tries, we all hit the target.

James walked behind us and said, "I'm going to miss on purpose this time. I want Charles to think he's better than me. You two go kick his ass."

James then fired and missed.

"Well, that is too bad, James," Charles said. "I thought a man like you would do better than that."

"I guess you're a better shot than me, Charles," James lied.

Charles, Joshua, and I all hit on the next three. We could see Charles was getting a little upset at us, but we weren't going to back down. He finally said, "It seems that you two are pretty good. Now what if we fire at ninety feet for...let's say...two hundred dollars a hit."

The men standing around smiled. One said, "I'm sure you'll show them now, Charles."

Joshua smiled and spit on the ground. "Why don't we shoot at a target that's...let's say...one hundred feet away for five hundred dollars a hit?"

Charles nervously looked at us and then at the crowd.

"Do it, Charles!" one man cheered. "There isn't a man around who can shoot that far and be as dead on as you."

Charles was suddenly feeling cocky again. "All right then," he agreed. "We'll see how damn good you two mountain boys are. But let's see the money first."

I reached into my leather pouch again and took out ten fifty dollar gold coins. I threw them on the ground and said, "Shoot your butt off, Charles."

The tension was high. Charles was really mad deep inside, which was exactly how we wanted him to feel. We knew he would miss.

"Shut up, damn it!" he yelled as he took aim.

We could see he was moving just enough to miss the target. Sure enough, he fired and missed by about one foot to the left. He was really mad now and swearing like hell. He turned to us and said, "The wind came up and moved the target. I never miss at this range."

Joshua smiled and said, "Well maybe, but I don't think so."

I took aim and fired. The ball hit the target. Everyone heard the hit and saw the target move. The men standing around clapped and then fell silent.

Joshua was about to fire. He then lowered his musket and said, "I tell you what, Charles. If I hit this target, you can either pay us five hundred dollars or you can give us two slaves—but they have to be husband and wife."

Charles thought very hard on this. The men who were watching started to talk among themselves. Charles had a look on his face that we had never seen before. He walked toward Joshua and said, "All right then. If you hit the target, you'll be given a married couple, although I don't know why you'd want a husband and wife."

Joshua smiled and said, "We need a strong man to help us, and we need a woman to cook and clean for us. It is getting too much for Lily."

Charles laughed and said, "That is fine with me. I can always get two more niggers."

I could tell Joshua was as mad as a hornet. I just hoped he was still calm enough to hit the target.

Joshua took a steady aim and fired. When the smoke from the musket cleared, we all knew he had hit the target. We saw it move and heard the sound when the musket ball hit the metal. The crowd let out a cheer of excitement. Charles stared at the target. He couldn't believe Joshua had hit it.

He walked toward Joshua and me and said, "I have never seen anyone fire a musket as well as you two. Whoever taught you to shoot must have been some damn good men."

Joshua lowered the musket and said, "Our grandpas taught us to shoot when we were seven years old. There wasn't a man or Indian back home that could outshoot those two men."

Charles said, "Well, let's go to the cabins and find your husband and wife."

When we led the way to the cabins, Lily was standing between a man and a woman. They looked like they were in their early twenties. They were both very strong-looking people. Charles walked up to Lily and said, "I see you have already picked your prize."

"When I heard about the bet you had with Joshua, I came here and found the ones I wanted," she told him. "I knew he would hit the target. I also asked these two Negroes if they wanted to leave with us if Joshua won the bet. As you can see, they are ready to leave now."

Charles was getting red in the face. I could tell that this wasn't over yet.

"You just can't come in here and pick who you want, Lily," he stated firmly. "I'll pick which ones go with you."

James walked over to Charles and said, "Come on, Charles, you never said anything about who was leaving. We all heard you, didn't we, gentlemen?"

One of the men stepped forward and said, "A bet is a bet, Charles. They won and you lost. Let it be. You can always find more slaves and even better than these two."

We knew we had Charles but good. He would never be respected again if he didn't pay off the bet fair and square.

"All right," he announced. "A bet is a bet. I lost and now you have two fine slaves."

The men cheered for Charles. He smiled, but we knew he was mighty mad deep inside.

Again, Lily told the couple that they now belonged to us. They were scared, but deep down they were happy to be leaving Charles Franklin's plantation forever.

We got the wagon and put them in the back. Charles said goodbye to us and then turned to James. "You come back real soon, James," he insisted. "I want to talk to you more about this riverboat steamer."

"I sure will, Charles. Again, thank you for having me here. I surely enjoyed your hospitality and all your wonderful friends."

When we got back home, Sam was sitting on the porch. When he saw the couple in the back he said, "Lordy, Lordy, what have you gone and done this time?"

"You wouldn't believe it, Sam, even if you were there. It was a hell of a day. We won and old Charles lost his bet."

We all yelled in delight. We told Sam all that had happened and what we had planned for these people.

That evening we all ate the supper that the woman made

for us. Neither one of them had said a word all this time. I stood up and said, "Now you two come and eat at this table with us. I want to talk to you."

They looked at each other and the man said, "We ain't never sat at a table with white folks before."

Lily smiled and said, "Tell us your names first."

The man was quiet and then he said, "My names is Ben. My wife is called Mindi. We were married on Master Charles's plantation almost two years ago."

"What did you do at the plantation?" I asked.

"I was his best field hand," Ben told me. "Master Charles tolds me that a lot of times. Mindi was the slave's midwife. She knows alls abouts babies and taking care of the peoples."

James smiled and said, "Well, looks like we've hit the jackpot. We sure hit Charles hard in his pocketbook, didn't we?"

We all smiled and laughed.

"The first thing you must get used to hearing is that we are not slave owners," I said. "We don't farm and we don't have whips or damn chains. You two are as free as old Sam here is. We want you to stay around here and help us for the summer. Then we all will go to Kentucky where we have a big trading post. But you must never leave this place without us. There are men out there who will take you back to Charles or resell you, and you won't be together ever again. As long as you two stay here, we can protect you."

Ben and Mindi looked at each other and then smiled at us.

Ben said, "We sure does understands you. We will stay

here, and does what you say. We is very happy about living heres with youse all."

Joshua said, "Tomorrow Sam and Ben can build a nice place for the two of you in the barn. We'll put in a new wood stove for you. We can make a nice bed too."

Mindi finally spoke. "Why is youse doing all these nice things for us?"

Lily reached for her hand and said, "What we are telling now is for your ears only. No one must ever know what we do or anything."

"We promise, Miss Lily," Mindi agreed.

Lily told them what we were doing and why. They told us they had never heard of such things, but they promised they would never speak of it to anybody except us.

Ben smiled and said, "We knows of many of the slaves on Master Charles's plantation who wants to run away, buts they is scared of being caught and hung."

"What are their names, Ben?" James wanted to know.

Ben swallowed and said, "There is Cottonseed, Tyrone and Maggie, and their two little children. Theys was brought here alls together about last fall. Theys tried to escape once, buts was caught. I heard Master Charles say to them, "You had all run away once on Master King's plantation and he sold you to me. Now if any of you run away again, I'll hang you from that tree over there and let you hang there for a week in front of all your homes." I knows them all very good. Theys would come with youse if theys could."

James said, "I'll remember their names. Next time I go over to Charles's home, I'll see what I can do."

"You had better be very careful, James," Lily warned. "Charles is a sly fox."

James smiled and said, "Don't you worry, Lily. I'm an even smarter fox than him."

The next day we showed Ben and Mindi where to hide if they ever had to. They were very smart and learned right away. Sam and Ben built a nice small room for them in the barn. They had more than they ever thought of having. All day long they thanked us for everything. I had a few dresses that I gave to Mindi, and Ben was given new clothes and his first pair of shoes. It was so darn funny watching him trying to walk with them on.

"I just can't gets used to these shoes," he kept saying.

Sam told him, "You'll get used to them, Ben. It took me all summer to get used to my first pair."

We didn't have one visitor for a whole month. It was the end of September when Charles rode in with some of his men. We didn't know what to expect, but we were ready for anything.

Charles got off his horse and said, "I figured I had better come over for a visit. I haven't seen any of you around lately. I wanted to see if you all were all right."

Lily said, "We all are doing just fine. The people that we got from you are working out real good."

Charles saw them working around the house and said, "I see you have them housebroken. You even put shoes on their feet. You should never do that."

"Why is that, Charles?" I asked.

"If they plan to run away, they can go a long way with shoes on."

Lily was mad and she showed it. "Let me tell you this, Charles," she growled. "They belong to us now and we don't treat them like animals. They ain't going to run. They like it here and they like us."

"Well, I hope none of you are starting to be nigger lovers," Charles remarked. "If you start, they will control you. You'll never get any work out of them."

Joshua spoke quickly because he knew that Lily was about to say the wrong thing.

"We ain't no slave lovers, Charles," he said. "We think if we take care of them better than you, they will stay here—they know I can shoot a target a hundred feet away and not miss."

"So you're going to throw that in my face, are you?" Charles scoffed. "That's all right. You did outshoot me. I know none of you are nigger lovers. I guess I'm still a little upset that you took my best field hand, but I did buy a few more, and they are doing fine in the fields. The other reason I came by was to see James. Is he still living here with you?"

"Here I am, Charles," James announced. He was just coming back from a ride he took down the road. He got off his horse and shook Charles's hand. "I've been thinking about coming over to see you. I was wondering if you have thought more about our business deal."

"I have," Charles confirmed. "I have talked to some of the local men, and we would like to invest in this steamboat in St. Louis. How much would it cost for…let's say…four men to invest?"

"I have been doing some figuring," James answered,

"and I think it'll be about two thousand dollars each. This would give us a fine riverboat and a good chance to start a trading route to New Orleans."

"Well, that sounds like a fair price for each man," Charles agreed. "That would be about eight thousand dollars total, right?"

"That would get us started. Then we have to buy the cotton and labor and take care of the other expenses. I was thinking close to fifteen grand total."

"We agreed that we could all put in five grand each, so your numbers are fair," Charles said. "When do you want to get this in the works?"

"I would need the money in one month," James stated. "I plan on going to St. Louis this fall, and hopefully by December I'll have the steamer heading to New Orleans. I want more than just cotton. I want to get furs that come from the far north. They'll bring a good price in New Orleans. England is still buying all they can get. The other thing is that many new settlers who want to go to St. Louis are coming into New Orleans. The fastest way to get there is up the Mississippi River. They'll pay top dollar for passage there."

"It seems to me, James, that you know what you're talking about," Charles approved. "I'll have the money for you in one month. Then by spring or sooner we'll all start making money."

"We are also leaving at the end of October," I added. "We have to get back to Kentucky and restock our trading post there for the winter. We want to get to St. Louis ourselves so we can get some furs for our next trip to Atlanta in the spring. We have a trader there who wants all our pelts."

Charles said, "It'll be lonely not having you all here, but I know we'll see you in the spring. Well, I'd better get going; I'll see you all in a month."

Charles left and James smiled from ear to ear.

Lily said, "You men sure can pull the wool over his eyes. The man is not so smart is he?"

James laughed and said, "Oh yes, he is. He knows he can make money from us, and that's why he hasn't bothered us yet. He'll plan on being nice as long as he can use us— and we'll do the same. We'll take his damn money and keep him hanging. In the meantime, you had better get some of his slaves. In two years the game will be over, and we'd better be long gone from here or any place south of Kentucky. All hell is going to come upon us when he starts putting two and two together. We'll have all their money and, hopefully, many of his slaves."

"That's what I figure," I said. "We've got two years to do what we gotta do. We'd better get thinking real hard about taking some people on this trip, but we'll have to have them in our hands and leave that same damn day. He'll have his damn hunters out in this countryside looking for them. The only thing we've got going for us is that Charles and his men know us. They'll know we are heading back to Kentucky. That is why we told him now that we are heading home or to St. Louis. If they figure we have them, they'll have to split up and follow each trail we may have taken."

"They sure will," Joshua agreed, "and all they'll find is a

trail of broken chains."

The next two weeks went by quickly. We got a plan together for how we would get the slaves from Charles.

It was Sunday, October 20. Halfmoon was lying on the porch. It was hotter than hell for October. We were all just sitting around when Halfmoon stood up very quickly and ran toward the trees. We watched him for a minute, and then he let out a howl like we'd never heard before. We grabbed our muskets and saw a man riding alone through the trees. Then we heard his voice.

"Halfmoon, what in hell you doing, old boy?"

Halfmoon started to bark like crazy. Then we knew it was Adam. He slowed down and got off his horse. He and Halfmoon rolled around on the ground like two kids. They walked toward us, and we all hugged him. He looked so different. He had gotten rid of his regular clothes and was wearing buckskins from his head to his moccasins. He had his long bowie knife at his side and another one strapped to his back. He was also carrying a new musket. He had let his beard grow, and he had some colorful feathers in his hat. Around his waist he wore some beautiful beads, the best I had ever seen.

"What in hell happened to you while you were gone?" I asked.

Adam smiled. "I got married," he announced.

Lily screamed. "You got married? Who did you marry? And where? Why?"

Adam said, "Slow down, Lily. Let me just show you."

Adam turned and let out a whistle. Then out of the woods came a beautiful Indian woman. She was riding a black horse, and she also was covered in buckskins. She was in her early twenties. Her long black hair went down to her waist, and she was smiling.

Adam said, "I want you all to meet my wife. Her name is Two Moons. I met her in Boonsboro."

Joshua said, "Boonsboro? What in hell were you doing there? I thought you just took the freight to Henry's."

"I did," Adam replied. "I just felt I should take them to Lily's aunt's place. I wanted to be damn sure our first freight would be safe."

"How are my aunt and uncle?" Lily wondered.

"They are fine," Adam assured her. "The business is bigger than ever. Henry is doing real well with our place. More people are moving in, and he is busy all the time. Everything is going great there. When I came back through from your aunt's, I met Two Moons near the place where we met Daniel Boone. I was all set up and was cooking some supper. Then off in the distance I saw this woman riding toward me. She was alone and I thought to myself, She is just going back home to Boonsboro. When she finally arrived at my camp, she asked, "May I have some food? I have been riding a long way, and I must rest before going into Boonsboro. I looked at her and said, "You can help yourself. I'm just staying for the night. Tomorrow I'll be heading south to Kentucky." She was so beautiful. I couldn't stop looking at her. She asked, "Why do you keep looking at me?" I said, "I ain't never seen such a beautiful woman as you, that's all.'

We all laughed.

"Then she said, "My father lives in Boonsboro," Adam

continued. "He is a tracker, and scout for Daniel Boone. Do you know Daniel?" I said, "Yes, I do. I met him over a year ago right here at this place. My friends and I were heading south to our trading post." She then suggested that maybe in the morning we both could go into Boonsboro. I said, "I really don't have the time to do that, but if you want me to, then I will."

"This is amazing," Joshua commented. "So what happened?"

"The next morning we rode into Boonsboro and she went and saw her father," Adam told us. "I met him and we hit it off real well. He was about ready to go west across the Mississippi River with Daniel Boone."

"I guess old Daniel finally needed to head out west to new land and get away from everyone," I said.

"That's what he told me," Adam replied. "He needed to find a new place for his family. He told me he felt cooped up there, so he decided to head west."

Lily asked, "How did you two fall in love so quickly?"

Two Moons broke her silence. "I knew at first sight that Adam was the only man for me," she said. "I could feel in my heart and soul that he was a kind and honest man. We talked most of the night about ourselves and about everything. I told him about my father and his plans for leaving Boonsboro to go with Daniel. I never wanted to go, but I knew he would never come back there to live. I had a big fight with him a few days before. That's why I left and was going back to see him. I needed time to think alone. Then I met Adam. My spirits had answered my prayers. I knew they had given me Adam."

"I told her father that I wanted to marry Two Moons and move back to our trading post," Adam added. "He knew it was best for her and that I would take care of her. So here we are."

We all hugged and kissed Two Moons, welcoming her into our family. James took her hand and kissed it like a gentleman. She blushed and didn't know what to say to him.

Joshua let out a yell and said, "Well, I believe it's time to celebrate. We'll have a hell of a wedding party right here and now."

We all yelled with him and got the wedding party started.

Mindi went into the house and made a special supper for all of us. Ben gathered up wood from the forest for a big fire we'd have later in front of the house.

Joshua said, "Robert, remember when we were little and our grandfathers had a huge bonfire after the war?"

"I sure as hell do," I said. "We stayed up all night playing with Coppernol's grandsons. It was a hell of a day or two that it went on. Let's forget all our troubles tonight and really enjoy our new family."

Sam stayed with us for the night. Lately he'd been with us more than he'd been with Victor.

By the time we had the bonfire going, we were all feeling a little drunk. Two Moons and Adam were hand in hand all night. Neither one of them drank, but Joshua, Lily, James, and I sure poured it down. We were laughing and having a great time.

Finally, when all of us were sitting around the hot, glowing fire, Joshua told Adam, "We've decided to let you sleep in the house tonight until we can build a cabin out back. Mindi and Ben are living in the barn in a nice place we fixed up for them, but now we'll have to build another place for you two. The four of us will sleep outside until we get one built."

Two Moons smiled and said, "No, that is not right. Adam and I have been given some fine canvas by my father. We will not be here much longer, so we'll do it next time we come back here. For now, we love sleeping outdoors. We have a spot all set for it already."

"If that's what you two want then it'll be fine with us," I said. "We just want you two to be happy."

Suddenly, Halfmoon let out a bark and howled like he knew something or somebody was near.

Joshua said, "Halfmoon senses something. Get your damn muskets ready."

We always carried our muskets close to us, and we were damn glad we did that night. About a minute later, a crowd of men rode like hell onto our place. The moon was full, and the night was still.

The riders came in very fast on their horses. Halfmoon ran in between them and us. He stood there, not letting one man come any further. Joshua and I stood up with our muskets. James just sat there, cool as could be. Adam sat with Two Moons, but we knew he was ready.

"Good evening," one of the men yelled to us as he walked his horse closer to the fire. "What have ya' got going on here? A party?"

James walked toward them and said, "I guess you can

call it that. Our dear friend Adam here has just married his beautiful wife, Two Moons."

The men looked around at all of us. One said, "What the hell kind of people are you? Hell, I see niggers and god-damn Indians and poor white trash."

With that remark, we all stood up, ready for hell to break loose.

I said, "We own this land, and this is our home. You just can't ride in here and talk like that to any of us."

"Ain't we invited to this here party?" the man asked.

Adam stepped forward and said, "Hell no, you ain't. We all want you to leave now and just let us be."

"Hey, fellas," one of the men cracked. "Did you hear this nigger slave tell us to leave? Maybe we don't want to leave. Maybe we want some of these fine women you got here. Just maybe we'll chain your ass up, nigger, and take you with us along with that damn Indian you got there."

I could feel the blood boil in my veins. This was the worst assault we had faced yet. We all had talked about such a day coming for a long time, and we'd discussed what we all must do if we had to fight. I looked around and didn't see Sam or Ben or even Mindi. I hoped they wouldn't walk in on the trouble that was brewing.

I don't know if was the heat from the fire or if I was about to explode, but I had never sweated so much in my life before. I could see the sweat pouring out of all our faces. The dancing flames from the fire and the clouds passing beneath the full moon made it look like the devil himself was standing in front of us.

I counted six men altogether. They could be smelled

twenty feet away from where we were standing. They walked another few feet toward us, and one grabbed a pitcher of ale that was on a small table. He smiled and started to pour it into his mouth. He swallowed it and said, "I hope that nigger and Indian didn't drink from here. Hell, I would get sick for sure."

I knew sooner or later that Joshua would make his move. He stepped forward within one foot of the man drinking and said, "You've had your fill of our ale. Now I want you to get your asses back on your horses and get the hell out of here."

The man still had a mouthful of ale, and he spit it into Joshua's face. Halfmoon saw this, lunged at the man, and grabbed him by his throat. The man went down yelling. We suddenly saw three musket blasts coming from behind the other men. All three of the men fell forward off their horses and fell onto the ground. The other two men turned around and fired. By that time, James had shot one of the men off his horse. Adam and I fired at the two remaining. Adam missed the man, but he reached over his shoulder and grabbed his bowie knife. He threw it and the blade found its mark in the center of the man's chest. The man looked at Adam and swore until he couldn't speak any longer.

The last man tried to escape, but he never got twenty feet from us. Lily fired and hit him in the back. The man fell forward and dropped to the ground. The wind had taken the black smoke away, and we could see who had fired the first three shots. It was Sam, Ben, and Mindi. Sam was lying on the ground, and we all thought for sure that he had been killed. We ran over to him, and old Sam sat up and smiled.

"Did I get that bastard?" he asked.

"You sure as hell did!" I yelped. "Are you hurt bad?"

"No," I replied. "I just caught a ball in the upper arm. I'll be fine once you dig the bastard out."

Mindi fell to her knees and studied the wound. "Help me gets him into the house," she said. "I can take care of this. I done it a lot of times before."

Ben and Adam carried Sam into the house. Meanwhile, we all looked through the dead men's pockets to see what we could learn about them. None of us could find out who they were or where they were from, but we all knew that they were slave trackers and just damn thieves.

Joshua called Halfmoon. Halfmoon ran for him, and Joshua checked him over to make sure he was not hurt. "Good boy, Halfmoon. You sure gave that bastard a good thrashing, didn't ya?"

Halfmoon barked, and we were grateful that he was not hurt.

I said, "Here we go again. It seems like we always have to bury this scum. I wish it was out in the damn woods somewhere, and I'd leave them there for the buzzards to feed on."

James said, "I'll get the wagon. We'll take them out by the trees over there. We'd better bury them now and hope no one comes around looking for them."

Lily took the horses and put them in the corral. Now we had more horses to feed and take back with us to Kentucky or try to sell further north. This way no one would recognize the horses.

It was getting dark, and we finally buried the men. We were so tired and worn out from this day. The rest of the evening we stayed in the house and drank ale.

The next morning, Victor finally came out to see us. He hadn't been there since his wife died. He rode up and just sat on his horse, looking all around the place.

"I see that all of you have been busy," he remarked. "The place has never looked so damn good before."

I began to tell Victor what happened.

"Yesterday six men came riding in here and got a little pushy. Well, anyway, all hell broke loose. Now they are all buried out there in the woods. Sam caught a musket ball in his arm, but he'll be fine."

"That's why I rode out here," Victor replied. "I saw them fellas asking questions about you and about any slaves that may have run away. They must have decided to come by here and take a look for themselves. I'm glad you killed them all. They were nothing but trouble. I knew they would get into a fight with somebody for sure. They sure stopped at the damn wrong place, didn't they?"

Victor smiled and then said, "I have news for all of you. I had to go to Charles's plantation yesterday and do some work. One of the slaves I know there told me that five slaves are going to escape tonight. Charles is in Atlanta, and he took two of his meanest overseers with him. There is only one man left there to keep the peace and watch for trouble, but he'll be sleeping and not doing what he's supposed to do."

Joshua asked, "What should we do?"

Victor gave a little laugh and said, "Well, if I was you, I'd be getting ready for some freight tonight. You see, they will come to my place, and then I'll have Sam bring them here. You'll have to hide them for a few days, but don't wait one week to move them north. Charles will be back in six days, and he'll be on every damn road there is in this county, so you best get ready to head back to Kentucky. I'll tell him that you all decided to leave earlier than you planned. I'll say that something came up back at your trading post, and you needed to get back as soon as possible."

I asked Victor, "Do you think he'll believe you?"

"I think so. He ain't that smart. But he knows you'll be back in the spring, so he won't think you're running slaves north."

"I'll stay here until Charles gets back," James said. "I'll make sure he knows we had nothing to do with this. Plus I want to get that money from him that we'd talked about. I'll tell him that you headed back to Kentucky, and I'll be going to St. Louis to get the riverboat business going."

Lily thought about this for a minute and then said, "This is perfect. We'll be on our way with the freight, and you'll be going to St. Louis. He'll believe this for sure. You can stall him here and try to calm him down for a few days. We'll need to get north as fast as possible. I don't want to have to kill any more men for a while."

It was all agreed. We all had plenty to do to get ready to leave within two days. Sam went back with Victor; they would handle the freight for that night. All of us would be awake throughout the night and be ready for them and maybe another bounty hunter.

There was not a minute during the day and early evening that any of us sat down. We started to get the wagon back in shape and made sure we had enough food and supplies for the journey north. It was almost two in the morning when Sam came driving a wagon with not six but twenty slaves in the back.

I yelled, "What in hell are all these people doing with you, Sam?"

"It is crazy, Robert," he answered. "All hell broke loose at the plantation. The man on guard was killed by some of the slaves. They slit his throat and hung him from a tree. The people went into a frenzy there. They even set fire to the main house. Charles ain't there, but his wife was. She is dead now too. I had to shoot two men who tried to steal my wagon. Victor is coming right behind me. They tried to steal some of Victor's horses and wagons. They are crazy. Victor grabbed what he could, and he is coming here. He is scared as hell like me, Robert."

"Everybody, get your muskets and stand guard," I ordered. "Hell, we ain't got to worry about bounty hunters tonight. Now we have to worry about these slaves."

Joshua said, "Damn, Robert, it's an uprising now. We'd better stay here until it's safe to leave. They will be all over the roads, and they'll kill anybody to get a horse or wagon."

Ben and Adam were in shock. Adam said, "This ain't normal. I know how these slaves can get when they go crazy like this. I saw it happen once, and it wasn't pretty. They will kill each other or anybody who stands in their way. When I saw this before it was terrible. The plantation owner and his men ended up killing fifteen of their own slaves. Two white men were killed trying to stop them. Once they all get away and stay together, they are deadly."

We heard Victor's wagon coming up the road.

"I know that Sam has told you what happened tonight. I tell you all right now," he said, "I ain't staying here. They can have my damn place. I'm going with you back to Kentucky. I'm getting too damn old for this. The times are changing to damn fast for me. It is only going to get worse down here. I grabbed all the money I had and left everything else. Hell, by morning there won't be a damn thing left anyway. What they don't steal, they'll burn."

James said, "So much for St. Louis and the money. This man will be hunting whoever helped theses slaves escape and all the ones who killed his hire men, and his wife."

Victor had a frightened look on his face and said, "You don't have any idea how mean this man can become. He'll catch most of them, and then he'll find out that Sam was there today and that I was there yesterday. He'll find the one who told me they were planning to escape. And that young boy ain't with Sam, so this is telling me this boy will tell him about me and how I helped him. I tell you all right now, we'd better get our asses north tomorrow."

Lily said, "What about this place and all our plans to help more slaves go north?"

"Miss Lily, it is over," Victor stated. "The Underground Railroad and the freight—it's all over. We have no one here who will help us now. If we stay or come back, we will be killed. Let's just get the ones we have now and get the hell out of here quickly."

James said, "We must do as Victor says, Lily. It's so bad here now that they may even bring soldiers to stop this and any other possible outbreaks on other plantations. I know damn well I'll be long gone from here. Once the word spreads about this uprising to the other plantations, the slaves there may try to do the same damn thing. It may turn into a wildfire with these runaway slaves."

Joshua said, "Let's burn the house and barn. They'll think we had to leave because looters burned us out. I don't want to, but James and Victor are right."

I was thinking of all possible ways to stay here, and what we should do now or next year. I finally said, "I have thought it over. I agree we must all get out of here tomorrow. We'll burn the place down, and we'll go home as quickly as possible. We can only hope they don't come after us up in Kentucky. I don't think they will. There is too much for Charles to do here now. He must regroup and start his crops again. If he does, we'll cross that bridge when we come to it. Let's feed these people, get them some clothes, and let Adam talk to them and calm them down. Please, Adam, tell them anything, but calm them down so they don't go crazy on us here."

Adam, Ben, and Mindi took care of our new people. They talked to them at great length and explained what we were going to do and where we were taking them. They finally realized that we were helping them. They all cried and were scared, but they knew they would be protected from here on.

Kentucky Bound

It was a long, busy night. We all took turns guarding the house and the barn. We tried to get some rest, but it never came for any of us. When the first morning light appeared, we had three wagons loaded, and everyone had a horse.

Lily walked through the house for the last time and said to Joshua and me, "Let's burn them. Damn it, I hate doing this, but I know it must be done."

We set fire to the house and barn, and we all felt as if we were losing a close friend. No one said a word. We just started down the road. The flames took the buildings to the ground. We heard the timbers falling, but not a single one of us turned around to watch.

We traveled for nearly four hours before we saw anyone else on the road. It was a young family going south with all their children and two cows. We said hello to them and kept on going. Adam and Two Moons knew a better route to travel. They took us higher into the hills and away from any towns and people. It was a hard ride, but we knew it was the only way to go.

After five days, we started into the foothills, and soon we could see the mountains far ahead of us.

Adam yelled, "We'll be all right now. There won't be a soul up there. We are getting there just in time."

"What do you mean?" James wondered.

Two Moons said, "The snow will come soon, and it'll become very cold at night, but we will be out of the mountains before it starts."

Victor came alongside of us wearing a smile.

"What are you so happy about, Victor?" I asked.

"This is the first time in my old life that I feel young again," he replied. "Hell, I ain't got a home anymore. All I have is what I got on my back plus plenty of money. I feel damn good. No more plantations and looking at the poor slaves in the fields. I can start a new life on that mountain with Henry."

"You could build a blacksmith shop, Victor," I suggested. "You and Sam can work it together. There is a need for one by our trading post. There isn't one close by."

Lily said, "I just feel bad about not being able to go back and help more of those people."

James said, "You can't save them all, Lily. We did the best we could. Just look around you here. We have twenty-three Negroes with us who will now live free. They'll have children who will be free. Damn it, be happy for what we were able to do in such a short time. There is a day coming when there will be a long bloody war between people like us and the ones who want slaves. I see it coming, and I sure as hell don't want to be a part of it."

I said, "That's what my grandfather told Joshua and me

many years ago. He had this vision of a big war. He said it might even be between brothers and families. I never knew what he meant by that before, but now I know exactly what he was saying. We have just seen the tip of this in the South. I know that I ain't about to get in it either."

Joshua smiled and said, "Well, that makes two of us, Robert. If that war comes, I'll just cross the Mississippi and disappear into the West somewhere."

Adam directed us up to the side of the trail. "We'll make camp here for the night," he said. "There is water and good protection from anything."

"Whatever you say, Pathfinder," I answered.

Adam yelled back, "I like that name, Robert. Maybe I'll change my name to Pathfinder."

Two Moons laughed and said, "I'll call you that, Adam. It is a good name for you. My father would be proud of that name."

Joshua yelled out, "Then it is done. Adam will have a new name: Pathfinder. Hell, we are all starting new lives it seems. Victor has no blacksmith shop. James is all dressed up with no place to go. Sam has never seen mountains before and neither have the others. I'll tell you what. This must be a sight. If we did meet anyone on the trail they would just shake their heads at us. Not one of us has a clue what in hell we'll be doing in another week."

Halfmoon let out a howl.

"Now that ain't true, Joshua," I countered. "Old Halfmoon knows what he is and what it is all about. Just listen to him howl!"

We all laughed, even the Negroes. They were happy and

felt safe with us. They started to talk to one another about us. We knew they liked us, and they were grateful for what we were doing for them.

That night we all could finally breathe a lot easier. We had plenty of miles behind the hell that was letting loose down in Atlanta. The thought of never going back was starting to set in.

James was still uneasy about the riverboat business. He sort of was telling us that he would be leaving soon.

"I think when we get to your trading post I'll stay a few days," he said, "but I've decided to head to St. Louis. I don't belong with you wonderful people. I need to get back to doing what I know best."

"What is that, James?" Lily asked.

"I need to get on one of those steamers and play some cards," he told her. "I like the challenge, and I know I could win some good money. Maybe I'll invest in a riverboat and see what happens. Like I said a while back, the people will need to come up river and start heading west. I know I can do well if I find the right person to invest with."

"I know one damn thing," said Joshua. "I'll be staying at the trading post for a few years. I like it there and the area is just beginning to grow. There is money to be made there. Maybe someday I'll go to St. Louis and look you up, James."

Sam and Victor had already decided to build a black-smith shop near us, but we weren't sure what Adam and Two Moons would do. I kind of felt they would head west also. They were the type of folks who enjoyed open land, so maybe they would go find her father. We knew Daniel had already left with her father and his family to find new land to settle, but life is funny, and there were many turns and hills to climb.

The next few days were slow but with no problems. We knew in another day we would be back home, and we were all getting excited about seeing Henry and our friends again. The weather was turning colder by the time we were a day away from home. We decided to make camp early and get ready for a storm that was brewing in the north. We'd been watching the clouds all day, and the north wind was really starting blow. It was about noontime when we found a good spot for the night. We had made a few lean-tos to protect against the wind. By the time we got them done, the snow started to fall. It was cold as hell, and we knew we were in for a Blue Northern.

The wind and snow never let up all afternoon and night. We had the wagons close together, and we even laid canvas over them for more protection. It was really hard on the Negroes. They had never been in such cold weather. Lily took all the blankets we had and wrapped them up the best she could. Sam and Victor had plenty of wood to keep the fire going all night. Halfmoon just lay there. I think he liked it.

The next morning, just as the sun started to come up over the hills to the east, the wind finally stopped.

"Look at all this damn snow," I said to Joshua.

Everyone came out from the covers and looked around. They were all swearing and laughing.

Joshua said, "Looks like we got six inches from this storm, Robert."

"It sure as hell does," I agreed. "I could go for some hot coffee now."

Lily smiled and said, "I heard you, but that is all we'll have this morning."

The Negroes reached down, grabbed the snow, and tasted it. They had never seen it before. They were like children playing in it. They were laughing and in good spirits, considering how damn cold it was. Within the next hour, we had the teams of horses all ready, and we started to move up the pass. Late in the day, we saw the last of the snow.

Adam yelled out, "We'll be there in two hours."

We all let a cheer of excitement. We kept going until dark and finally made camp.

Victor jumped down and said, "It has been many years since I've seen old Henry. I can't wait to see his face when we all pull up there tomorrow."

Lily said, "I sure hope he can handle all of us. He'll think a wagon train is stopping by for supplies."

After we got done eating supper, one of the Negroes came to where we sitting and said, "We all been talking about this new place we is going. Well, we was wondering, is there land up there wheres we can live on?"

I smiled and said, "There is land there, but I don't know if you'll be able to live there. Some of the people there are not like us. We can send you to Pennsylvania where Lily's aunt lives. She can get you to Ohio. There you can live free, and we know there are many others like you who live there."

"But we ain't got no money or anything, Robert."

"Don't worry," I said. "We'll give each of you one hundred dollars to get you there, and I'm sure you'll be able to get a place to live."

A big smile came across his face, and he thanked us.

After the man had left, Adam smiled and said, "Just give them time. I bet you sooner or later they'll have their own railroad running. There is one of them that I talked to once back on the trail. He is damn smart. I figure he'll be doing what we are doing in a few years. They will survive. They are strong, and they will know all the routes and how to get as many people free as possible."

Joshua said, "That would be good. Hell, we can hide them out at our place and send them to Lily's aunt later on."

James laughed and said, "You see. You people are already thinking about how to keep this going. You don't know it yet, but you will be the major station on this Underground Railroad. Let them bring the Negroes to you from the South. You can just stay at your place and guide them farther north. It'll be a hell of a lot safer for you here than down South. Sooner or later, all of us would have been caught or killed."

"You're damn right on that, James, I said. "They would sure figure us out real soon. Hell, how many people look like us anyways? The odds would be against us."

By the time we all went to bed, we felt damn good about our new plans. We now knew what we had to do. We would help finance the freed Negroes and then guide them farther north.

The fall weather felt great. The last turn in the road was

ahead of us. We could see smoke up on the hill coming from our chimney. We knew old Henry had something cooking in one of his big pots. He sure could cook up a storm.

We were about to start up the hill when Halfmoon jumped off the wagon and ran like the wind toward the trading post. He barked like he was chasing the devil. When we got to the top of the hill, Henry and Hans were standing on the porch.

"What in hell is all this?" Henry gasped at the sight of our four wagons. "Did you bring the whole South up with ya?"

We all jumped off the wagons and ran to Henry. We hugged him, and everyone was trying to talk at once.

Henry yelled out, "Slow the hell down! Now, just one of you talk. You'll drive me crazy."

I walked up to Henry and said, "Just get out a keg of ale, my old friend. We have the rest of our lives to tell you what we all went through."

Sam gathered the twenty-two Negroes and led them around the house to get water and food. He was already thinking about where to house them all.

Henry brought out the keg of ale and set it on the front porch.

"Here is the ale," he said. "Now, please, one of you tell me all about this wagon train you've got here."

For the rest of the day and late into the night, we all drank and told Henry everything.

Victor and Henry got really drunk. They were like two young boys talking and swearing about the days long ago.

The rest of us went into the kitchen. There we felt like we were finally back home.

Sam came into the kitchen and said, "My people are all set for the night. They have bedded down in the wagons, and we put the horses in the meadow out back. Now I'll have a drink with you. I see old Victor and Henry are having a hell of a good time. That is good. Victor needed to get away from down there. Now he can start a new life with his friend and away from the bastard Charles."

James stood up and said, "I see why you love it here so much. The place is beautiful and peaceful. Unfortunately, I had better leave in a day or so."

"Why so soon?" Lily wondered.

"If I stay here too long, I'll never want to leave."

Joshua said, "Well, just stay here then. You can build your own inn and have a bar and card tables. Hell, with all the people coming and going this way, it'll be a great way for you to set down some roots. You can do it, James. We'll all pitch in to help you."

I added, "There is some fine land along the river down below. If you build an inn at the corner of the two rivers coming together, you'd have a perfect location. That old dirt road would pass right by your new place. What else could you ask for?"

James smiled and thought about it. Then he said, "You know, you're right. Why should I go to St. Louis to start a business? It is just as good here. Then it is settled. I'll buy some land down there in a few days."

Lily smiled and said, "Now that is a load off my mind, James."

It was the first time any of us had seen Lily act this way. We all started to wonder what was going on in her mind.

Two Moons giggled, and Adam said to her, "What's so funny, Two Moons?"

Two Moons smiled and said, "I see two people here are in love—and neither one of them will admit it to the other."

The kitchen fell silent.

Joshua finally threw up his hands. "So *that's* what's been going on!" he said with a laugh. "We all should've known."

James stood up again and said, "Well, I'll be damned. Two Moons, you are right. It is about damn time I said it myself."

He took a long drink of ale and finally came out and said it.

"I do love you, Lily. I have been in love with you since the first time I laid eyes on you. I know this isn't the right way to say it, but nothing is normal with this bunch. To hell with all of those formalities. Miss Lily, will you marry me?"

Lily's face turned red.

I said to Joshua and Adam, "Look at her. This is the first time I have ever seen Lily blush."

"Oh, shut up, Robert," she said with a scowl. "You men have been with me for a long time, and now you'll have to take care of yourselves."

Adam laughed and said, "What does that mean, Lily?"

"It means yes," she declared. "I will marry you, James. I do love you, but you have never even kissed me."

James walked over to Lily, took her into his arms, and

kissed Lily for the first time.

"So," he then said, "what type of inn and house do you want, Lily?"

We all cheered with excitement. Henry and Victor came stumbling in and Henry said, "What in hell is going on in here?"

Joshua said, "Get another keg, Henry. There is gonna be a wedding here real soon."

Henry looked at Lily and started to cry. He hugged her and then Lily said, "Henry, will you give me away? Since my father is gone I need you to be my father now."

Henry sobered up real fast. "Darling, it'll be my damn pleasure to be your father," he replied. "I will be very proud to give you away."

We all had tears in our eyes. Halfmoon barked in celebration. Our family was about to become even larger.

Victor brought out another bottle of brandy. He set it on the table and said, "The way we've been drinking, and Sam and I will never get that damn blacksmith shop started."

We all laughed. None of us ever went to bed that night. At dawn we all walked out onto the porch and watched the sun come up.

Joshua said, "Just look at that sunrise. Another new day, and now we have one another here together. It's a new beginning, and we all must be proud of what we have done so far."

Adam put his arm around Two Moons and said, "Two Moons and I have decided to stay here also. We'll build a place out back in the meadow near the spring. There is way too much work to do for all of us now. We have to build a blacksmith shop for Victor and Sam and the inn for James and Lily. We'll also have to build some cabins for any slaves that can get here."

I said, "Adam is right. There is a lot of work to do come spring. Maybe we can start this fall and work when the weather is warmer. We'll have to make do with what we have here for the time being. Maybe we can take the loft and make a few rooms."

Sam came from the back of the house and said, "I have been in the barn, and I think we can make a nice place in the back. Hell, I can live in there. I can build anything."

Victor staggered off the steps and said, "Well, I know one damn thing. We drank all the ale and the brandy. I guess I'll help Sam build a place for us until spring."

Henry laughed like hell and said, "If there ain't no more ale then I guess I'll help ya."

James held Lily's hand and said, "Why don't Robert, Joshua, and I go into that town you were telling me about? We'd better get stocked up with supplies for the winter."

The rest of the day everyone was busy. We finally made a long list and got the wagons ready to go. Adam stayed to watch the place. We knew there would be no one looking for runaways here yet, but we would always be on guard for them if they came.

We left and told everyone we would be back by dark. We hoped we could find everything we needed. We had to watch what we said to anybody in town. We could never trust strangers again.

1800-1801

It was early spring in the year 1800. The winter months passed very quickly. A day didn't go by when we didn't get something finished. We had taken the loft and made a nice place for Adam and Two Moons. Victor and Sam made a great living area in the barn. Sam was a damn good carpenter. He had made an open space nice and warm, and a room to do whatever he wanted. Victor liked it just as much as Sam did.

James and Lily were making plans for the inn they wanted to build. James bought a few acres from Hans's father. The land was located about half a mile from the bottom of the hill. James hired some of the German farmers to build it. He knew that they were the best people around to do the job. It was going to be a grand place to stay. James had seen so many nice places that he knew exactly what he wanted. Lily was very happy, and we were so glad for her. She needed a man in her life. It was time for her to have children and settle down.

Joshua and I, on the other hand, were different. We loved the place, and we were happy for everyone, but deep down we knew that there was more for us to see and do.

The spring of 1800 was the time for us to finally send the Negroes north to Lily's aunt's place. During the winter, we had gotten to know the one Negro who had become the leader of the group. He was a very smart man. He wanted to learn to read and write, so Lily taught him. He learned quickly, and he wanted to lead his people further on their journey. From Lily's aunt's place, he said he might go back south to help others, but first he wanted to take his people to Ohio and see what was there.

When the day came for them to leave, Ben and Mindi came to us.

Ben said, "We want to stay here with you folks. We love you all, and we want to help. Maybe we can work at the inn when it is built."

James and Lily were very pleased to hear this.

James said, "We would love to have you here. You can sure help us at the inn. We'll pay you well, and we'll build a nice cabin for you."

Ben and Mindi were so pleased. They needed to be with James and Lily. They never had children and now they felt as if they had people to take care of, and just maybe Lily would have children some day.

Joshua and I gave the twenty Negroes a wagon and one hundred dollars each, just as we had promised. As they left and we all watched them go down the hill, we knew they would be safe on their journey to a new land.

It seemed so quiet around the trading post once they

were gone. They had been with us for six months. It would take time to get used to them not being around, but we hoped that someday they would bring us more of their people from the South.

June arrived with all its warmth and beauty. James and Lily finally set a date to be married. The wedding would be held on the fourth of July. We all thought that this would be a grand celebration not only for us, but also for the local farmers. They had been trading with us since we had first arrived.

The inn was almost completed. James and Lily were hoping they could open by the end of July. Sam and Victor had also built a large blacksmith shop just down the river from the inn. It seemed as if everybody was doing fine and had a bright future ahead of them.

Henry was tending to the trading post and spending a lot of time with Victor and Sam. The three of them were a hell of a bunch. They were always talking and laughing about something. Joshua and I enjoyed talking to them. We were always asking Henry what was beyond the Mississippi River.

It was a few days before the big wedding when Henry and Joshua and I were sitting on the porch, watching all the people coming and going below us on the river and road.

Henry asked, "You boys sure have been asking a lot of questions about what is across the Mississippi River lately. I get the feeling that you two and your wolf Halfmoon are getting itchy feet again."

I said, "Well, it has always been Joshua and my dream to go out that way, but when we met Lily and Adam, it all seemed to change."

Joshua took a long drink of ale and said, "Its true, Henry. We've been thinking real hard on this for quite a spell now. Now that Lily and James are getting married and settling down, and Adam and Two Moons are planning their life together, we feel like we are out of place here. The Underground Railroad is almost dead. Hell, we ain't freed a soul since we brought those folks up this spring."

Henry smiled and said, "Don't you two worry. There will be many folks coming this way. I've been hearing from people who've been coming up from the South. They say it's getting worse down there. Many of the slaves are running away and heading north."

"I wonder who is doing it now," I said.

"They said that some free Negroes have been going back and forth, helping the slaves break free," Henry explained.

"I guess Joshua and I will just see what happens around here this year, and then decide what we'll do come spring."

Henry looked at us and said, "You do that, and don't feel like you have to stay on account of all of us. This old trading post will be here whenever you want to come back. Hell, I'll probably die here, and then Adam can run the place. If you both want to travel about for a few years, then go. You'll kick yourselves in the ass for the rest of your lives if you don't."

That evening, Joshua and I took Halfmoon past the meadow in the back and climbed up to the highest boulder. The sun was just beginning to set. We sat there as the warm southern breeze brushed against our faces. The view was so beautiful. We sat back and drank our ale.

"Robert, I've been thinking about what Henry said to-day," Joshua said. "He's right. We should go west for a while and see this country."

"I agree with you, Joshua. You remember when our grandfathers used to tell us how they and Coppernol went into the mountains toward Lake George?"

"Yes, I do. They said they were on the mountain there. The three of them were watching the fort and saw the Huron coming up the lake. They told us that only a few men had ever been where they were, and that it was exciting to see the fort and the large lake below."

"Well, that's how I feel now, Joshua," I stated. "I got this damn feeling in my gut that is pulling me west."

"Then let's just do it," Joshua replied. "We'll take Half-moon and the wagon and just go. Maybe we can find Daniel Boone and see where he is now. Hell, it won't be hard to find him. Everybody knows him."

I thought for a moment and then turned to Halfmoon. "What you think, Halfmoon?" I asked. "Do ya think the three of us can go and do what we talked about so long ago?"

Halfmoon stood up and howled with excitement.

Joshua smiled and said, "Well, there's our answer, Robert. Halfmoon says it is fine with him."

"Then we'll do it," I announced. "We'll head out in the spring. We'll go to St. Louis first and see that town. Then we'll cross the Mississippi River and follow the sun west. We may never get back here again, but we'll go and do what we've always wanted to do."

The sun was setting in the west. The stars were coming

out, shining brightly in the sky. As we drank our ale, Joshua yelled, "Look up there, Robert! Two falling stars!"

I looked up and saw them. "There is our sign to go west. I tell ya, Joshua, I got this strange feeling that our grandfathers have given us this sign to do it."

Halfmoon had also seen the falling stars. He let out a howl that lasted for a minute.

Joshua put his hand on my shoulder and said, "Now we know what we have to do. There isn't any damn doubt in our minds. This is what our grandfathers wanted us to do, and damn it, we'll do it together—you, me, and Halfmoon."

The next morning, Joshua and I sat around the kitchen table with everyone.

James asked us where we went last night after supper.

"Joshua, Halfmoon, and I went clear up onto the boulders beyond the meadow," I told them. "We were watching the sunset and talking about leaving here."

A dead silence took over the kitchen.

Lily asked, "What do you mean by 'leaving here'?"

Joshua stood up. "Robert and I have always wanted to go across the Mississippi River and see the West," he announced. "Now is a good time to go. You're getting married, and you'll have your life with James at the inn. Adam and Two Moons are settled here now. This is the right time for us to go. Maybe someday we'll come back."

Adam looked up at us and said, "You two won't come back here. Once you see the West and all the beauty that they say is out there, you'll never come back."

"You may be right," I agreed, "but we have to go and

see it for ourselves. Maybe we'll do some trapping or start a trading post there. I know you all think we're crazy, but that's how our grandfathers were also. They went all over the place during the wars. They came back home to our grandmothers and their children, but Joshua and I ain't tied down, and we probably never will be."

Lily smiled and said, "Don't say that. Look what happened to me. I thought I'd never find a man as nice as James."

"When are you leaving?" Adam asked.

"We will leave a day or so after the wedding," I told him. "We'll take four horses and, of course, Halfmoon."

Henry said, "I wish I was thirty years younger. I'd go with ya, but I'm too damn old now, and I have to stay here and keep Victor in line."

We all laughed and then Victor said, "He's got that wrong. I have to watch *him* or he'll drink our entire supply of ale."

Everyone agreed that we had to do what we wanted to do.

Lily said, "Adam and I will buy your share of the business. It is only fair to you. That way you'll have money and you won't have to worry about trying to get any while your roaming around God knows where."

Joshua and I were thankful for the offer. We knew we sure could use the money along the way.

Henry stood up and went to the hidden compartment in the false wall. He brought back the map that Luke and he had made years ago.

He laid the map on the table and said, "You two are now

the owners of this map. Guard it with your lives. I also found this wampum belt with my belongings that were in the trunk I brought. I forgot all about it until the other day. Once you get in this area here," Henry pointed to a line of mountains drawn on the map, "you will be in Blackfeet country. You will be spotted many days before you even see one of these proud Indians. When you do, do not fire at them. You'll be dead within minutes. Wait until they approach you. I know their language very well. I'll teach you as much as I can before you leave. Show them the wampum belt."

Joshua and I listened closely, and I asked, "What does all this different color beadwork mean?"

Henry answered, "Every shape and color of these beads mean a name, place and over here is telling them who ever has this wampum belt is their friend."

We looked at the fine workmanship that was carefully done.

Two Moons said, "I can read most of it. It is sort of like my people's wampum. I have heard stories about these Blackfeet people from my grandfather. They say many tribes live out on the plains and in those mountains. They also say they are great horsemen and mighty warriors. There are Crow, Apache, and other tribes that roam that vast open land."

The more Two Moon talked of what she has been told, the more Joshua and I were intrigued about this land west.

The day of the big wedding finally arrived. The inn was completed, and it sure was a fine place. There were four rooms upstairs for guests and a large bar filled with the fin-est whiskey James could get. There was a small dinning room for maybe twenty people. People already wanted to stay there, but James told them it wouldn't be open until two days after the wedding.

Almost thirty people came from around the area. Henry got all dressed up in his finest clothes and gave Lily away to James. We had the party at the inn; Mindi cooked up a feast for all of the guests. She and Ben had a nice cabin just down the road on property that James had given them.

The party went on all day and night. There was not one unhappy person there when first light finally arrived. Joshua and I were standing out in front of the inn when everyone came out.

"Well, we are packed and ready to go," I said. "We ain't gonna get down from these horses and hug and kiss you all one by one. We'll say our good-byes from up here. This is hard enough for us, so we'll make it quick."

I looked around for Adam and Two Moons, but I didn't see them. I asked Lily where they were.

"Just turn around and see for yourselves."

Joshua and I turned and saw Adam and Two Moons with the big wagon. Adam yelled to us, "What in hell are you two thinking? We sure ain't gonna let you leave without us!"

Joshua smiled and said, "Why are you coming?"

"We talked it over and decided somebody has got to watch your backs," Adam explained. "Plus we are better off going with you two. Just look at us: a black man and an Indian woman. You know sooner or later we would have trouble knocking at our door if we stayed here. At least out West the Indians will accept Two Moons and maybe a black man too. Out there we'll have our own lives, and you never know. Maybe we'll start a trading post with you two."

Joshua smiled and said, "We were hoping you would come along. We will need Two Moons to read this wampum belt and maybe understand some of the Indians' language. Robert and I have a hard enough time just reading damn English!"

Adam whistled loudly. "Come on, Halfmoon, get up in this wagon with us. You can't walk the whole West. You ain't getting any younger."

Halfmoon barked as he jumped up into the wagon with Adam and Two Moons. He loved Adam, and we knew that it would be better for him to ride than walk.

I looked at everyone and said, "We'll never forget any of you. We love each and every one of you. And don't be surprised if we all come back someday."

They all waved as we left, wishing us luck and praying for God to watch over us.

Lily yelled, "You'll be back someday. I just know it. Maybe by then I'll have a house full of children."

Joshua yelled back, "I sure as hell hope so. Name them after Robert and me."

Joshua and I started down the road with Adam and Two Moons behind us in the wagon. Halfmoon didn't stop barking until we were over the hill and out of sight.

We stopped for a moment and Adam pulled alongside of us. Joshua said, "Together we four and Halfmoon will see places that few men have ever seen."

Two Moons said, "My father gave me a map of where he and Daniel Boone and his family were going. Would you two like to come with us and see them?"

Joshua and I looked at each other and smiled.

"We were hoping you'd say that," I replied. "We would love to see Daniel again. He reminds us of our grandfathers, and we sure would love to stay with him for a spell."

Adam said, "Let's go find him and Two Moon's father. Between the two of them, we can learn all about the West and what is out there. Then we'll decide which trail we'll follow."

"Maybe once we find Daniel and your father, we all could stay with them through the winter," I suggested. "Then by spring we can go looking for that gold mine of Harry's. Just maybe we'll strike it rich and come back to Round Knob and see all our family again. Heck, maybe we'll buy that steamboat for James."

Joshua said with a smile, "Maybe, just maybe, Robert we'll strike it rich and buy our own steamboat. We could really have a way to hide any runaways on that steamer. We could use it as a front. They say the Mississippi River is long, so we could start in New Orleans and run north with the Negroes. We could always tell anyone that they are our slaves and deck hands."

I said to Adam and Two Moons, "Here we go again. Joshua is already planning our next adventure. I swear, Joshua, you never cease to amaze me with your ideas. It sure sounds like a good plan. When we get to Daniel's home, we'll sit down and talk about it. I do like the idea.

I'm sure Lily and James would really like this new twist."

Adam let out a little laugh and said, "You may have a good idea there, Joshua. I think that Two Moons and I would look mighty fine on a fancy steamer going up and down the Mississippi with you two. I can see us now. Lily all dressed up in some fancy dress and James with his fancy coat playing cards."

Joshua and I pictured this in our minds and then Joshua laughed and said, "I can't see Lily in a fine dress. Maybe her old buckskins."

We all laughed and smiled. Halfmoon let out a happy bark.

"Well, we'd better get going," I said. "It sounds like Halfmoon is telling us to quit talking and get riding."

"Well, Robert," Joshua said, "It's time to start planning another chapter in our lives. I'm sure we'll have all our old friends back at the trading post in this new chapter."

"I believe you're right, Joshua. I can see us all together again in the near future."

About the Author

I was born in a very small village known as Stark-ville, New York. The total population was nearly two hundred people. I was raised in a fourteen-room farmhouse dated around 1860 and grew up in the Mohawk Valley, where the French and Indian War and the American Revolution were fought. I learned from an early age about all the rich history that surrounded me. Every dirt road, as well as the Otsquago Creek that flowed near my home and would finally meet the beautiful Mohawk River, held its own history and its own stories.

I graduated from a very small but beautiful school in 1968. Needing to see more of this amazing world, I joined the Navy. I completed four years in the Navy, including two tours of Vietnam on a Navy minesweeper. Traveling the South Pacific to many countries, I would always think back upon the Mohawk Valley and its history.

I have had my own construction business since 1976 and have been a carpenter since 1972. I enjoy restoring old homes and finding the history about each one I work on. I also enjoy reading pre-1840 history and doing reenactments of this time frame. My hobby, or should I say passion, is reading and researching early American history of New York state.